American Royalty

Suzy Langevin

This is a work of fiction. Names, characters, places, and incidents either are the product of the author's imagination or are used fictitiously, and any resemblance to actual persons living or dead, business establishments, events, or locales, is entirely coincidental.

© COPYRIGHT 2026 by Suzy Langevin

All rights reserved. No part of this book may be used or reproduced in any manner whatsoever without written permission of the publisher except in the case of brief quotations embodied in critical articles or reviews.

AI was not used to write this book, to create the cover art, or in formatting.

NO AI TRAINING: Without in any way limiting the author's and publisher's exclusive rights under copyright, any use of this publication to "train" generative artificial intelligence (AI) technologies to generate text is expressly prohibited. The author reserves all rights to license uses of this work for genAI training and development of machine learning language models.

Warning: Not intended for persons under the age of 18. May contain coarse language and mature content that may disturb some readers. Reader discretion advised.

Cover Art Design by: Kelly Moran/Rowan Prose Publishing
Photo Credit: Adobe Images/Deposit Photos
First Edition
ISBN: 978-1-961967-78-6
Rowan Prose Publishing, LLC
www.RowanProsePublishing.com
Published in the United States of America

Get this other romance from Suzy now!

Dedication

For the idealistic ones, who believe that leading with love will always win in the end. And for everyone still mentally in the Bartlet administration. **West Wing** *fangirls forever!*

Chapter One

It was absurdly early, but Jasmine been awake for at least a half an hour, scrolling through the Sunday morning show lineups. She hadn't dared to flip on the light, afraid of waking her boyfriend, who was still asleep beside her. She made do with the first bits of sunlight bleeding in around the cheap roller shades in their tiny bedroom. She was used to this—angling her laptop away from Danny, working at the crack of dawn. She couldn't seem to turn her grind off, even though they'd gotten in pretty late the previous night. One of Danny's friends from college had just moved back to town to start law school at Georgetown the next month, so they'd gone down to the Navy Yard for a housewarming party.

Her boyfriend spent the whole Uber ride back complaining that another one of his friends was going the 'sellout' route.

"I remember when he hated corporate America, now he wants to cozy up to it."

Jasmine had drunk a little too much wine to handle that kind of a conversation. But when Danny had some whiskey and a weed gummy, he almost always ended up ranting about integrity.

An unfortunate side effect of living in D.C.

"Maybe he thinks he can actually affect change from the inside," she reasoned. "That's why I'm working on the Hill."

Before she'd even graduated from Georgetown that spring, Jasmine had accepted a job on the communications staff for Senator Jack Ashworth, of the storied Ashworth political dynasty—an old money, old power family rivaled only by the Kennedys themselves. Since mid-May, she'd been crafting press releases and tracking headlines for the entire Ashworth clan, always on the lookout for the best way to position the Senator in the media.

"And once you do your time, we can get the fuck outta D.C. and you can do some real good out there," Danny slurred as they climbed the stairs to their third-floor walkup apartment.

Uninterested in getting into the debate about staying in D.C. with Danny when he was like this, Jasmine simply washed her face, wound her long box braids into a knot onto top of her head and covered them with her silk scarf and collapsed into bed, hoping he'd be in a better mood by morning.

He let out a groan when Jasmine's phone began to vibrate on her nightstand. She got up quickly to grab it, tossing her laptop to the side to retreat to her corner of the room so she wouldn't disturb him. The screen lit up with two pieces of bad news: it was five-thirty in the morning, and the call was from Gwendolyn Jacobson—her boss at Senator Ashworth's office. If she was calling this early on a Sunday, it couldn't be good. Maybe she'd gotten wind of something that was going to dominate the Sunday morning shows, a warning to tune in to *Face the Nation* or *Meet the Press* for some kind of bomb to drop.

Jasmine fumbled to swipe the screen to answer the call, speaking in hushed tones. "Gwen? What's going on? It can't be good this early."

Gwen's voice came through rushed and close to frantic. She operated at a constant caffeinated buzz under normal circumstances, but this was intense even for her. "Jasmine, we have a problem. A big one."

"Is Martinez announcing an exploratory committee already? Before the midterms?" Senator Ashworth was eyeing a presidential run, so news about every other potential primary challenger sent Gwen straight into the stratosphere. Governor Ramon Martinez of New Mexico was the latest source of panic, and for good reason. Young, Latino, and a self-made green energy executive, he'd gotten into politics almost as a hobby and rocketed to the governor's mansion. His telegenic, happy family was a far cry from the once-widowed, incredibly white Jack Ashworth—not to mention his younger trophy wife and adult son who could be a press liability thanks to his playboy reputation.

"No, it's Trip."

Speaking of that particular liability...

"Another post from some girl he took home last night?"

"Oh, honey, if only. Do me a favor, hop onto TikTok, watch Mariana DaSilva's most recent post and call me back."

Her stomach dropped. Mariana DaSilva was a pop princess, with a reputation for highly personal, almost confessional song writing, and legions of rabid fans that followed her every move. Every single she released got dissected to death on Tumblr and Instagram, trying to parse just which of her exes she was singing about.

So, of course, Trip, Senator Ashworth's son, had decided that she was the perfect option for a summer fling.

They'd been photographed together all over New York City and down the Jersey Shore where the Ashworths had a famous summer retreat. There was even a rumor that Mariana had been looking at real estate down there, considering purchasing her own home in Stone Harbor. And then, just as quickly as they seemed to catch fire, they burned out about a week ago, amid a swirl of rumors that Trip had cheated.

Whatever Gwen was directing her towards on TikTok, it couldn't be good for Trip... or for the Senator.

"I'll call you right back."

Jasmine ended the call and opened her TikTok. She searched Mariana DaSilva, and tapped on the most recent video she'd posted. The caption on the bottom read:

"Last min addition to the new album out October 9. Fire in more ways than one."

Jasmine turned the volume up. Mariana was dancing to the track, but the lyrics immediately caught her attention. She replayed the video several times, wanting to catch every word.

I learned the hard way,
American royalty
The playboy prince
Not who you want him to be
It's a game, it's a shame
Earned that notoriety
Guess you just can't trust
American royalty

"Shit," Jasmine cursed, loudly enough that Danny lifted his head across the room.

"What's going on?"

"Trip fucking Ashworth making my job a goddamn nightmare." She darted into their small living room to call Gwen back while Danny flopped back down.

"Did you watch it?" Gwen asked as soon as she picked up.

"Yeah, this... isn't good."

"Isn't good? That's like saying the Titanic took on a little water, honey. This is a fucking disaster."

"How soon do I need to be in?"

"Crisis meeting at seven a.m. You able to get here before to strategize?"

"Sure thing, who will be..."

"Just the inner circle. Me, Ben, Addison, Trip and the Senator."

"Are they going to be comfortable with me being there?" Jasmine was the newest member of the staff, and she knew neither Senator Ashworth nor Trip warmed up quickly to new people. Ben had been with the office for years, and Addison was family. She didn't want it to be awkward—or worse, unproductive—if they held back.

"If I'm there, I need you there. This is a communications nightmare. We both need to be up to speed."

"Okay, then." Jasmine exhaled. "I'll see you soon."

She went back into the bedroom to get ready, unwinding her head scarf and letting her braids down, laying her edges quickly. She groaned when she realized she was going to have to text Bailey and tell her she wasn't coming to the hairdresser's after church to get her hair done. Hopefully these braids could hold on for another few days because this week was shaping up to give her no free time at all.

She changed into her typical weekend work outfit: wide leg linen pants and sleeveless top that she'd add a cardigan to from the collection on the back of her office door. Despite the relative swamp-like atmosphere in the city in August, the air conditioning gave the entire office suite an arctic level chill. She added enough concealer and mascara to hopefully cover up the fact that she was running on only three hours sleep. The Metro didn't start running until seven a.m. on Sundays, so she ordered an Uber and began to scroll through the comments on Mariana's TikTok while she waited for her pre-coffee coffee to finish brewing.

"Oop. Guess Ashworth isn't Prince Charming."

"Go OFF girlie"

"That white boy is trash."

"Do we need to unalive him bestie?"

"We ride at dawn, MariNation!"

"Ok, but you still look flawless? Drop the post breakup glow up skin care, bestie!"

"Savage. We love to see it."

In addition to being a PR nightmare, the Capitol police were going to have to investigate some of these comments as actual death threats. Great.

There wasn't enough caffeine in all the world to make this morning not a giant headache.

She filled her favorite pink glitter tumbler with coffee, grabbed her beloved plum colored Kate Spade bag already packed with her laptop and tablet, and went downstairs to wait for her ride on the already sweltering sidewalk in front of their building.

Gwen's texts started as soon as she got into the white Honda. Her driver was predictably and blessedly silent, knowing that anyone going up to the Hill at this hour on a Sunday wasn't having a good morning.

Ben and I just got in and he's already breathing fire about this. Hope you're ready for your first crisis campaign.

She thought the pictures from earlier in the summer of Senator Ashworth's wife cozying up to a lobbyist at Le Diplomate should have qualified as crisis, but what did she know? This apparently was a much bigger deal, especially if Ben's back was up about it.

She swiped into the building, nodding to the familiar security guard. The elevator doors slid shut, and she pressed the button for the third floor, her stomach tightening with each floor number that ticked up. As she exited the elevator, the familiar hum of the fluorescent lights made her heart beat faster.

When she walked into the main waiting area in the outer part of the office, Jasmine could already hear Gwen's voice going a mile a minute, sounding higher pitched than usual, and Ben's rumbling baritone sounding less than pleased in response. She ducked into the small office she shared with Addison and grabbed a sweater before taking a deep breath and entering the conference room. She went to the sideboard and started making coffee, wanting to avoid interrupting the current heated exchange.

Ben looked more disheveled than Jasmine had ever seen him. He wasn't even in a tie—just a plaid shirt open at the neck. From what Addison had told her, there had been a minor turf war over dress code when Gwen joined the office last year. Ben wanted the staff in business dress one hundred percent of the time, even on weekends. Gwen favored a much more casual approach when they weren't in session, to make staffers seem more 'accessible' and less stiff, a deliberate effort to counter to the old money connotations of the Ashworth name. With her patented blend of charm and iron will, Gwen had prevailed.

Unfortunately, Ben was as stiff as they came. Jasmine sort of understood him, at least better than the rest of her officemates. As a Black man that came up more than a decade ago, he'd had to fight harder for respect. Even after fourteen years, though, he hadn't figured out how to let his guard down. He stuck to his ties, just as neat as his always impeccably fresh lineup, while the rest of the team dressed down. Today, though, was clearly an exception.

"Gwendolyn, how does this *happen*? The kid's off limits, we've said this a thousand times."

Gwen flicked her wavy blonde ponytail and sighed with exasperation. "This isn't *media*, Benjamin. It's *social* media. We can't very well tell a 23-year-old pop star what she can and can't post on her own TikTok page."

"Didn't she sign some kind of NDA?"

Gwen scoffed. "Are you serious? Do you really think that would work? She's a songwriter, she wrote a song, that's her job. Besides, in the clip so far, she doesn't say his name, doesn't mention any details. There's nothing there that would be covered by an NDA anyway."

Jasmine wasn't exactly sure what she was supposed to do in this situation. Finally, Gwen greeted her.

"Morning, Jasmine, dear. Things are a little tense at the moment."

"He didn't ask for this, you know," Ben interjected.

"He didn't not," Jasmine mumbled as she poured some coffee into a navy-blue mug emblazoned with a picture of the Capitol building to hand to Ben.

"What was that?" Ben asked sharply.

Jasmine froze. She wasn't afraid of Ben—not exactly—but as the chief of staff, he had the power to fire Jasmine instantly. Getting canned from Senator Ashworth's office all but guaranteed no other Democrat on the Hill would touch her. His famously flat affect made him hard to read under the best of circumstances, and she felt even less certain now that he was actually fired up. Jasmine had to tread carefully with her response.

"Sorry, sir, but Mariana DaSilva has a history of writing about her exes. I mean, I think it's unfair the flak she gets, honestly. Male artists do the same all the time, and it's not a big deal. But when she does it, people say she's using them for clout. Trip had to know when he started seeing her that this could happen. So, while he didn't ask for it—I'd never say that—he also should have been aware that it might."

"She's not wrong," Addison's voice said from the doorway of the conference room. Senator Ashworth's niece and constituent services liaison came in and sat down next to Jasmine. She was dressed even more casually than Jasmine in jeans and a t-shirt with her long chestnut brown hair coiled into a messy top knot and last night's mascara still smudged under her eyes. Ben eyed her disapprovingly but said nothing. Even with the considerable power he wielded in this office, his last name wasn't Ashworth, and that was always going to be the most significant credential in the room.

"Where's Trip?" Ben asked. Trip and Addison shared a brownstone in Georgetown, so they usually drove to the Capitol together when Trip had to put in an appearance at the office.

"Parking the car. He dropped me off so I could check to see if Uncle Jack was here yet."

Gwen shook her head. "The Senator won't be joining us until after church."

"So, we've got about three hours to fix this thing and prevent Uncle Jack from murdering Trip right here in the Russell office building?"

"Fix is a relative term," Gwen said. "The song is coming out whether we like it or not. It'll be more brand management."

"Brand management? Really, Gwen?" Ben asked incredulously.

"I don't know Benjamin, I think that sounds better than *damage control*, don't you?"

"He's gonna love that," Addison said under her breath. Jasmine wasn't sure if she was referring to Trip or Senator Ashworth. "Jazz, can you pass me a cup of coffee?"

Jasmine filled another mug and handed it to Addison, also wordlessly passing her the caddy of sugar packets and creamer, having learned over the three months that they'd shared an office that she liked her coffee very light and sweet, unlike Jasmine who drank it black.

"Well, no matter what we call it, we need a plan," Gwen huffed. "Anyone have any ideas?"

"Ignore it?" Trip Ashworth joined them, leaning defiantly against the door frame.

Chapter Two

Jasmine had been working for Senator Ashworth's office since the end of May, but could count on one hand the number of times she'd actually seen Trip Ashworth in person. He'd spent most of the summer out of the city, so it was still a little startling every time she saw him in the flesh, this guy from the cover of *People*.

Tall like his father, Trip was in every other way a carbon copy of his mom. She was the dark-haired youngest daughter of a minor Italian noble that Jack had met at Oxford when he was there on his Rhodes scholarship. She was pursuing a PhD in literature. Their whirlwind romance, engaged in just weeks and married in under a year, was a fairytale that added another layer to the Ashworth mystique, and meant that gossip about Trip's love life ran rampant. Everyone wondered if he could recreate his parents' magic.

It also meant he was infuriatingly handsome—better looking in person than he was in the countless photos every website ran proclaiming him *America's most eligible bachelor*. Impossibly fit, with striking green eyes and summer-tanned skin, Jasmine couldn't deny that the headlines were right. Even his slightly crooked smile, also inherited from his mom from what Jasmine could tell from the family photos lining the walls of the office, only added to his charm—imperfect yet somehow flawless.

But right now, he looked like he hadn't slept, a plaid button down haphazardly thrown on over a t-shirt and joggers. His chin was covered in stubble, and his much-discussed green eyes looked heavier than usual. It seemed like Trip would have preferred to be anywhere else in the world than in this conference room right now.

"Trip, how are you, son?" Ben asked with compassion in his tone, the harsh anger mellowing a bit. Ben had an enduring soft spot for Trip and was more protective of him than Senator Ashworth ever was.

"I mean, ready to chuck my iPhone in the Potomac with my mentions blowing up everywhere. If she was gonna call me out like that, I just wish she'd done it during daylight hours on the east coast. But this isn't my first rodeo."

Jasmine stayed quiet, still trying to get a read on the situation. She poured two more mugs of coffee, setting one down for Trip beside Addison before taking the other for herself. She eyed the empty chairs at the table, then slipped into the seat next to where Gwen stood. Pulling out her tablet and stylus, she got ready to jot down any action steps from the conversation.

As Trip came up to sit beside Addison, she reached over and grabbed Trip's phone out of his hand. "Why don't you let me take this for a while?"

"The Senator isn't going to like not being able to reach him," Ben said coolly.

"And I'm not letting him out of my sight for at least twenty-four hours, so I can run interference again." Jasmine didn't know what Addison meant by 'again,' but Ben clearly did, as he gave a grim nod.

"I'm not a child, Addison, I don't need a chaperone," Trip protested.

"No, but you do need a friend."

Trip's face softened into a smile. The two cousins were incredibly close, and everyone on the staff knew that getting in between Addison and Trip was a non-starter.

"So now can we start talking strategy?" Gwen chirped.

"What's there to talk about?" Trip asked. "We can't do anything about it."

"There must be something," Gwen countered. "We can't just let this go unaddressed."

"We absolutely can," Ben said. "The people of the commonwealth of Pennsylvania didn't vote for John David Ashworth III to represent them in the Senate, they elected Jack Ashworth. The public isn't owed any information about Trip's private life."

"And that's a fine quote for the press release we're going to be forced to issue, but it's not going to do a damn thing to stem the tide on socials, and you know that," Gwen bit back.

"Some other sound will trend on TikTok eventually," Trip said, his eyes glued to his coffee cup.

"But then the album is going to come out. Or if she decides to release it as a single and this starts to get radio airplay, we're looking at a few months—at least—of your relationship with Mariana staying front and center on the gossip sites."

"Not like that's anything new," Trip muttered under his breath. For a second, Jasmine really did feel bad for him. Even though he sometimes seemed to court the attention, it must suck to have your dating life constantly examined by people who don't actually know you.

"Listen," Trip continued. "Isn't it better to just like, let her have her truth? The press release about my private life being private, fine, whatever. I think my entire life is documented in press releases, I'm pretty sure there was one announcing I was fucking potty trained." Jasmine had to stifle a giggle as he continued. "But anything else coming from me is going to sound like I'm calling her out as a liar, and that'll be even worse with her crazy fucking fandom."

Gwen's face grew tight when he said the word *liar*, and she hesitated, choosing her words carefully. "Look, this is uncomfortable, but I have to ask the question before we proceed—"

"I'm certain you don't, Gwendolyn," Ben said warningly.

"I can't protect him if I don't have the truth, Benjamin," she shot back, before taking a deep breath. "Trip, did you cheat on Mariana with Teresa Kensington?"

"Absolutely not," Trip replied instantly, and Addison nodded emphatically beside him. "Not with anyone else, either, for the record, but no, definitely not with Tess."

"So, the photos were..."

"Taken out of context."

Jasmine had seen the photos. They'd popped up on a couple Beltway gossip blogs and got picked up by Drudge Report. The ones that showed Trip and Tess drunkenly stumbling into his townhouse, and Tess leaving again the next morning in very much the same clothing that she'd worn the night before. News of Trip and Mariana's breakup started to circulate just days later, and obviously Mariana had believed whatever 'context' those gossip pages wanted her to have.

"Can we just get Tess to come out and say nothing happened?" Gwen asked.

But both Trip and Addison shook their heads. "Not gonna happen. I decided a long time ago, this office doesn't get to ask my friends to do shit," Trip said. "It's not their fault I'm who I am—I won't have them offered up for media scrutiny."

"But with her father, Tess understands..."

"Senator Kensington isn't an Ashworth. You know it's not like this for anyone else. And I'm not going to ask her to open herself up to even more speculation than she already gets."

"I just thought someone who's been friends with you for so long would want—" Gwen started, but Trip cut her off again.

"All the more reason for me to say hell no. I'm not jeopardizing a decades-long friendship for some momentary mediocre pop music crisis."

"To be fair, it's not *not* a bop," Addison said, a smirk on her face. Trip shot her a faux murderous look before chuckling.

"I really wish you two would take this more seriously," Gwen huffed at the pair of them.

"How can they, Gwen? This whole thing is patently absurd!" Ben cried.

"And if you think it won't matter to voters, you aren't a very capable politician."

"I'm not a politician. I'm a policy wonk."

"And that's why Jasmine and I are here." Gwen gestured to Jasmine sitting at her right. "Because if the last three election cycles have taught us nothing else, it's that people don't vote for policy, they vote for personality. Especially in statewide or national campaigns," she emphasized. "And Trip is a part of the Senator's brand, whether you all want to acknowledge that or not."

Ben closed his eyes and sighed, pinching the bridge of his nose as he always did when he was stressed. "Since addressing this directly seems to be out, what are our options?"

"I repeat, do nothing," Trip said defiantly.

"I'm afraid your father isn't going to accept that answer, son," Ben said with a grimace. Trip fell back in his chair with a sigh, seemingly conceding that Ben was correct.

"Jasmine, what did you just write?" Gwen asked, peering over Jasmine's shoulder at her notes on her tablet.

Jasmine looked up and met Trip's eyes. His gaze sharpened slightly, as if he'd just registered her presence. They'd spoken—maybe—a handful of times. She got the distinct impression Trip didn't care much about connecting with his father's congressional staff, despite the level of involvement they had in his day-to-day life. Except she spent hours each week monitoring media mentions of the whole Ashworth family. So, she felt a weird sense of intimacy, even though she was almost a stranger to him. She knew his patterns better than he knew her name.

"Oh, um." She glanced down at her tablet. "It just says 'pivot the narrative,' that's all."

"What do you mean?" Ben asked.

Jasmine fidgeted with her stylus. Ben's gaze was steady on her, waiting. "It might not work, it may be too simple, but instead of addressing this directly, maybe we just—Look, the story is always about Trip's romantic relationships, right? Because that's the most public-facing part of his life, when people see him out and about with women."

"I'm right here," Trip grumbled from the end of the table. "You can talk *to* me, not *around* me."

Heat flooded her face as she looked up at him. "Sorry. But what I'm getting at is that we should think about a media push that highlights something other than your dating life. Like the fundraising you do for cancer charities, or some kind of policy initiative that your dad backs that you could get behind. Start to paint you in a more serious light."

"Ooh, that's good," Gwen said. "Not a direct response, just shifting the conversation beyond the playboy image, to show that he's more than just a vapid pretty face."

"I graduated *summa cum laude* from Princeton and was recently named editor-in-chief of the *Georgetown Law Journal*. Do people really think I'm vapid?" Trip asked, shaking his head.

"I don't think those credentials mean much to the crowd reading *Seventeen*," Addison laughed.

"*Teen Vogue* might be a good place to start, though," Jasmine offered. "They've gotten into a lot more serious journalism over the last several years. From there, we can probably pitch an exclusive profile to a print publication like the *Atlantic*."

"And this isn't all just a little bit transparently in service of a presidential campaign that hasn't been formally announced yet?" Trip said.

Jasmine's jaw tightened. Why did he act like every media strategy move was some kind of deception? His dad had been in Congress since before he was born, he had to understand the game, the balance they needed to strike between authentic and aspirational.

"Any move this office makes for the next six months is going to be seen that way, so we might as well give it a try," Ben said. It was exactly what Jasmine was hoping he'd say.

"What's the angle we're pushing then?" Gwen asked.

"Not the cancer thing," Addison said quickly. "Sorry, guys, that's personal." Trip nodded beside her.

"Environmental anything looks like it's a direct shot at Martinez, and we can't compete, record-wise, so we can't even attempt to engage on green energy," Ben said.

Jasmine looked directly at Trip. "What matters to you, Trip? It'll be best if it's something you're authentically passionate about."

He furrowed his brow at her, clearly not expecting anyone, least of all a junior communications staffer, to ask him that kind of question. But his expression softened into something thoughtful, before looking like wasn't sure if he should say what he was actually thinking. "I don't really know if it's a good—I mean I have an idea, but—"

"Why don't you sit with Jasmine and go through the policy books until we hit on something you can champion?" Gwen cut him off firmly. Trip's expression flattened—the first spark of interest he'd shown all morning, snuffed out. Jasmine opened her mouth to protest—educating Trip on his own father's policy positions wasn't her job—but Gwen's look stopped her cold.

"I don't think I need someone to..." Trip tried to interject, but he too was silenced with a look from Gwen. "Fine," he sighed, his face slipping into a scowl once more.

"And we need to think about your overall image," Gwen continued.

"What, 'hyper privileged white frat boy' doesn't do it?" Addison joked.

"I was never in a frat, thank you very much," Trip said with a roll of his eyes. "They're not really a thing at Princeton, plus Dad thought being in something 'exclusive' was bad for the tiny bit of populist clout he could possibly claim as a child of the second most famous political dynasty in the country."

"Don't you both belong to Ivy Club?" Addison snorted, citing the most exclusive and prestigious of the famed Princeton 'eating clubs.'"

"Yeah, but no one outside of Princeton actually knows what that means."

"Then my sentiment stands," Addison said, sticking her tongue out at him.

"I think what Gwendolyn is getting at is that it would be better for you to not be photographed with any more pop stars or other assorted Hollywood types," Ben said, giving Trip a pointed look.

"Who makes the cut for 'staff approved social contacts,' then?" Trip asked.

"Well, classes start in like two weeks, right? So, you'll be back in D.C. for the most part?" Gwen asked.

"Already am. Law Journal stuff started up again mid last week, I don't expect I'll be out of the city much at all this fall."

"Then we need you to start being seen with Hill staffers—policy wonks. Make it look like you actually care about the work."

"I live with a Hill staffer," Trip said, jerking a thumb at Addison beside him. "That doesn't seem to have helped."

"Maybe find someone you aren't related to?" Ben suggested. "Or, you know, don't have the net worth of a small European principality."

"Oh, Jasmine!" Gwen said, looking over at her. "Why don't you introduce Trip to some of your friends? Getting him seen at Union Pub with a bunch of anonymous, normal young Congressional employees would be a good look."

"Are you saying I'm not normal?" Addison asked, full of mock offense.

"At least she got that part right," Trip cracked while Addison swatted his shoulder.

Through their banter, Jasmine just stared at Gwen. How had this gone from her merely suggesting a change in strategy to somehow being single-handedly responsible for rehabbing Trip Ashworth's image? What would her mother have to say about this, that she was wasting her prestigious—not to mention expensive—Georgetown education on something that Mary Lewis would summarily dismiss as "media nonsense"?

It probably didn't say anything good about Jasmine's relationship with her mom that her probable disapproval made the whole project more appealing.

Trip caught her eye and smirked. "Guess we're going to get to know each other a little bit better, then."

"Looks like it," Jasmine said with a weak smile.

"Just promise me there won't be any wardrobe consultation," he quipped. "I know how you media staffers operate. I'm not giving up my hoodies."

Jasmine's smile faded. "Believe me, I'm not concerned about what you do or don't wear."

Trip raised an eyebrow, and Jasmine felt a rush of heat bloom across her cheeks. She silently cursed herself for saying anything with even a hint of suggestiveness. The thought of Trip Ashworth wearing nothing had *never* crossed her mind. Trip seemed like the type that, if you gave him an inch, he'd take a mile—and Jasmine hated giving up any ground at all.

Addison looked back and forth between Jasmine and Trip, trying to get a read on the vibe. She obviously knew Trip better than anyone, and she'd gotten to know Jasmine well, though they didn't hang out much outside the office—not that Jasmine had much of a life outside of work to speak of over the last few months, anyway. The look on her face didn't give Jasmine a warm and fuzzy feeling about this plan being successful.

"Okay, great, let's work on getting this mapped out on a calendar," Gwen said briskly, and they snapped back into business mode.

They took a break a little after nine-thirty, and Jasmine made another pot of coffee while waiting for the Senator to arrive. Trip's eyes were on her back, intense enough to practically feel his stare penetrate her shoulder blades. She knew he wasn't thrilled about being stuck with a stranger, but she wasn't exactly eager either—so she wasn't in the mood to stroke his ego and lie about the whole arrangement.

She was filling her mug when the chatter in the room fell silent. The Senator had entered the room. His imposing voice rang out across the wood-paneled room.

"What kind of fucking mess has my son gotten us into now?"

Chapter Three

"I can't believe you let this happen, Trip! I told you when you got involved with that singer that it was a terrible idea. It was fucking foolish to date someone in the public eye again when you keep insisting that you want your personal life out of the press. But you just *had* to ignore me, like some kind of petulant child. I swear to Christ, the minute I tell you *not* to do something, it makes you ten times more likely to go ahead and do it!"

"So does that make this your fault, then?" Trip shot back, his eyes ablaze with anger.

"John David..." His voice held a clear warning, but Trip waved him off.

"Sir, I think we should focus on the path going forward," Gwen interjected. "Thanks to Jasmine here from the communications team, I think we've got a solid plan to change the conversation the media is having around Trip."

"Should there even be a conversation around Trip?" Ben asked.

Gwen looked affronted. "Benjamin, I thought we were in agreement that..."

"Well, the Senator has a point. Trip's been public about wanting to keep his private life private. Are we working against that by going along with your charm offensive?" Jasmine watched Ben as he spoke. He wasn't grandstanding—his tone was too even, too deliberate. He was offering Trip an exit.

"It's the exact opposite of a charm offensive, Ben, it's about giving Trip more substance," Gwen said. "And Trip agrees, don't you, dear?"

Trip just sat there fuming, arms crossed tightly across his chest. Addison spoke up for him. "Yes, Gwen, you're correct, that *is* what we discussed," she said, nudging Trip sharply.

He glared at Addison for a second. "Yeah, the plan makes sense to me."

"Shall I go on, then?" Gwen asked. Ben grunted in vague agreement. "We're not going to react in the immediate aftermath, other than a boilerplate press release about how we're not going to comment. Then, Trip's going to work with my communications staff"—pointing to Jasmine—"to identify a policy priority he's passionate about and aim to get a feature interview before the midterms with a youth-centered publication. Even though the Senator's not up for reelection this cycle, we can get a little goodwill from the party for it. And then we use that energy to pitch a longer-form piece about Trip's upcoming graduation from law school and defining the next generation of the Ashworth legacy over the winter."

"I already said if that's the angle we're taking, it'll be me and Addison," Trip said. "She's just as much a part of it as I am, probably even more since she actually does the work."

Gwen skated over it for now. "We've got time to work out the specifics. But basically, we want to give them something to talk about that *isn't* about his relationship status and bone structure—though the latter is lovely, dear."

"In the lead up to the announcement, that makes sense," Jack agreed. "But what are we doing in the meantime? I've previously suggested locking him in the brownstone until he can learn not to be a distraction, but somehow that doesn't go over well."

Jasmine nearly winced, but she smoothed it quickly, hopefully before anyone else noticed.

"That's also where Jasmine comes in," Gwen said. "We're going to have her introduce him around the Hill, have Trip make friends with some of the staffers. When he's seen out, it'll be with a different sort of crowd."

"And the situation with Tess?" Jack asked, casting his glance between Trip and Addison.

"It's handled, Dad. I won't let them ask her to say anything."

Jack gave a curt nod. Jasmine bit back the questions forming in her mind—she had no idea what was actually going on with Tess, but she'd learned not to ask. If they wanted her to know, they'd tell her.

Jack turned to Jasmine. "So, you've been tapped to babysit the pampered prince here, then? Has Benjamin offered you hazard pay?"

Behind the Senator, Ben's jaw visibly tightened, but he stayed silent.

"Oh, I'm happy to do it, sir," she said with a smile that she hoped didn't seem too fake. Trip might have been difficult since day one, but watching his father talk about him like this—right in front of him—didn't sit right with her. She kept her mouth shut. Whatever she said would only make it worse for him.

"I see you're an actress like your boss," Jack deadpanned. "Well, all the same, we appreciate you taking on this little side project to rehabilitate my son's unfortunate image." He turned to Trip. "Don't sleep with this one, please? I've barely recovered from having to bury the thing between you and that congressional page."

"That was seven years ago, Dad," Trip protested. "Believe me, I am not interested in revisiting that particular bit of your wrath."

Heat prickled at the back of Jasmine's neck. She turned her attention back to her tablet.

"It's nothing like that, Senator," Gwen assured him. "Jasmine is someone of the highest integrity, I made sure of that when I did her backgrounding. She understands that working for the Ashworth family requires a different level of discretion and decorum than the average D.C. job."

Gwen's comments, despite sounding like praise, troubled Jasmine. It was her job to keep Trip from hitting on *her*? That seemed wildly regressive, especially for someone like Gwen who had all the makings of a female power player. But Jasmine was learning the Hill wasn't as progressive as she had hoped it might be. Old patterns of power apparently die hard.

"Not to mention Jasmine's got a boyfriend," Addison pointed out. "Which the rest of you would know if you spent five seconds talking to anyone about anything other than optics."

"Fine, then, move this forward," Jack agreed. "But Trip, I'm warning you. You're on a short leash. One more scandal, and we're going to revisit you heading to Italy for a while after graduation."

"Because banishing me to Europe with Mom's family is a good look for a presidential campaign?"

"It's a better look than you being a fixture on *Drudge Report*," Jack countered, before turning to Ben. "Can you send me everything we've got on the Ninth Circuit nominee? I know we've got a couple more weeks until we're back in session, but I need time to craft some substantive questions—something that puts daylight between me and the current administration on something progressive."

And just like that, he'd moved on. Trip—dealt with. Next item. Jasmine blinked, still catching up. She glanced at Trip, his expression was stony, unreadable. Clearly this wasn't a new experience for him—no matter what Jasmine thought.

After the Senator and Ben walked out, talking rapidly in hushed tones, Gwen gave Jasmine a nod—the meeting was over. Jasmine flipped the cover over on her tablet and began to pack up. She'd work from home for the rest of the day, combing through the policy books to pull some options for Trip, cross-referencing which other members were already co-sponsoring related bills in order to narrow down who should be on the list of staffers for Trip to connect with—and most importantly, not contradict.

Danny was going to hate her being glued to her laptop for the rest of the day, but it just was what it was. At least she wouldn't be at the office, and she could probably head over to the pizza shop to grab dinner and see him between delivery runs.

Jasmine collected everyone's mugs and placing them on a tray to take them down the hall to the kitchenette. She needed to get them washed before she headed out. Gwen and Ben were holed up in their respective offices, and Addison and Trip were talking quietly at the end of the table. Jasmine tried to slip out as inconspicuously as possible.

As she pushed up the sleeves of her sweater to wash the mugs, she heard someone moving around behind her. She turned, surprised to see Trip toss his flannel over one of the chairs and head to the sink.

"Oh, I've got these, you don't need to..." she started, but Trip had already turned on the water and grabbed the first mug off the tray.

"It's not in your job description to do my dishes," he said, reaching for the sponge and soap.

"It's in my job description to do whatever Gwen asks me to do."

"And that's how you get stuck having to deal with me and my bullshit," he sighed. Without looking her way, he handed her a navy-blue mug, and she ripped off a paper towel to dry it.

"It's not a big deal." She tried to sound nonchalant, as if image doctoring her boss's son was obviously a part of what she signed up for.

"I saw your face in there, I know you're not thrilled about this. And for what it's worth, I'm sorry."

"I really don't mind…"

"You don't have to lie to me, save that for the Ben and Gwen show."

A tug of sympathy for him was bubbling up again. "I'm not lying, I swear. It's a *little* awkward since we don't know each other—like at all—and now I'm supposed to be your Hill tour guide or whatever. That's the job sometimes."

Trip snorted out a laugh. "Which is hysterical, considering I literally used to ride up and down the halls of the Capitol on a Razor scooter. But I guess my steadfast refusal to engage on anything related to my dad's career since prep school makes people forget I grew up here."

"I didn't mean to imply—" Jasmine started, but he cut her off.

"Not your fault Gwen seems to think I need someone new to D.C. to show me the ropes."

"Hey, I'm not new to D.C."

"Oh, yeah, you went to Georgetown, right?"

Jasmine was surprised he remembered, given that they'd only had a very brief conversation about it one day when he noticed the Georgetown mug holding her pens on her desk. "Well, yeah, but I also grew up here. I've lived in the District my entire life."

"Really? I feel like I so rarely meet anyone who's actually from D.C. who wants to work for Congress."

"Tons of them do," she said icily. "Like every single person who cleans the buildings or staffs the cafeteria."

Trip had the decency to look embarrassed. "Okay, you're right, sorry. I just meant—"

"You meant the people that matter," she bristled. Typical for someone like Trip not to notice or care about the workers that hovered around his bubble of privilege.

And typical of Jasmine to judge him for it and not be able to keep her mouth shut.

"Hey, that's not fair."

She sighed. "Look, I get it. It's just—the people who are most overlooked in this building? They tend to look like me."

Jasmine didn't often bring up her biracial background, preferring it to be a footnote rather than her whole identity, even if her hair usually gave her away in a way her tawny complexion didn't. But she wanted to make sure Trip knew exactly why his comment got her back up, even if it made him uncomfortable.

Maybe especially if it did.

Trip nodded. "Yeah, I get that." He fell silent as he finished washing the last mug. Jasmine wordlessly dried it and placed it back on the tray to take them back into the office.

As she walked out of the kitchenette, she looked back at Trip, leaning heavily against the sink with his head bowed, seemingly letting the weight of the morning finally catch up with him. "Thanks, though, for helping with these," she offered.

Trip didn't turn around, just gave a slight wave of acknowledgement, and Jasmine made her way back down the hall to Senator Ashworth's office suite.

Addison was sitting in the waiting area, scrolling through Trip's iPhone. "Jesus, people say some nasty shit online, huh?" Addison said as Jasmine walked back in.

"Is that why you took his phone?"

"Part of it," Addison nodded. "But it's less the anonymous online hate and more screening the texts and calls he's going to get from everyone and their brother that he's ever met looking to get a comment from him they can leak to a gossip site."

"Seriously?"

"Jazz, you have no idea. It's ridiculous. There's, like, five people I'm willing to let him talk to right now. He's just not careful enough when he's like this."

"Like what?"

"Sick as fuck of being Trip Ashworth."

Jasmine had so many more questions, but Trip walked back in, his flannel thrown back on and his car keys in his hand. "You ready, Addie?"

She nodded, holding up his phone. "I ordered in Shake Shack from Door Dash. It should get there just after we do."

"Great, I give you my phone and you use it to spend my money," he joked.

"You had to expect that," Addison cracked as she got to her feet.

"Jasmine, I guess I'll text you so we can set up a time to start *Operation Make Me Not Look Like a Douche*. Addie has your number?"

Jasmine nodded.

"Perfect. Then I'll talk to you later." He turned and left before she could think of a response.

"Sorry, this was a lot for him," Addison said apologetically.

"It's okay, really," Jasmine assured her. "I'm going to pull together some high-level summaries from the policy books today, so we'll get started later this week when things aren't... quite as intense."

"Sounds like a plan. Text me your coffee order for the morning?"

"You don't have to..." Jasmine began.

"I know," Addison smiled. "Text me your order." She ducked out and followed Trip down the hall.

Chapter Four

Once the Ashworth cousins had departed, Jasmine double-checked with Gwen that she was good to go, and shouldered her bag and headed down to Union Station to catch the Metro home now that it was running. She never wasted cash on an Uber unless absolutely necessary. On the way, she noticed a text she'd missed from Danny. He'd gotten called into work early to cover the lunch rush. Delivering pizzas wasn't his dream job, but it kept money coming in, supplementing his slow trickle of freelance writing gigs, and gave him time for his novel—good enough for now. Plus, working for his best friend's family shop meant plenty of time goofing off with Eddie between runs. She was relieved he wouldn't be around to give her shit for working all afternoon. She texted him back, letting him know she'd come in to say hi and grab dinner at some point.

Once she was back in the apartment, she got to work. What Gwen and Benjamin called the "policy books" were actually huge folders on their shared server, filled with PDFs of bills, supporting documents, and memos various legislative aides and committee staff had written to convince the Senator to take one position or another. There were also reams and reams of polling information, trying to ascertain how certain policy positions would go down in various zip codes across Pennsylvania.

If Jasmine had criticism of her boss, it was that Gwen relied way too much on polling data. Her first gig in politics after abandoning her barely-there acting career had been for a House member, where every decision was about surviving the next election. Senators were different—especially Senator Ashworth. He'd been re-elected with more than seventy percent of the vote two years ago, and hadn't faced a legitimate challenge to his seat in years. He could probably coast on name recognition alone. Jasmine knew he had room to take bold stances, to actually push ideas instead of tiptoeing around public opinion. But no one was ever going to ask her what she thought. So, putting things onto Trip's priority plate for this "project" was the smartest way to nudge an edgier position forward.

Jasmine began pulling key phrases into a new document to give Trip a high-level overview of each of the policy priorities. She got so engrossed in what she was doing, she didn't notice that she'd skipped lunch until it was four in the afternoon and her stomach growled in protest at being fed nothing but coffee and a granola bar she'd grabbed out of her desk drawer while waiting for Senator Ashworth. Jasmine slipped her laptop and tablet into her bag and headed over to the pizza place to grab an early dinner and get some work done there.

Potomac House of Pizza was an Adams Morgan institution—Eddie's family had been running it for three generations. Mac House was where she and Danny had met, when Jasmine was a junior at Georgetown showing her transfer roommate the quirkier side of D.C. They'd stumbled into open mic, and found Danny playing and singing. Jasmine had been instantly smitten by the attractively disheveled redhead—white boys with guitars always her weakness. She scrawled her Snapchat handle on a napkin to hand to him before slipping out into the night without exchanging a word. He'd added her that same night, and they'd been together ever since.

Jasmine waved hello to Eddie behind the counter as she walked in, sliding into her usual booth in the far back corner. Within minutes, Eddie appeared at the table with her two slice and salad combo. "Thanks," she said with a smile. "Is our boy out on a run?"

Eddie nodded. "Just one, though. He should be back soon before the rush picks up."

"Tell him I'm here when he gets back?"

Eddie nodded again as the front doorbell jingled with another customer and retreated back behind the counter.

Jasmine ate without taking her eyes off her laptop screen as she continued to work. She abandoned policy analysis to Google Trip to see if she could find anything that would give her any insight. Unfortunately, for as much as was written about Trip, almost none of it came from him. Speculation on his love life abounded, but very little about who he was beyond being rich and attractive.

She was reading an *US Weekly* article from three years ago entitled "They Have Our Vote: Next Gen Political Heartthrobs" and willing her eyes not to cross at both the terrible writing and ridiculous content when Danny dropped down into the booth next to her.

"Political heartthrobs? Should I be worried?" he joked as he pressed a kiss to her temple.

"Please," Jasmine snorted. "I'd be a terrible political spouse, I'm allergic to the 'shut up and smile' routine."

"So, this whole Mariana DaSilva situation... is it as bad as it looks?" He plucked a chunk of chicken off of Jasmine's pesto slice and popped it in his mouth.

"The TikTok has over nine million views, so it's worse, actually."

"I mean, to be honest, the guy always seemed like a dick. I'm not sure anyone is actually surprised he's also a cheater."

Jasmine picked at the crust on her pizza. She'd believed Trip's denial earlier that day—not that she should be repeating anything from that meeting to Danny. "Who ever really knows what happens in a relationship except the people in it?" she said. "And it's not like the truth really matters anyway. We're going into full image rehab mode either way, and guess who's leading the charge?"

"How'd you get stuck with him? Rite of passage?"

"Nah, they just want someone who speaks Gen Z helping him figure this out. Honestly, the strategy was kinda my idea in the first place, so it makes sense that I need to make it happen."

What Jasmine wasn't saying was that as the day had worn on, she'd actually started to get excited about the prospect of leveraging Trip to advance progressive policy. If she could pull this off, it would prove she was good for a lot more than drafting press releases, and maybe convince Gwen to give her more of her own portfolio, which would go a long way towards securing a campaign role.

She pursed her lips when she remembered the other half of this assignment, though. "I wish I'd realized it would mean I'd also have to hang out with the guy socially, too."

"Wait, what?"

"To make him look more, I don't know, substantial? They want him hanging out with Hill types," she parroted from Ben's description earlier. "Gwen asked me to introduce him to some Congressional staffers I know, the more straightlaced and serious, the better."

"Dude's twenty-five, he can't find his own friends?"

"Apparently the ones he finds aren't good for business." She gestured to one of the photos on her laptop screen. "Like this guy. He went to Princeton with Trip. That's the son of Congressman Riviere from California, and he's got an even worse reputation than Trip when it comes to sleeping with beautiful women. Though he also comes with a nice little cocaine habit that their staff have to manage."

"Hard to believe our political class produces such illustrious offspring," Danny said, his voice thick with sarcasm. He glanced back at Jasmine's screen, where the article she was reading contained a photo of Trip in his impossibly tight Princeton crew uniform that showed off every inch of his muscled frame. "Of course he rowed crew. And what the hell kind of a name is that, anyway? Trip?"

"Like short for triple," Jasmine explained. "He's John David Ashworth the Third."

"Cuz that doesn't sound like the name of a natural-born douche, he decides to make it worse by going by 'Trip'," Danny scoffed.

"I mean, his grandfather was John, his dad goes by Jack, you're sort of out of other nicknames at that point."

"Isn't JD like, right there?"

"Except one of his cousins already goes by JD. And *his* full first name is Jedidiah, so I think he automatically gets nickname preferences, who wants to be called that?"

"Because that's what you should be focused on, learning the family's nicknames," Danny said with a roll of his eyes. Jasmine gritted her teeth, knowing exactly what was coming. It was the same debate they'd been having for a year now. "I still don't understand the appeal of all this for you. You could be working for an NGO, making a real difference, not sucking up to some pampered political prince." Jasmine nearly grimaced at Danny's description, remembering how uncomfortable she'd felt when the Senator described Trip almost the exact same way.

"I'm not sucking up to Trip, I'm doing my job so I can make a good impression on the Senator. We've been over this a million times. A recommendation from Senator Ashworth will go a long way to getting me into any law school I want." Law school had been the plan for years, one of the few paths Jasmine's mom actually approved for her daughter. But when she'd started the application process during fall of her senior year, she just couldn't get excited enough about it to actually follow through. So, she'd made a deal with both her mom and Danny: she'd work on the Hill for a year, get some real-world experience, and try to parlay that into acceptance to a top tier law school.

"And that will hopefully finally get us the hell out of D.C."

Jasmine just nodded with a tight smile, unsure as usual about how to broach the subject that she might not be quite as ready to bail on the city as he was. She was saved from having to decide whether she should do it right now when Eddie came out from the kitchen. "Dan! Got four orders to go out."

"That's my cue," Danny said, rising to his feet. "You sticking around for a bit?"

Jasmine shook her head. "I think I'm going to head to bed early tonight. I need to do something to make it through this week."

Danny leaned in and kissed her quickly. "Don't work too hard, he's not worth it. Hopefully I'll make it home before you're asleep tonight." She pushed his unruly red hair back off his forehead and out of his eyes. There was something she loved about that, setting him just a bit more right.

Jasmine returned to her article before finishing her pizza and packing up. She waved goodbye to Eddie on her way out and walked back to the Metro stop. When she checked her phone before the train pulled up, there was a text from an unknown number.

Hey, this is Addison on Trip's phone. Here's his number for when I give him back phone custody tomorrow morning.

She tapped on the contact to save it, calling him 'John' to keep things discreet and slipped her phone back into her pocket as the train arrived. She sighed as she climbed aboard the train to head home, the day finally catching up with her. She was exhausted.

She had a feeling she should probably get used to it, because managing Trip Ashworth's reputation was already promising to be a full-time job.

Chapter Five

"It's only been four days, Gwen, we need to give it time to blow over," Jasmine said, attempting to soothe her boss's rapidly fraying nerves.

"The video is up to seventeen million views," Gwen said, frantically pacing the floor.

"Which is only like seven million after the first day!" Jasmine said brightly.

"So, we're still averaging well over a million a day. And the sound's been used more than half a million times!"

Jasmine had no response for that one.

"Benjamin is absolutely apoplectic about it," Gwen continued. "I thought I was going to have to talk him down from the ledge this morning, when—"

Ben hadn't been in the office at all today. He had taken a six a.m. flight to Pittsburgh with the Senator for a constituent event. So, the only way she'd seen Ben that morning was...

Jasmine looked down at her tablet quickly.

Gwen was saved from making an awkward explanation when Addison walked in, balancing a tray of drinks and scrolling her phone.

"Trip's on his way up—just got out of a law journal meeting." She passed Jasmine her iced dirty chai, gave Gwen her cappuccino with two extra shots, then took her own iced mocha and dropped onto the couch next to Jasmine.

"Do we have a plan for the weekend yet? I think everyone's expecting him to lay low. It would make a statement that he's unbothered if he's seen out and about, but it has to be with an anonymous crowd," Gwen said. "And especially not with Tess."

"Tess's classes are about to start up again, so she'll be in Cambridge until early October at least," Addison confirmed without looking up from her phone.

"Good," Gwen nodded.

"Good that I'm basically banned from seeing one of our closest friends?" Trip said from the doorway. "We seem to have different definitions of 'good.'" He grabbed the last cup from the drink tray and retreated to the doorway, seeming to want to be ready to cut and run at a moment's notice.

"I don't mean it like that, dear," Gwen said. "I just think all of you could use a break from that particular bit of speculation."

Trip let out a low, disgruntled sound as Addison shot him a pointed look. Jasmine stifled a sigh—she was forever left trying to decode the cousins' wordless conversations.

"So anyway, back to the task at hand. What's the plan for the weekend?" Gwen asked.

"I was thinking Union Pub for Happy Hour Friday after work," Addison put in. "A guy Jasmine and I are friendly with from Senator Timlin's office is planning to go with his boyfriend."

"Timlin's good optics with the Colorado thing, we'll need to shore up support in the west before the primaries. And he's gay?"

"Gwen!" Jasmine cried. "Alex is a real person, not a photo op. Can we not?"

"Sorry!" Gwen exclaimed. "But yes, that sounds good. What about Saturday night?"

"Really? I can't just stay home?" Trip protested.

Gwen ignored him. "Doesn't need to be a bar or club, probably better if it's not."

"No clubs," Addison said. "Last time I went to a club with this jackass, some girl threw a drink on me because she thought he blew her off to go home with me."

"I was," Trip smirked.

"Because I'm cursed with the world's worst roommate. I'm not getting my new boots ruined by some crazed Mariana DaSilva fan, emboldened by a dark club and too many vodka sodas."

"My boyfriend is playing a set at the pizza place he works at in Adams Morgan," Jasmine offered. "It'll wrap up by eleven—we can call it an early night."

Trip looked at her for the first time since he arrived. "Your boyfriend works at a pizza shop?"

Jasmine didn't love the vaguely dismissive edge in his voice. "He's a freelance writer," she said, a little defensive. "Delivers pizzas for a friend's family business on the side." The fact that the delivery job brought in more money than Danny's writing wasn't something she felt compelled to share.

"Whatever, fine," Trip said. "Gwen, do you need to vet my order in advance? Is Hawaiian going to start some kind of pineapple-on-pizza controversy in the Scranton polling?"

"I know you're being sarcastic, which I don't appreciate," Gwen said, "but since you asked... if you could be photographed with a bottle of Yuengling, it wouldn't be the worst decision you could make."

"Pennsylvania beer, got it. Any other instructions?"

"Yeah, can you actually *look* like you enjoy it? Not like you're being marched to the gulag? The only thing that will look worse than you hiding is you looking miserable."

"We're not all actors, Gwen."

"I don't know—enough girls seem to buy your 'nice guy' act. At least long enough for you to sleep with them," Addison said.

Trip shot her a dirty look but said nothing.

"Are we good here?" Addison asked. "I have about a thousand calls to return about some widow's power getting shut off near State College."

"I've got to go over some new correspondence from the judiciary committee staff," Gwen said. "Jasmine, you and Trip good to start looking at policy points?"

Jasmine nodded. "We'll use the conference room so Addison can take the office."

Trip headed to the same conference room they'd used over the weekend while Jasmine stopped to grab her laptop. He was sitting by the door, scrolling on his phone, looking disinterested.

"Did you get the position summaries I sent on Tuesday?" Jasmine asked.

"Mmhm." He didn't bother to look up from his phone.

"And anything jump out at you?" A hint of annoyance crept into her voice.

"That my father's so-called positions read like they were written by focus group, instead of him?"

Jasmine had privately thought the same thing, but bristled at his dismissal of the policy team like that. "It's important that he be attuned to the perspective of an average Pennsylvania voter—" she began, but as usual, Trip cut her off.

"There's no such thing as an average voter anymore. Everything is so polarized, candidates pander to the extremes to get elected, then feel like they can't compromise without getting crucified on social media. It's why nothing ever gets done."

"That's an awfully cynical view."

"Really? I think it's even more cynical to believe that you need to change with the tides just to stay electable."

"For someone with no interest in politics, you've got a lot of opinions about how to be a politician."

"You're right, I have no interest in politics. But I have plenty of interest in policy—and the distance between the two is truly frightening."

This wasn't at all how Jasmine expected this to go. She'd wanted Trip to read her summaries, pick a cause, and move on—not critique the entirety of the current US political climate.

"I mean, I don't think I'd say any of that in an interview," she said. "Unless your goal is to sound like an asshole."

Trip finally looked up from his phone screen. "Did you just call me an asshole?" he asked, though he seemed bemused rather than angry.

"No—just that you'd look like one if you say that to a reporter. And since it's my job to make you *not* look like an asshole, I'd appreciate you choosing your words a bit more carefully when you're on the record."

"Fair enough." A smile threatened to quirk up the corners of his lips. He set his phone down and leaned back in his chair. "Still, I'm not sure how I'm supposed to be... how did you describe it? 'authentically passionate' about something that's been workshopped and sanitized within an inch of its life."

"It's not sanitized, it's digestible," Jasmine countered. "Some of these bills are so opaque they're not even about the issues anymore, the position papers at least cut through all that."

"Policy is supposed to be nuanced. Reducing it to the length of a social media post is disingenuous, and sometimes even dangerous."

"If you can't communicate your point in a few sentences, you don't actually understand your point."

"Spoken like a true Gen Z media staffer."

Jasmine blew out a frustrated sigh, fingers hovering over the laptop keyboard. "Did you even read the summaries?"

"Of course, I did. But for the record—I didn't need them. I know you all think I'm some kind of idiot, but I'm not completely uninformed."

A heat crept through her face. Her hands hovered over the keys a beat too long as she tried to figure out what to say. "I—I don't think you're an idiot. Just... you don't always seem the most engaged."

"Not being engaged in making my dad look good is different than not being engaged."

"Around here, that's the only engagement we care about."

"Not you," he said instantly.

Her stomach tightened. What the hell did he know about her? "Excuse me?"

"You don't just care about my dad. You care about the issues. It came through in every single one of those summaries you sent me."

"I don't know what you—"

Trip picked up his phone. "Like your healthcare summary. Whatever he believes personally, my dad's never publicly supported a single-payer option. But you wouldn't know that reading this—it's a love letter to Medicare for All." He paused. "Your position is right, by the way. But it's certainly not my dad's public one."

Jasmine stared him down for a moment, unwilling to admit he was right. After a long beat of silence, Trip continued. "Anyway, I'm specializing in criminal law at Georgetown, so criminal justice reform is probably the easiest place for me to land that won't look like I'm straying out of my lane."

"Really? I assumed constitutional law."

"Because Daddy could guarantee me an SJC clerkship?" he said dryly. "Nah, I prefer to do the real work, not just sit around and wait for cases to come to me."

"So what, am I looking at D.C.'s next district attorney?"

"More like the other side. I want to be a public defender. I'm in the criminal defense clinic and the street law program."

"Street law?"

"Teaching about the law to kids who've gotten in trouble, helping them understand their rights within the system."

Jasmine's eyes widened. "How long have you been doing it?"

He shrugged. "Since I was a 1L, why?"

"Why does the office not know about it?"

"Ben does, but I specifically asked him not to say anything. I volunteer under the name David Torelli," he explained, citing his middle and mother's last name. "And most of those kids don't seem to follow *US Weekly* that closely. I'm sure some of them have figured out who I am, but in their world, it's safer to just mind your business."

Jasmine was quietly impressed but tried not to show it. "You know, it'd be a lot easier to manage your image if we knew about the good stuff you're doing."

"Which is why you don't," he said flatly.

"Do you enjoy making my job more difficult?" she asked, her exasperation fully on display.

"I don't particularly enjoy any of this."

"Okay, then," she said, getting back to the task at hand. "Criminal justice reform. Any particular areas you want to focus on?"

"Discretionary sentencing for drug crimes and funding for treatment."

Jasmine winced.

"What?" he said. "It's what I'm passionate about."

"And that makes sense. But every time someone from his camp talks about substance use..."

"It's a reminder that my dad is an alcoholic?"

"Pretty much."

"And he got access to world-class treatment when he needed it. That seems like something we should be championing for everyone—not just those of us with money."

Jasmine closed her eyes. Trip was right, of course, but *right* and *good optics* were rarely one in the same.

"And it's more than just that," Trip went on. "If you knew how much weed I smoked in prep school with zero consequences while there are guys my age doing twenty in prison for it..."

"Yeah, let's not lead with that," Jasmine said, shaking her head. "But if this is definitely what you want to do, I'll run it by the Senator."

"Then what?"

"We find a house member or senator who's vulnerable in the midterms that has this as a policy priority, and we offer you up for a campaign appearance. Get *Teen Vogue* interested from a 'get-out-the-vote' perspective, so it doesn't look like blatant image rehab."

"Even if it is."

"Perception is reality."

"You and I both know that's bullshit."

"And we also both know it doesn't matter that it is."

Trip looked at her intently. She got the impression that his dad's staffers didn't often talk to him like she did. But she had a job to do and wasn't about to let him stop her.

Even if he sort of was the job right now.

"Fine," Trip sighed. "We good here then?"

Jasmine nodded and pushed her chair back. "See you tomorrow? Addie told Alex we'll meet him and Nigel at four-thirty. We're still in recess, so everyone should be able to get out of here by then."

"I've got another editorial board meeting at three, I'll head there after." He collected his phone off the table and left with a wave. Jasmine watched him go and then made her way back to the office she shared with Addison, who was currently typing furiously on her laptop while her speakerphone blared hold music.

"I've been on hold with the power company since our meeting ended," Addison grumbled. "Did it go any better with Trip?"

"Depends on your definition of 'better,' I guess? We narrowed it down to criminal justice reform, specifically on drug treatment vs. incarceration."

"Think Uncle Jack will go for it?"

"Gwen's going to hit the roof about it. She won't want the reminder that..."

"But I mean, it makes sense..."

"That's exactly what I said. I'm willing to go to bat for him on it."

"Good luck," Addison said, as a voice came through the speaker.

"Thank you for calling West Penn Power, how can I help you?"

Jasmine settled down at her desk while Addison turned on her best 'do you have any idea who you've fucked with here' routine for the poor customer service rep on the other end of the line. Jasmine started an email to the legislative aides for both the House and Senate whips, seeing if they could point her towards someone championing criminal justice reform in their districts. She figured someone from the Midwest might be the best bet, maybe Indiana where the opioid epidemic had been particularly hard-hitting, so she fired off a similar message to the Democratic rep from District 7 in Indianapolis. She picked up her coffee, now severely watered down from the melted ice, but the caffeine was a necessity at this point.

Addison hung up with a look of smug satisfaction on her face, having browbeaten the power company into getting the widow's power turned back on. "And that's on constituent services!"

Jasmine laughed. "What time is Ben back from the Pittsburgh event?"

Addison consulted her texts. "Flight touched down about thirty minutes ago, they're on their way back. He's going to want a status update on Trip. Should we order dinner? Probably going to be here awhile."

"Yeah, wanna do Pho 75 tonight? I cannot look at another slice of pizza. Danny's been bringing stuff home from the shop all week and I feel awful wasting it, but I literally can't eat any more cheese."

"I'm excited to finally meet the elusive Danny this weekend and sample this pizza you're always talking about."

Jasmine gave wan smile. She'd been putting this off for months—introducing Danny to her officemates. His filter when it came to politics was nonexistent. But if working with Trip meant socializing with him, she couldn't avoid it anymore. At least at a show, they'd have something to talk about besides work.

"Is the Senator coming back to the office?" Jasmine asked, changing the subject.

"No, *the Missus* is in town tonight, so he's taking her out for dinner. But he'll want an email summary about tomorrow's bills by the time he's home."

The Missus—Addison's derisive nickname for Jack's second wife, Elizabeth. She'd been devoted to her late auntie Chess and had no intentions of replacing her.

"Find out what Ben wants, and I'll order online," Jasmine offered, pulling up the menu on her phone. As she debated between chicken and rare beef, she received both a text and an email.

The text was from Danny.

Danny: What do you want me to bring home for dinner?

Jasmine: Sorry, babe, going to be at the office till late. Sen had an event out of town, need to brief the COS for tomorrow.

Danny: Again?

Jasmine: Literally every night this week. She took a deep breath before replying.

Jasmine: Crisis mode.

Danny's equally fast comeback wasn't any more understanding.

Danny: Is it ever not?

She sighed, left the text unanswered, and swiped over to her email. Trip had sent a message with an attached file.

See attached for my position summary on CJR re: mandatory minimums, discretionary sentencing and court ordered treatment. Fwd to anyone who's thinking about taking you up on the campaign appearance. This is what I'm selling.

He attached a four-page document entitled "Criminal Justice Reforms in Drug Offenses,"

with another three pages of citations. There were lists of bullet points organized under headings like *Efficacy of Drug Court Programs, Financial Implications of Incarceration vs. Treatment*, and *Racial Disparities in Sentencing and Time Served*.

Everything had detailed notes after it, citing the relevant case law that was listed in the reference pages.

Jasmine shook her head as she scrolled through it. The analysis was intricate, thorough—her policy summaries suddenly felt like amateur hour by comparison.

And he'd fired this off in about an hour.

Turns out the whole Princeton thing wasn't some kind of legacy fluke. He really did have the book smarts for an Ivy.

She scrolled back up to the top to start reading in more detail.

At least they'd have something to talk about the next night.

Chapter Six

"And that's when I told them that Timlin wasn't ever going to vote for a green energy package that didn't include wind incentives. We need to stop thinking offshore is the only place you can plant a wind farm!"

Jasmine nodded along, catching maybe half of what Alex was saying about the green energy bill getting batted around the Hill. His back-up glasses—the thick and unfashionable ones he kept in his desk—sat crooked on his nose, and his sandy blond hair was badly in need of a cut. Senator Timlin's reelection was grinding everyone in his office to dust. On top of the sheer volume of work, the Mountain time difference meant Alex probably hadn't seen his bed before two a.m. in weeks.

Addison came up behind where they were standing, a cluster of shot glasses in her hands. "$5 Fireball Fridays!" She held them out to Alex and Jasmine.

Jasmine groaned. Cinnamon whiskey shots were practically religion at Union Pub on Friday nights, but she'd never grown to like the burning amber liquid. Still, she dutifully accepted the glass from Addison and clinked it together with her and Alex's before gulping it down in one go.

"Getting started without me?" Trip's voice rang out behind Jasmine. "Or is this just saving me from myself?"

"Don't worry, dear cousin," Addison said with a smile. "Shots stay on special 'til six, we got plenty of time." She leaned in to hug Trip, who nodded a hello to Jasmine over Addison's shoulder.

"I don't know, I doubt Gwen would approve of shots this evening," he drawled, a smirk on his face.

"Which just means you're even more likely to do it," Addison pointed out.

Trip looked over at Jasmine. "You gonna rat me out to your boss?"

"Of course not. Didn't you hear? I understand *discretion*," she said with a smirk of her own.

"The shade!" Trip laughed. "Is working for Gwen not all it's cracked up to be?"

"Gwen's a great boss," Jasmine demurred. "But she tends to get a little over dramatic sometimes."

"I mean, she was an actress for like ten years before she got into politics," Addison offered.

"And politics is mostly acting anyway," Trip snorted.

Jasmine couldn't bring herself to joke along. Maybe politics was a joke to Trip, but it was her life. She glanced over at Alex, who looked mildly starstruck, so Jasmine had to jump in. "Alex, this is Trip Ashworth, Senator Ashworth's son. Gwen asked me to help him make nice with some Hill staffers as a part of an image rehab campaign."

"After the whole TikTok thing..." Alex said with a sympathetic nod. It had basically been the talk of the younger staffers for the last week, which Jasmine knew because every time she walked into Cups & Co in the office building, the chatter stopped. She'd done the same thing dozens of times—automatically clamming up when the staff of whoever she'd been gossiping about turned the corner. It sucked even more on this side of things.

"Turns out dating someone known to write songs about her exes isn't the best move—who knew?" Trip deadpanned.

"Literally everyone," Addison said. "But again, someone tells you not to, and..."

"It's basically pathological at this point," Trip agreed with a shrug. "But hi, anyway." He extended his hand to Alex to shake, along with his charming megawatt smile.

"Hi," Alex said, looking a little flustered.

"Should I be worried, Alexander?" a distinct British accent asked from a few feet away. Jasmine turned to laugh as Nigel, Alex's boyfriend, approached. "I know this is basically your closeted adolescent fantasy."

Alex groaned, dragging his hand over his face while the other kept a loose grip on his beer.

"I'm sorry, what?" Trip said, clearly amused.

"He kept a copy of *People* magazine with your picture on it under his bed for months, pretending it was because of the *politics* of it all," Nigel continued. "I'm Nigel, by the way, Alex's boyfriend." He looked Trip up and down. "Though *you* can call me anything you like. You're even better looking in person."

"Nigel!" Alex cried. "Could you be slightly less mortifying, please?"

"Hey, I'm flattered, really. And, uh, straight. Like, incredibly straight. Sorry about that," Trip said, and Jasmine stifled a laugh because Trip sounded genuinely apologetic.

"Honey, they'd figure that out the second you tried to dance," Addison said with a light laugh.

"Well, that's reassuring," Nigel said. "To what do we owe the pleasure?"

"Trip's been sentenced to hanging out with us after getting put on blast by Mariana DaSilva," Addison explained before taking a swig from her own bottle of beer. "Gwen thinks we're serious and boring enough to be able to make people forget Trip fucked a pop star."

"Well, I for one would be happy to disabuse Gwen of the notion that we are serious *or* boring," Nigel said. "I'm a research fellow at the IMF, and a proud British national. Play your cards right and we just might be able to cause an *international* incident."

"I think my dad would finally have that coronary he's been threatening for years—not that I'm saying that means it's a no, mind you."

"I think TikTok is high profile enough," Jasmine put in, slightly exasperated already. "And in addition to keeping my job, I desperately need to get my hair done tomorrow, so can we keep the incidents—international or domestic—to a minimum, please? At least for tonight."

Trip held up his hands. "Best behavior, I swear."

"Coming from you? That means very little," Addison snorted.

"Can only work with what I've got," Trip said with a shrug. "So, about those Fireball shots, everyone in?"

This was already promising to be a long night.

After the two shots of Fireball, Jasmine nursed the same pint of cider for over an hour, determined to keep an eye on Trip and make sure there were in fact no incidents. She was unable to shed the slightly anxious edge that Trip was bound to do something Gwen disapproved of, and this time it would be *her* fault.

By six, when happy hour ended, the bar was packed. Several groups had recognized Trip, and a few were not at all subtle about taking photos. When she went to the bar for a second pint, she caught Trip's eye as he was talking animatedly to Nigel about God knows what. He flashed her that same brilliant smile he's turned on Alex earlier, then wove through the crowd to join her.

The bartender set her drink down just as Trip reached the rail. Jasmine was digging through her purse for a ten when Trip said, "Just add that to my tab," pointing to her glass. The bartender nodded and turned to enter it into the POS system.

"You really don't have to do that," Jasmine protested, still looking for cash in her wallet to hand over to Trip.

"Please, you're only out tonight to babysit me, the least I can do is buy your drinks. I wish you'd let me get the last one, too."

Jasmine wanted to protest that she wasn't just 'babysitting' him, but she found she didn't have it in her.

"It's fine."

"It's really not. You look wound tighter than when I got here—that's sort of the exact opposite of the point of happy hour."

"Well, this is still work for me," she pointed out.

Trip's face fell a little, but he recovered quickly. "Hey, if you're still working, let's actually work." He drained his bottle of Gwen-sanctioned Yuengling before motioning to the bartender. "Let me grab another beer, and we can head out to the patio and talk about the position paper I sent you."

It was a little pathetic that talking about Trip's position paper felt more exciting than watching Nigel and Addison dance while Alex frantically tapped at his iPhone, chasing end-of-day updates from the home office in Denver. So, she picked her pint from the bar and took a careful sip, waiting for Trip to collect his beer.

He placed his hand on her back, just below her shoulder blades, to steer her towards the patio. There was nothing remotely romantic about it, but Jasmine still stiffened, her media-trained mind immediately spinning to the worst-case scenario—someone snapping a photo and posting it online. She could already see the headline: *Trip Ashworth Mystery Rebound*. All hell would break loose.

If Trip noticed her reaction, he didn't make mention of it. He simply moved his hand away and reach for the door handle.

They sat opposite each other at a small square table in the corner.

"So," Trip began, regarding her seriously. "What did you think of my summary?"

"I mean, you proved your point—you know what you're talking about. I won't patronize you with my little policy book blurbs anymore."

Trip cracked a slight smile. "I'd be lying if that wasn't a little bit of the point," he admitted. "But I'm also genuinely curious about your opinion. I write for substance over style, and I'm not sure how that plays in primetime."

"So, you're saying I'm all style and no substance?" God, why did everything about this guy just immediately get under her skin?

"No, that's not—Sorry, I didn't mean it like that," Trip said quickly, rubbing the back of his neck. "Addie told me you're really good at, like, message crafting. You cut to the heart of something, you know? Better than Gwen even. And I could use the help."

Jasmine exhaled slowly. Maybe she shouldn't jump to conclusions so quickly. Her mom and Danny liked to point out she had a temper, so she could probably make more of an effort to keep it in check. That didn't mean she wasn't still going to sneak in a little dig.

"No offense, but hearing you describe yourself as substance over style... that's not exactly your public image."

"Believe me, I know. That's why I overcompensate for it with shit like this. It's not exactly easy to get anyone to take you seriously when they see your shirtless photos in *People* like Alex did."

"So, is that what yesterday's little speech about nuance was about? Trying to get *me* to take you seriously?"

"I mean, it's also true."

"Of course it's true, and there isn't a single communications expert in this town who would disagree. But think about where people are getting information—Instagram, TikTok, even on conventional news outlets—it's all soundbites. You've got fifteen seconds to capture someone's attention, maybe thirty if you're really good looking," she said with a wry smile. "If you can't hook them in that time, you've already conceded defeat. There's no space to care about the complexities if you can't get them to listen in the first place."

"So how do you take something as controversial and complex as the drug enforcement policy and distill it down to a fifteen second sales pitch?"

"You already did." She tapped on her phone screen and opened up the draft of Trip's paper she'd been annotating, stopping on a highlighted passage on the second page.

He took the phone and read that section out loud. "The 'war on drugs' isn't actually that. It's a war on those who use drugs. And it's time to fight the real enemy: addiction." He looked up, surprise evident. "Really? You think that's it?"

Jasmine nodded. "It's simple, it's elegant, and it takes conventional wisdom and turns it on its head. That's it—that's your message. And, aside from a few blue dogs who can't abandon their tough-on-crime stance, it plays in every time zone. I can't think of anyone who's life hasn't been impacted in *some* kind of way by substance use."

Jasmine avoided Trip's eyes, sure he'd think it was because of his dad's history. The truth was a lot more complicated than that, but there was no way she could unpack her past in the corner of the pub patio.

"So, if that's the line, how do we move this forward?"

Jasmine gave a slightly conspiratorial grin. "It's no accident Addison wanted us to come out with Alex. Timlin is our target. He's in a tight race, but popular nationally, with that 'future of the party' energy. Even if he loses his Senate seat, he'll stay in politics—probably just announce a run for governor in the next cycle. And anything pro-weed is a hit in Denver."

Trip laughed for a moment, before he grew quiet. "Do you..." he cut off abruptly.

"What?"

"Do you really think this is going to work? That people are going to stop focusing on the whole Mariana thing?"

Jasmine played with her glass. "I mean, my honest answer?"

"Won't do me much good if you lie to me."

"This is going to be news for a while, but whether it's a footnote to a larger narrative or *the* story? I'd say it's a toss-up."

Trip sighed and leaned back in his chair. "That's what I thought." He rubbed the back of his neck, the toll this whole thing was taking on him since their initial crisis summit on Sunday becoming obvious. "I have to hand it to Annie. She knows how to get people talking."

"Annie?"

"Mariana's childhood nickname," Trip explained. "That's how she introduced herself to me when we met, and she said I could keep calling her that. It was nice, kinda felt, I don't know, significant? That she wanted me to do that."

Jasmine hadn't really considered before this moment that the breakup could have been weighing on him as much as the whole post-split song situation.

"I'm sorry it ended," she offered. "Breakups always kinda suck."

"I know everyone thinks it was, like, a publicity thing, but I really did care about her." He toyed with the edge of the label on his beer. "And that's not—I mean, you know that's not really my thing. I don't do a ton of, like, actual relationships."

"I know. It's literally been my job to stalk your mentions on the internet since May."

Trip legitimately winced. "May, huh? Yeah, I should probably apologize for the comment thread from those sorority girls at American during their Senior Week..."

"The one with the, uh, detailed descriptions of your junk? Imagine reading that to Ben and Gwen." She decided to keep it to herself that she'd staged a dramatic reading of thread for her best friend Bailey the last time she got her hair done, and that her curiosity was unnecessarily piqued about just what her boss's son was packing.

"At least it was complimentary. But because of shit like that, I thought maybe me and Annie would actually be able to make it work. She understood a lot of the media bullshit I go through. The faceless internet trolls have treated her pretty shitty over the years, too. But it didn't work out."

Jasmine felt that tug of sympathy rear up again. Trip was emphatic that he hadn't cheated, and it must have been a pretty devastating blow that Mariana didn't believe his denial.

"For what it's worth, I believe you. That you know, you didn't..."

"Thanks," he said with a small, insincere smile. "We should probably—"

"Yeah, Addie is probably wondering where we went."

They picked up their drinks and headed back inside. Addison and Nigel were currently both dancing with Alex, clearly trying to get him to relax. "Jasmine!" Addison cried. "Come dance with us. You're such a good dancer and you never want to come out with us. You need to dance with us tonight."

"She's drunk," Jasmine said with half a laugh.

"Is that true?" Trip asked. "You don't come out a lot?"

"I mean..." Jasmine wasn't quite sure what to say. "Every once and a while, sure. Gets expensive, though, even with happy hour specials." She decided not to mention that Danny didn't love socializing with 'Hill types' after hours—considering it a waste of time when they weren't sticking around beyond a year. She didn't always love it either. As a biracial woman with a single mom and zero clout, she couldn't afford to not be taken seriously.

"Well, all the more reason I'm happy to pick up the tab tonight," he said with a more genuine smile. "You need another, by the way?"

"You're not going to come dance?"

"If you think my image needed rehab before, if anyone puts a clip of me dancing on TikTok, there would be absolutely no coming back from that."

"That bad, huh?"

"Whatever you're imagining, it's worse."

And with their laughter still hanging in the air, he turned to weave through the crowd toward the bar.

Chapter Seven

"Girl, what did I tell you about leaving braids in this long?! These roots are a mess!"

"I know, I'm sorry!" Jasmine cried as Bailey unwound another braid and then picked through the grown-out hair at the top. Jasmine was perfectly capable of taking her braids out herself, but she liked having an excuse to sit in the chair for a couple hours and catch up with Bailey during their marathon styling sessions.

Jasmine had worn long box braids trailing halfway down her back for the past couple years, ever since she got her first internship at the Labor Department her junior year at Georgetown. Her natural curls were beautiful, but high maintenance, and with fourteen-hour workdays, braids were far easier to manage. Sweeping them up into a bun or ponytail also made her less conspicuous. She wasn't trying to hide that she was biracial—her curls clearly inherited from her Black mother—and her protective styles didn't obscure that, either. But one of the earliest lessons that she'd learned in politics was simple: unless you're the one running for office, drawing attention to yourself rarely helped. Braids were the best way to fly under the radar and blend in.

Bailey tried to encourage Jasmine to be more adventurous with her hair, but Bailey was an aspiring fashion designer, working at her mom's salon for now. Her aesthetic could be a lot more creative than Jasmine's life of suit separates and dry cleaning.

"How long was this set in?" Bailey admonished as she clipped out another.

"Um, maybe nine weeks?" Jasmine lied. It was actually way longer than that, but Bailey got on her ass over anything over eight, so she wasn't going to make it worse.

"Jazz..." Bailey said warningly. "There's going to be a bunch of breakage in here—I'm putting you in timeout for a month."

"A month?! You always reinstalled for me after two weeks!"

"And I can't responsibly do that right now. I'm not about to have your plaits snapping off in the shower."

"What if I promise to deep condition it for the next two weeks?"

Bailey snorted. "Girl, you know you won't keep that promise."

Jasmine couldn't argue with that. Her beauty maintenance was the first thing to go out the window whenever she was short on time—which seemed to be always lately.

"Fine," Jasmine grumbled as Bailey worked more detangler down her braids. "Do you have time to do a twist out, so it'll at least be fresh to go out tonight?"

"I got you," Bailey assured her. "So, what's good for tonight?"

"Danny's playing a set at Mac House," Jasmine said. "You coming?"

"Hmm, honey, I would... but you know how I feel about white boys with guitars."

"C'mon, please? I could use the moral support—work people are coming."

"Work people? You couldn't possibly mean that fine ass heir to the throne who you're currently responsible for, now could you?"

"That's exactly who I mean," Jasmine confirmed. "Plus, Addison."

"Why did you invite them to Danny's gig?"

"Because Gwen said Trip needed to get out this weekend, and there's no way I could miss Danny's gig, I'd never hear the end of it."

"Can't Addison handle babysitting duty?"

"She can, but Gwen asked me to take a bit of personal interest in this situation. The Senator needs this whole Trip thing to blow over." The look on Bailey's face said exactly what she thought about Gwen's request.

"I know, Bay, but she's my boss. I'm not exactly in a position to say no if I want to keep this job. Or be considered for a role with, you know..."

"The campaign," Bailey said bluntly.

"Ssshh..."

"No one here cares about me talking about Senator Ashworth running for president," Bailey said, shaking her head while she worked the tail of her comb through another one of Jasmine's braids.

"And you know this isn't about his privacy but *mine*."

"Then maybe you should tell your mama you don't want to go to law school right now, so you don't need to pay no mind to whether a church lady is gonna overhear you at the beauty shop."

"Listen, you know that my mom has certain expectations of me," Jasmine said carefully. "And I'm just not ready to commit to that—not yet. Not when this is the thing I'm passionate about."

"Installing another privileged old white man as president?"

"Getting someone electable on the ballot that I believe can reliably be nudged to the left."

"You really think so?"

"I do. And right now? That feels like the best way I personally have to make a difference."

"Then you do you, girl. But you gotta tell her. And Danny." She didn't respond, so Bailey kept going. "And what's up with Danny's gig tonight? You sound like you'd rather go to the dentist."

"It's not that I don't want to go. He needs me, and the support. Especially this week. He got another batch of form rejections on his novel." She paused a moment, before spilling what was really on her mind. "It's just—I don't even know. It's like I've been watching him play the same covers at gigs at Mac House since we first got together, and that was when we were barely halfway through college. So much has changed since then."

"I mean, his setlist has been updated, right? He's added a lot of Ed Sheeran over the years. I think the red hair makes him think they're long-lost brothers or some shit."

"Ha. It's just like—I don't know, we feel stuck? Like, since I graduated, my job has basically taken over my life. It feels like I'm making real progress in my career, you know? So, to spend Saturday night at Mac House just like we always have? It's a reminder that he's still doing what he's always done. Delivering pizzas, playing guitar, and waiting on me."

"Well, that's kinda the truth, isn't it? I mean, he still thinks the deal is on. One year in this job to secure a great recommendation, and then get the hell out of D.C.?"

"And I haven't decided that isn't the plan yet," Jasmine said defensively. "I just didn't expect that I would get a job with the de facto front runner for the Democratic nomination when I made that deal."

"And you need to tell him that."

"He'll freak out, you know how he gets, after the shit with his mom."

"You knew he had mommy issues when you started dating."

"I know, and it's not—I love him. Which makes it, you know, not the easiest thing to bring up, especially when it might not even matter. If this Trip thing is any indication, a lot of shit can go down between now and the spring that might change the game. I don't want to throw away a good, stable, loving relationship over a huge maybe."

"You might love him, but if you can't even talk to him, how are you going to do life together?"

"We talk!" Jasmine protested. "But this is the kind of thing I need to decide for *me*, you know? I just—I need to sit with it a little longer before I bring him in on this, really know where my head's at and be prepared either way."

"Well, then, you've gotta do what feels right to you," Bailey said, looking unconvinced. "But I hope you do a better job putting on a happy face tonight for your new work friends than you're doing right now."

"They don't know me like you do. We've been friends so long, you can read me like a book."

They had twenty years of history, of running around in Bailey's mom's shop after school, or on Sunday afternoons after church when Jasmine's mom getting her hair done. Jasmine glanced at Bailey's hands working through her curls. D.C. might not be forever, but leaving Bailey? That was harder to imagine.

"It also means Imma give you shit when you don't take care of this crown!" Bailey exclaimed as she freed the last braid. "We've gotta clarify and condition before I can think about twisting you out, but I'm gonna sweep up first, you shed enough for a damn wig back here. Go wait for me at the shampoo bowl, I'll be there in a minute."

Jasmine walked to the other side of the salon, pulling out her phone to check her messages while Bailey swept up all the hair she'd teased out of Jasmine's braids. She had three emails marked *Urgent* from Gwen—none of which were actually urgent, texts from Danny, and a group chat with Addison and Trip. She swiped open Danny's messages first.

Danny: Heading in early to do the lunch deliveries, will just get ready at Eddie's for tonight. See you there at eight.

Danny: Your regular table will be reserved.

Jasmine smiled. Danny always made Eddie hold a table for her right up by the stage. It was kinda cheesy, but that was one place that Jasmine didn't mind things always staying the same.

Her nerves start to grow when she swiped over to the other conversation.

Addison: Super hyped for tonight! Is Danny going to have time to hang out, or...

Trip: Damn, Adds, don't pressure the poor dude.

Trip: Or Jasmine, for that matter.

Trip: Lord knows we're... a lot.

Addison: I just want to meet the guy who's in the cute pic on her desk, JOHN DAVID!

Trip: Oop, she busted out the government name. Shit's getting serious. Jasmine, don't let her make you nervous.

The truth was that she was nervous.

At first, inviting them to Mac House—home turf—had felt like the smart move. Familiar ground, Danny performing, something to focus on besides work. But now it felt like a mistake. Adams Morgan was trendy, sure, but Mac House wasn't really like that. It was a family joint that happened to sit on hot real estate. What if Trip or Addison look down on it? It felt like she was revealing too much about herself. Not to mention Danny and Eddie would both be tied up all night. She was navigating this alone.

As she sat down at the shampoo bowl, Jasmine let out a deep breath. Whether she was ready or not, this night was happening.

Chapter Eight

When the car came to a stop, Addison emerged first, laughing. Trip followed, looking less amused.

"Jazz! Hi!" Addison said, snickering so hard she barely noticed when her foot caught on the curb.

"Don't mind her, she's a little high. I tried to warn her that there's a decent chance of cameras around tonight, but…"

"Oh, live a little, Johnny boy," Addison said with a smile. "Jasmine, tell him to lighten up."

"I am probably the only person inside the Beltway who would definitely not suggest Trip lighten up," Jasmine said with a laugh.

Trip smirked. "I know, I know, you don't want to be seen with a liability. I see how it is. Wouldn't want to damage your brand for when you run for office someday."

Jasmine shook her head. "I have no desire to run for office. Opening yourself up to that bloodsport takes a certain level of masochism and ego I don't possess—no offense," she added quickly, not wanting either of them to think she was passing judgment on the Senator with her estimation of electoral politics.

"Nah, we're on the same page," he assured her. "Despite a lot of pressure to the contrary—and, you know, being 'the Third', I'm not interested. That's Addie's future, not mine."

Jasmine blinked. Trip was widely regarded as the heir apparent—everyone assumed he'd follow his father to the Senate, eventually. Addison's dad left politics after a single term in the Pennsylvania General Assembly to run the family's charitable trust, redistributing the Ashworth fortune one grant cycle at a time. Different path, same dynasty. Jasmine never questioned which kid would follow which father.

"Really, Addie?" She turned to the younger Ashworth. "I didn't know that you wanted to run, I just thought you liked the work you did helping constituents." She had never seen Addison get particularly involved in policy, despite having the Senator's ear and his last name.

"Why let the straight old dudes have all the fun?" She paused, before she added. "And I do like the helping people part. After all, isn't that the whole point of politics?"

Trip snorted, making his opinion clear. "Now I *know* you're high as shit if that's what you think about politics."

Jasmine was about call out his cynicism when Trip cut her off with a casual glance her way. "Your hair looks great like that, by the way."

Heat crept up her neck. Was he like this with every woman? Damn that charm. He may hate politics, but he could turn it on like a politician for sure. "Should we go in and grab a seat? This thing kicks off at eight, yeah?"

Jasmine smiled. "Don't worry, we have reserved seating."

She led them inside, waving to Eddie who was swamped behind the counter before leading the way to her usual table.

Eddie had added an additional chair into the small space so there would be room for all three of them to sit.

"Oooh, is this the VIP spot?" Addison cooed, looking at the 'Reserved' sign next to the small bud vase with a fake plastic flower in the center of the table. Jasmine couldn't tell if she was being sincere or sarcastic.

"The staff always make sure I've got the best seat in the house."

Addison laughed, bright and uninhibited while Trip glanced at his phone, already calculating his exit time. The goodwill Jasmine had extended him over complimenting her hair was fast evaporating.

Jasmine grabbed the menu cards and gestured to the wall behind them. "Regular menu is here, including the drink menu. Specials are up on the board."

"Great, thanks." His eyes stayed on his phone. She forced her expression to neutral—the last thing they needed was for someone catching her snapping at him in public.

"Well, I'm starving," Addison said eagerly. "What's good?"

Jasmine pointed out the items she really liked on the menu while Addison listened intently, seemingly carefully weighing her slice options. Trip had all but tuned out the conversation and was tapping away on his phone while Addison hemmed and hawed over what to order. "I don't know, I can't decide!" Addison finally cried. "Trip, what do you want?"

"Hmm, what was that, Adds?"

Addison's annoyance was obvious. "Wanna put your phone down and join us?"

"Sorry," he said without a single note of apology in his voice. "It's Tess."

Addison's face immediately softened. "Oh, what's going on?"

"Got into it with her dad again tonight. He's worried about anything coming out before the election."

Jasmine's stomach dropped. What else could come out? Trip had denied the cheating rumors—had he lied? Something was going on, something they weren't going to explain. She flipped into communications staffer mode. "Uh, not to be a bitch, but maybe don't use her name when we're not sure who's around right now?"

"Oh, for fuck's sake, Jasmine, we've been friends with Tess since we were kids, we can use her goddamn name," Trip snapped.

She flinched at his tone. "Sorry, I'm just trying to—"

"He knows," Addison tried to reassure Jasmine, but his expression wasn't nearly as forgiving. She backed off while Addison and Trip debated pizza toppings, eventually deciding to just sample a bunch of individual slices and pints of beer.

They approached the counter to grab their slices, and Eddie had two slices ready to go for Jasmine, one white and one chicken pesto, with a side salad and a pint of Blue Moon, like always.

"You really do get the VIP treatment here," Addison commented as they waited for their slices to heat up.

"Must be what it's like to be an Ashworth pretty much everywhere else," she joked lightly, but it didn't seem to be a comment that Trip found funny.

"Comes with tradeoffs, that's for sure," he said half under his breath.

Once again, Jasmine had no idea how to read him or his mood.

They'd barely started eating when the lights went down a bit, and Danny emerged from the kitchen, guitar in hand. The makeshift stage at the back was a small platform they cleared for live music nights. He plugged in his hybrid acoustic into his amp before strumming a few chords to check the sound.

"Hello Potomac House of Pizza!" he said into his mic, brushing his perpetually messy red hair off his forehead. "Welcome to acoustic night here at the best pizza joint in the District. I'm Dan Wakefield, and I'm here to play a few songs for you tonight. How does that sound?"

Jasmine clapped enthusiastically, Addison cheered and Trip just continued to text. She almost nudged him—someone trying to discreetly snap his picture—but if he wanted to keep up the disinterested jackass act, she wasn't about to ruin the illusion. Job description be damned.

Danny began to play, running through his usual set list of covers—a mix of newer popular stuff, the Ed Sheeran songs that Bailey had made fun of, and some classics like the Beatles and Billy Joel. As much as Jasmine had complained about coming to Bailey earlier that day, she couldn't deny that she loved hearing Danny play. It was magic, the way he could command a room with nothing but his voice and a guitar. It was, at least in part, why she'd fallen in love with him years ago.

Tonight was predictable and safe, sure—but it was also still special. Despite her earlier protests, she was glad she was there for it. Which only made her more annoyed at Trip for not giving a shit.

When Danny stepped off stage to take a brief set break, Jasmine turned to him.

"You could at least pretend to be paying attention," she said. "It takes a lot to get up in there are perform. You could show a little respect for that—for me."

She wasn't sure what made her tack on that last part, and she regretted it the second it left her mouth.

"I live my whole life in front of an audience, I think I get it," Trip shot back. "And I didn't exactly plan to have a friend to in crisis when I agreed to this fucking charade your boss cooked up. So, sorry if I'm prioritizing that over your boyfriend's pizza-joint gig."

Jasmine's breath caught, and she lowered her gaze to the table. Before she could respond, he pushed away from the table and walked outside.

Addison got up to follow, but Jasmine stopped her. "No, Adds, it's—I'm the one who pissed him off, I should go try and smooth it over."

"You sure? He can be a little... well, he can be an asshole when he's like this," Addison finished bluntly.

"Yeah, I'll be right back." She ducked out into the night to find Trip.

Summer in D.C. held on until well into September, so the night air was still sticky with humidity when Jasmine pushed out of the aggressively air-conditioned restaurant. She walked around the building and spotted Trip leaning against the wall in the alley, his phone put away, staring at the ground.

"Hey." She approached, avoiding his eyes. "I'm sorry. I knew you didn't want to be here. I shouldn't have forced you to pretend to have a good time. I get it, this isn't how you want to spend your Saturday night."

He let out a long sigh. "It's not that. And for what it's worth, your boyfriend is legit talented. It's just—there's a lot going on with Tess right now, and I feel fucking helpless. I know I'm supposed to keep my distance, but I just want to be there for her. It's not fair for me to take it out on you."

"I get it. I'm a convenient target," she said with a slight smile. "I do represent the evil empire known as your dad's congressional staff."

Trip laughed. "You're just trying to do your job. I know Gwen is the real enemy." He looked her right in the eye. "But seriously, sorry about that. I know you're just trying to help."

She hadn't expected an apology like that from Trip Ashworth—sincere, direct, no deflection. "No big deal," she offered, but it actually did feel like a big deal in their relationship, that he was being this real with her.

They held each other's gaze. Finally, Trip cleared his throat and glanced away.

"We should get back in there before the music starts again, yeah?"

Jasmine nodded, and they made their way back inside. The tension between them had shifted, even if nothing was actually solved.

Trip held the door, his hand grazing her back as he guided her in. He'd done the same thing twice now—automatic, like muscle memory. She found herself not minding.

Intermission was over and Danny was already back on stage. He caught Jasmine and Trip walking back in together. His eyes narrowed, his lips pressing together for just a second before his stage smile snapped back into place.

Jasmine's stomach tightened. He wasn't the jealous type—not exactly. But Trip represented everything he despised: Inauthentic. Shallow. Privileged. The perfect candidate for Danny's ire.

Addison leaned in as Danny stepped back up to the mic. "Danny came over to introduce himself and asked where you were. I told him you were having a private conversation with Trip—and maybe I shouldn't have, based on the look he gave me."

"Oh, it's fine. He just gets protective when he thinks work is, like, interfering with my life. I'm sure he's concerned that I'm having to handle something on my night off."

The second set proceeded without incident, and to his credit, Trip left his phone in his pocket while Danny ran through some of the big crowd pleasers: Tom Petty and Pink Floyd, before wrapping up as always with "Good Riddance" by Green Day. He tossed his pick into the audience before he came off the platform and straight to Jasmine. He leaned down to kiss her, lingering there for longer than Jasmine felt was in good taste. She pushed back on his shoulders to get him to disengage.

"You sounded great, babe," she said, taking his hand. "Let me introduce you. I know you already talked to Addison. This is Trip."

Trip flipped into his public persona quickly, extending his hand to Danny. "Good to meet you, man. Jasmine's right, you were great up there."

Danny shook his hand a little warily. "Thanks. Good to meet you, too. I'd say it's nice to put a face to a name that I hear so often, but I think the whole world kinda knows your face already. Especially lately. Saw you on the cover of *People* this week."

Jasmine shot Danny a look, but he ignored it.

"Just an inset this week, thank goodness, and at least I had a shirt on in that shot." Trip tried to laugh, but it was tight and uncomfortable.

"Yeah, seems like you've been keeping the office busy with all the, uh, media attention," Danny continued, and Jasmine dug her nails into his hand, trying to get him to stop talking, but he continued. "Lots of late nights this week for Jazz."

"My father and I are both grateful he has such a dedicated staff," Trip said with an unmistakable edge to his voice.

"I bet you are."

Addison glanced back and forth between the two of them, picking up on the tension even through her buzz. "So... this is awkward."

Jasmine let out a nervous laugh. "First meetings usually are."

"Yeah, of course," Trip said. His smile didn't reach his eyes. He turned to Addison. "Hate to cut this night short, but Addie, should we get going so we can try to Facetime Tess before it gets too late?"

Danny's eyebrows shot up at the mention of Tess's name.

"Yeah, you ordering an Uber?" Addison asked.

Trip nodded and tapped on his phone screen while Addison kept rambling.

"Well, Jazz, this was fun, thanks for the invite. Danny, you're even more talented than Jasmine let on—thanks for having us tonight!"

Danny wrapped a possessive arm around Jasmine's waist. "Thanks for coming out. You too, Trip," Danny said, a small concession of a nod in his direction.

Trip gave a wordless wave and indicated to Addison they should head outside.

Once they'd left, Danny turned to Jasmine. "What the fuck was that guy's problem?"

"Um, not for nothing Danny, but you kinda started it. Why the hell would you go after him like that?"

"I didn't!"

Jasmine just stared him down for a moment.

Danny looked at the ground. "Okay, fine, maybe I did. But only because you had to go manage him in the middle of the show. Any other night, you would have been waiting for me to come out and say hey. What was that all about?"

"I went after him to apologize."

Danny scoffed. "What could you possibly have to apologize to the plastic prince for?"

"I was honestly kind of rude to him about something outside of his control."

Danny looked skeptical. "Did you really need to apologize for that, or did you feel like you had to kiss his rich white ass to get ahead at work?"

"Does that sound like something I would do?"

Danny pulled back. "Why are you defending him anyway? I'm not the *New York Post,* I know what a nightmare this guy is."

Jasmine's jaw tightened. She wasn't sure why she felt the need to defend Trip—he'd annoyed her through most of the first set. Maybe it was just her day job bleeding through, the automatic defense of anything Ashworth-related. Or maybe it was that apology in the alley, the way he genuinely did try after she'd called him out.

Whatever it was, hearing Danny tear into Trip felt wrong. She could criticize Trip herself.

"Because he's actually a real person, with real shit going on. He's not the cardboard cutout you're trying to reduce him to."

"That doesn't change the fact that he's been a huge fucking headache for you all week."

"The situation is, not him."

"You mean the situation *he* caused by cheating?"

Jasmine shook her head. "I don't…"

"What, you really believe your own bullshit about this guy now?"

She felt the spike of anger at "bullshit," but didn't bite. "He says he didn't do it, and I believe him," Jasmine said simply.

"Yeah, okay."

"I'm serious! Believe me, I didn't want to give him the benefit of the doubt, but I don't know… something about how he talks about it, I believe him."

Danny narrowed his eyes a bit. "You've never been naive about shit like this before. Sure you're not letting yourself act like a fangirl and get a little too charmed by him?"

"I'm absolutely sure of that. I'm a damn professional, Danny," Jasmine said, fed up with the whole conversation. "You ready to head home?"

Danny scratched the back of his neck. "Yeah, lemme grab my guitar and we can get outta here." Neither of them seemed thrilled with where this conversation had turned, but they weren't getting anywhere with it, it was best to just table it for now.

A couple hours later, after they'd silently agreed not to talk about the Ashworths anymore and had ten minutes of perfunctory sex, Danny was passed out while Jasmine stared at the ceiling. She picked up her phone and searched social media for Trip's mentions. A couple posts about the previous evening and tonight, but no pictures she could find. One person did ask if he was out "with that same girl from last night"—presumably her, but it went unanswered. Nothing was blowing up around her.

Not yet, anyway.

She glanced over at a sleeping Danny, placid and unbothered. She wished she could be more like him—able to shut it off, comment and critique from a distance without feeling driven to fix it all. But that had never been her, and probably wouldn't ever be. Normally, that was a good thing. They balanced each other out. But tonight felt different.

Her entire future seemed to hinge on her relationship with the Ashworths—DC, her career, everything she wanted. Would Danny come to accept it? *Could* he?

She wasn't going to get her answering the question tonight. She set her phone on her nightstand and rolled over, resting her head on Danny's chest. His heartbeat was steady, predictable.

Her eyes stayed wide open.

Chapter Nine

"Wait—can we go over the schedule again?" Jasmine rifled through the stack of printouts. "I just realized I didn't cross-check it to see if we're going on local time or sticking to East Coast."

Papers were strewn across the conference table in Senator Ashworth's office, along with both Jasmine's and Alex's laptops, half-empty cartons of Chinese food and several cans of Celsius. Even though Alex technically worked on the Hill, he was serving as liaison between the Timlin and Ashworth camps, and with his already full plate, that meant spending late Thursday evening firming up details over takeout. Senator Timlin's campaign had agreed to have Trip make an appearance at a youth vote forum in Denver over the weekend, so Jasmine would be accompanying him. They were flying out of Dulles entirely too early on Saturday morning, hitting the afternoon rally and then coming straight back. It was going to be an epically long day, but Trip's law school schedule and Gwen's demands on Jasmine's time didn't allow for much more than that.

She hated being away longer than necessary—especially when things still felt off with Danny. He'd been making an effort since the incident at Mac House, doing things like picking up her dry cleaning and leaving little love notes on her laptop inside her purple work tote. She appreciated it, she really did, but it only made the disconnect between them more obvious—especially with their opposite schedules. She chalked it up to growing pains, the awkward process of figuring out what a partnership looked like in the real life. But she didn't want this work trip to add more friction when they were still figuring it out.

Alex located the hard copy of the schedule before Jasmine did, handing it over to her with one hand and reaching for another spring roll with the other. "Everything's in local time, but I had the campaign put corresponding East Coast times to keep you both on track since you're flying back the same day."

"Bless you. Are there any more of those spring rolls?"

Alex looked guilty behind the thick glasses he wore when his contacts couldn't hold out any longer. "No, sorry. I didn't even think to leave one for Trip."

"Trip's over an hour late, so he gets what he gets." He'd texted that he was hung up with some law journal thing she didn't understand, but this was stretching the boundaries of acceptable. "Hand me the lo mein?"

Alex shoved the rest of the spring roll in his mouth and passed her the greasy paper carton. The noodles were now cold, but Jasmine still twirled her fork through them and took another bite as she looked over the schedule again. Ben had outright banned chopsticks from the office the night that Gwen had insisted she knew how to use them, but then dropped a roll covered in eel sauce on his suit pants when she tried to offer him a bite. He hadn't gotten angry—just shot her a look equal parts fond and exasperated.

"This looks like what we agreed to," Jasmine said. "But holy hell, this is going to be a long day. Do I have a list of the media that's going to be attending?"

"Outlets, yes, specific people, no. The campaign is coordinating that. Do you need that level of detail?"

"We've been talking with one particular *Teen Vogue* reporter, Lauren Wong, I think? Is she on for this event?"

"Credential confirmations went out this morning, so if you ask her, she should know."

As Jasmine texted the reporter, the door to the office flew open.

"Sorry I'm so late," Trip said as he rushed in, dropping both his gym and school bags to the floor before landing heavily in one of the chairs at the edge of the table. "Law journal editorial board went on forever. We were assigning out tonight."

Alex grimaced, but Jasmine had no idea what that meant.

Trip noted her confusion. "I'm the editor-in-chief, so it's my job to assign which editors are going to work on which articles. Which means I had an entire room of law students arguing with me about why they should get certain articles."

Jasmine wanted to stay mad at Trip, but frankly, that sounded miserable. "A room full of overachieving lawyer wanna-bes attempting to out-argue one another? I'm almost positive that's one of Dante's circles of hell."

"You have no idea," Trip said with a smile, visibly relaxing. "Alex, you're not also trying to do law school part time right now, are you?"

Alex shook his head. "One of my roommates is a 2L who just made law review at GW, so he's in it right now, too, and it's been an absolute slog to get through all the submissions."

"You both make it sound like so much fun, I can't wait 'til I go!" Jasmine said with faux enthusiasm.

"Didn't know you were thinking about law school," Trip said before he reached over and grabbed the container of noodles.

"That's my fork," she said, but Trip dug in with it anyway. Jasmine made a face but didn't push it. If he wanted her germs, oh well. "And yeah, that's the idea. Do a year here on the Hill and then parlay that into a great recommendation for law school."

"You want to be a lawyer?" Trip asked, mouth full. For someone who'd been raised in high society, his table manners left a lot to be desired. "But you're so good at the communications stuff."

Given how openly Trip disliked Gwen and her tactics, it surprised her that he would compliment her work.

Before she could reply, he added, "And you seem to enjoy it. Since you made it clear you didn't want to run for office yourself, I assumed a press-secretary-type gig was your goal."

"Oh...maybe? I don't really know yet. But it's always felt like if I wanted to do anything substantial in politics, law school is—I don't know—the thing to do?"

He laughed. "Trust me, if you don't absolutely need to go to law school, don't."

Jasmine was vaguely offended. "Why? You think media types can't handle it?"

"Oh, God, no, it's not about *you*—you're obviously smarter than ninety percent of the assholes I was arguing with an hour ago," Trip said. "It's about what a fucking racket it is: law school is a long, slow form of torture, and you get to pay thousands for the privilege." He stood to examine the rest of the takeout containers. "I want to be a defense attorney, so I don't have a choice. If you do, pick literally any other degree."

Jasmine glanced at Alex, giving him her best *Can you believe this guy?* look, but he just nodded. "My roommate would totally concur."

She felt a little unsettled. Law school had been *The Plan* for years. Even though she'd already been questioning the timing—especially if she could land a role with the campaign—this was about stalling, not changing lanes completely.

Still Trip and Alex had definitely given her something to think about.

As Trip poked into the containers of kung pao chicken and string beans, Jasmine snapped back into business mode. "Anyway, can we go through the details for Saturday? Since you were running late, Alex and I have everything sorted logistics-wise. You just need to sign off on your remarks and review the questions for the panel so you can figure out how you want to answer." She slid a small stack of papers in front of him with the details she and Alex had already hashed out.

"I hate how rehearsed these things can be," Trip said with a sigh, but dutifully began flipping through the papers.

"It's a tight race," Alex said almost apologetically. "The campaign is just trying to avoid any surprises."

"Do I have talking points on these?" Trip asked, holding up the list of panel questions.

Alex passed over another sheet. "These are Senator Timlin's position statements, pulled straight from his website."

Trip took them and looked at Jasmine. "Where are the notes from this office?"

"I don't have any. You know your dad's positions well enough to stay in line, and the criminal justice stuff is your area of expertise. Do you really need me to hold your hand?"

"I'm shocked Gwen trusts me enough not to script me within an inch of my life."

"Oh, she doesn't," Jasmine said with a smile. "But I convinced her that a youth voter forum will be able to smell inauthenticity from a mile away. It's better to just let you be you—just, you know, in a 'study Timlin's positions on the plane and don't contradict a damn comma' kind of way."

"I've been on campaign trails my whole life, got it."

"Hopefully you've gotten better at it than the great 'Jack hates cats' debacle of your youth," Jasmine said with a smirk, referencing the infamous YouTube clip of Trip as a kid, saying *"My dad doesn't really like animals, but especially not cats. He says the hair makes his suits itch."*

The clip was immediately weaponized by an opposing campaign, trying to paint Jack as some kind of puppy-kicking nightmare. The Ashworth Family Trust had to make donations to rescues throughout Pennsylvania just to quiet the outrage.

Just one more absurdity in the world of politics.

Trip groaned. "I was nine. Statute of limitations, people."

"You know better than I do—the internet never forgets."

"Speaking of things I'd rather forget, did you give the Timlin campaign the no-fly list?"

Jasmine nodded. The 'no-fly list' was exactly what it sounded like: topics off-limits for any interview or appearance that Trip was doing. For this round of image rehabilitation, Gwen allowed 'drug use' to come off the list, letting Trip talk about his past marijuana use in context. "Mariana DaSilva" had been added to the bottom, while at the top, as always, was Francesca, Trip's mom.

"Thanks," Trip said with a curt nod.

Alex got up and began packing his things. "If we're all set here, I'm going to head out. Nigel has some kind of networking reception thing this weekend while I'm out of town and he's been texting me pics of potential outfits all night. I need to help him choose before he has a fashion-induced panic attack."

Jasmine chuckled. If anyone would, it would be Nigel.

"Thanks for all your help, Alex. We'll see you Saturday morning," she confirmed.

Trip gave Alex a distracted wave goodbye as he continued to look over the papers Jasmine had handed him with his brief prepared intro.

"Gwen okayed this?" he asked, raising an eyebrow.

"What do you mean? She wrote it," Jasmine said carefully.

"Bullshit," Trip said definitively. "You wrote this."

"It's Gwen's message, I just—"

"Wrote the whole damn thing. It's really good, by the way. Actually sounds like me."

"Thanks." She felt a heat rise in her cheeks.

Trip got to his feet. "So yeah, looks like we're all set here, thanks to you. Let me help you get this cleaned up." He grabbed the cardboard flat everything had been delivered in to gather the empty boxes.

"Why do you do that?" Jasmine blurted out as Trip stacked the cartons.

"What do you mean?"

"Pathologically clean this office. Washing out mugs, clearing up takeout boxes. You've done it every time we go out, too—always returning all the empties back to the bar."

"What, you think I'm so pampered it wouldn't occur to me that someone has to clean up all that shit?" he asked, deliberately avoiding her eyes.

"I don't mean it like that, it's just—I don't know." She took a deep breath. "You'd be surprised how many people don't see that kind of stuff, or just expect someone else will be along to take care of it. It's unusual to see a member or their family to notice, let alone actually pitch in to help."

"Ask Addie—I'm kind of a neat freak. Makes me a pretty obnoxious roommate, obviously." He sighed, setting the cardboard box next to trash bin and started rounding up the cans for recycling. "Maybe when you create enough messes, you get a little obsessive about cleaning them up, too."

So, this had nothing to do with coffee mugs or takeout containers.

"Trip..." She started, but he waved her off.

"Sorry, it's not your job to be my amateur shrink," he said, cracking a smile. "Besides, Tess psychoanalyzes me for fun all the time. The perils of having one of your best friends doing a PhD in clinical psych."

"How's she doing, with all of this?" Jasmine asked cautiously. In the three weeks since their minor faceoff at Mac House, he hadn't mentioned Tess again in her presence.

"She's a lot better at letting the public side of it roll off her back than I am. But it really bothered her when she thought she'd caused problems for her dad. Once they got new polling data showing it didn't move the needle on his numbers, he's been a lot calmer."

"It must be so weird to have your relationship with your parents swing based on opinion polling. At least with my mom, it was just my report cards."

"Oh, come on, did you ever pull anything other than straight A's? You seem the type."

"Hey, I had a very touch-and-go relationship with chemistry there for a while. Though it was actually the 'needs improvement' in conduct in fifth grade that was my most scandalous."

"Jasmine Lewis, anything less than perfectly behaved? I refuse to believe it."

"I mean, when you publicly call out your male gym teacher for making girls in your class uncomfortable with comments about their changing bodies, followed by organizing a school-wide campaign to get him fired, not everyone's going to love you."

Trip's eyes grew wide. "Jasmine, that's...awesome! But, I mean, it does suck that they retaliated with your grade."

Jasmine shook her head with a snort. "Believe me, my mom hit the roof over it. Mary Lewis is a lifelong bureaucrat—she lives by the mantra of 'just put your head down and work.' I think she was embarrassed I made a big deal out of it at all. She thinks speaking up like that jeopardizes your chances of getting ahead in life."

Trip was silent for a minute. "Wow, that—I'm sorry."

"And I get it. That's how she's gotten as far as she has: work hard, don't rock the boat, play the game. When you're a Black woman in this town..." Jasmine trailed off, realizing how much her mother's advice had shaped her own strategy for staying under the radar. "But when I was unwilling to do the same, she wasn't happy."

"Well, for what it's worth, I think that's fucking badass. Makes sense that Gwen hired you."

"You don't really seem like Gwen's biggest fan," she said with an arched eyebrow. She wasn't sure if appealing to Gwen was good or bad.

"I mean, I have a tepid relationship with the media as it is," Trip allowed. "But I know enough to know she's incredibly good at what she does, and I respect that she hired someone who actually balances out her worst impulses rather than feeds into them. In my experience, that lack of ego is rare in Washington."

Jasmine blinked at him, momentarily caught off guard. He'd just complimented Gwen—and by extension, her. A small, satisfied thrill ran through her. Smart, perceptive, and apparently capable of noticing the little victories, too. She reminded herself not to get too carried away. But it was hard not to.

Before she could respond, Trip's face melted into a conspiratorial grin. "And I mean, Ben seems to appreciate her diverse talents."

Jasmine burst out laughing. "They're *so bad* at hiding it!"

"I'm trying to see how many comments I can make before Ben goes off on me. So far, he just starts to twitch a little."

"What's the deal with you and Ben, anyway? He acts like an overprotective big brother most of the time, and you definitely annoy him like a little brother."

"Ben's worked for Dad since I was eleven. He started as an intern when he was an undergrad at Catholic and just never left. He's basically family at this point, and I trust him more than I trust some of the rest of the extended Ashworth clan, to be honest. He's always been there for me, especially after..." His voice trailed off.

"It's a seismic thing," Jasmine said. "Losing a parent."

Trip threw her a sharp look. "How did you know..."

She met his eyes, and decided fuck it, it was just time to put it on the table. "My dad died when I was four. Car accident," she explained. "I hadn't seen him for a while at that point, my parents split before I could even remember them being together. So, it wasn't close to what you went through, but it's still—it leaves an impact."

Trip's eyes went soft. "Yeah, no matter how it happens, it's—yeah." A beat passed. "I'm sorry. About your dad."

"Thanks, and same. About your mom, I mean."

"Yeah," was all Trip said, before he finished tossing the cans in the recycling bin and changed the subject. "Sorry for keeping you so late, I know your boyfriend hates it. I feel bad about that, especially since we'll be gone all day on Saturday."

"How did you..."

"Addison mentioned that he's not always a huge fan of the hours that come with the job, especially when it's about me."

Jasmine's ears got a little warm at the edges as she glanced at the Post-it from Danny stuck to the cover of her laptop, a twinge of guilt rising. Why would Trip assume that Danny had a problem with him, specifically, did he think that she...

"You know," Trip continued, "because you don't actually work for me but need to deal with my bullshit anyway."

Jasmine hoped Trip didn't notice her small sigh of relief.

"Oh, I mean, he gets that it's part of the job even if he doesn't love it. His mom works in politics, so he's been around it forever." Jasmine couldn't bring herself to explain that part of the reason Danny disliked her job so much was *because* his mom worked in politics and what that had done to his family. It was one thing to spill her family secrets to Trip, but Danny's were another thing entirely.

"I mean, you can get it and still not like it, believe me, I understand that."

"Yeah," Jasmine agreed with a nod. "I guess I'll head out then, do you need to me to…"

"I've got this." Trip finished gathering up the trash. "Talk tomorrow to finalize the times for Saturday?"

"Sounds good." She slipped her things into her purple tote and headed for the door with a wave.

As she walked to the Metro, she wasn't sure what to make of tonight's interaction. Trip seemed to be full of contradictions—at once both aloof and disarming, guarded and distant one second and then sharing small, intimate details about his life the next. That puzzle made him hard to figure out, which made him even harder to position in the press. He wasn't as easily captured in broad brush strokes as people assumed.

It was making her job a lot harder than she expected, but the time they spent together was a lot more interesting as a result. And as much as she tried to shake it, she couldn't stop replaying the way he'd looked at her when she mentioned her father—that flash of recognition, of shared understanding.

By the time she got home, the apartment was dark. Danny was already asleep, turned away from her side of the bed. She paused in the doorway for a moment, that memory still lingering, unsure why it stayed with her at all.

Chapter Ten

It was ungodly early on Saturday morning when Jasmine got the text that the car service was downstairs. Danny was still sound asleep, nothing but his mop of unruly hair poking out from under the covers. He'd gone to Eddie's after their shift to play video games and smoke weed. She wanted to be annoyed that he ditched her the night before she left town, but honestly? It had been a relief. Her nerves had been ramping up since Gwen's interrogation about event prep yesterday morning, and spending the evening alone—watching videos of similar events, anticipating curveballs—beat listening to Danny's ongoing critique. It hadn't helped much. She'd still gone to bed early, imagining reporters asking Trip about his preferred style of underwear.

The driver grabbed her bag to put it in the trunk while she opened the door to the sedan, and was surprised to find Trip already inside.

"Morning." He held two cups of coffee, one iced and one hot.

"Trip, I didn't realize—"

"Seemed easiest to go together since we're under the same flight reservation. I had the office just arrange for one car, two pickups."

Jasmine sank into the seat next to him.

"I stopped at the coffee shop on our block, I hope this is right." He passed the iced coffee to her. "Addison told me what you usually get at Cups & Co., but I'm not confident this place knew what I meant when I showed them the text."

"Is it caffeinated? That's all that really matters."

Trip let out a genuine laugh, if a bit muted due to the early hour. "Yes, I made sure of that."

She took a sip. Close to her usual dirty chai—a little sweeter, probably more spiced syrup—but good. "Thank you. Seriously, this will do the trick."

He gave another light laugh before he took a long sip from his own cup. "Thank goodness. I had no idea what I was doing. Drip coffee, black is hard to get wrong."

"Oh, you're one of *those*," Jasmine said, slightly teasing. "Thinks you're morally superior because you only take your coffee black."

"Are you making fun of me? I genuinely can't tell because my brain doesn't work this early."

"Indeed, I am, Mr. Ashworth."

"Hey, no moral high ground here. I only drink it black because in prep school, I couldn't be bothered to remember to keep milk in my dorm room. Black instant was the only way."

"That sounds truly gross," Jasmine said, pulling a face.

"Oh, it was. It wasn't even good instant, but Starbucks Via wasn't a thing at the tiny little convenience store by campus. It was straight up Folgers crystals."

"A true man of the people," she quipped, placing her hand over her heart.

"You did hear the part where I said that's how I drank it at boarding school, right? Still firmly in the one percent over here."

"Of course, my mistake." A smile tugged up the corners of her lips. She was suddenly glad she got to spend the ride sipping coffee with Trip rather than in awkward silence with the driver.

They chatted about not much of anything for the rest of the ride to Dulles, and then met up with Alex once they were through security. He was waiting for them with an indignant expression behind his glasses.

"Trip, did you do this?" he asked, holding out his boarding pass.

"Do what?" Trip tried to sound innocent, but whatever Alex was accusing him of, it was obvious he'd absolutely done it.

"Did you upgrade my flight without telling me...? First class?"

Jasmine couldn't help but smile. Addison had a habit of doing sneaky nice things for her around the office—a new book appearing on her desk, bath bombs tucked into her work bag. Apparently, it ran in the family.

"It's the least I could do," Trip demurred. "Maybe this way you'll actually get some sleep on the flight. I'd bet good money you were on the phone with the district office 'til way past your bedtime last night making sure they're ready for me."

Alex's shrug was answer enough.

"Jasmine and I are in first, too, but I couldn't get you a seat near us." Trip had paid out of his own pocket for the flights, insisting that since it was his fault they were going at all, he wanted it to be as easy for them as possible. He turned to Jasmine. "Do you want me to swap seats so you can sit next to Alex?"

"Well, you and I should probably review some talking points on the plane." If she sat with Alex, he'd feel it necessary to entertain her, and he really needed some sleep.

Boarding started shortly after they found the gate. Their first-class status meant they were first on the plane. Jasmine ran her hand over the soft leather of the seats on her way by, trying not to freak out about flying first class for the first time.

As they settled in and buckled up, Jasmine joked, "So this is how the other half lives."

"Sometimes. We're lucky United flies to Denver. Their first class is pretty good, though it's better on their international flights," Trip said. "If the only option was American, there would be no reason to bother shelling out extra cash. There is barely a difference between coach and first class on those planes." Of course he had flown first class often enough to have opinions.

"Not as plush as flying private, though." The Ashworths could afford to charter, they'd done it plenty of times.

"True, but we're not going to risk being labeled 'climate criminals' on the way to a youth vote forum. Especially not while we're staring down a potential primary run against Martinez."

"I still don't get you, Trip."

He looked both a little taken aback and a little bemused. "What does that mean?"

"You're just—I don't know. You claim not to care about politics, but you know every move on the board. You say you want privacy, but then court publicity, even unintentionally, by dating famous women. You're so smart, but don't push back when all that's ever in the media about you is that you're rich and hot."

"You think I'm hot?" he asked, a smirk on his lips.

"Everyone thinks you're hot," Jasmine shot back. "It was a headline in *US Weekly* last week! And that's completely not the point!"

"It's not *not* the point." He shook his head a little. "I don't know, I guess it's just who I've always been. My life has always been a weird mix of public and private. I'm not actually important but at the same time I'm so important to how people think of my dad, and my family. It's strange, but..."

"I literally can't even imagine..."

"And that's all I've ever known."

She looked at him—really looked—when the flight attendant appeared by their seats.

"Good morning, Mr. Ashworth, and welcome back to United. Can I get you and your companion anything to drink?"

"Oh, this is Jasmine Lewis, my colleague," Trip quickly supplied. "And I'll just have a coffee, thanks." He turned to Jasmine with that slightly crooked smile of his. "Booze is free in first class, you might need it if you have to spend the day with me."

"I need to stay sharp to keep you on your best behavior." Jasmine smiled despite herself. "I'll also just take a coffee, thanks." The flight attendant nodded before moving onto the next row.

"You're not going to try and get some sleep?" Trip asked, something like concern appearing on his face.

"I've got some polling data to comb through before Monday, and I'd prefer not to work much tomorrow if I can avoid it, so might as well get to it while I'm trapped on a metal tube in the sky."

"I should work, too. I've got a truly obscene number of citations to proof, in addition to my actual class work, so I feel your pain."

"Didn't you assign the work to other people the other night?"

"As editor-in-chief, after we accept a submission, I go through everything twice. Once before it gets to the assigned editor to confirm it's in workable condition, and then again before we go to print."

"So... you, like, pre-edit? And then do a final copy edit?"

"I'm the first and last line of defense."

"That's an intense amount of responsibility."

Trip just shrugged. "At least I signed up for it this time."

The subtext was clear: he hadn't signed up for this whole dog-and-pony show they were currently taking to Denver. Or any of the rest of what came from being Trip Ashworth.

"Oh, I forgot," she said. "My laptop is in my other bag, do you mind..."

"Of course." He rose to his feet and stepped into the aisle.

Jasmine expected him to move aside so she could retrieve her bag herself, but he reached up and took it down on his own, setting it on his seat so she could get her laptop out. She unzipped it and pulled the computer from its sleeve. Trip waited patiently and then put her bag back up for her.

It was a small thing, but Jasmine's mind flashed, unbidden, to the last time she'd flown with Danny, on their trip to visit his mom in Illinois. Danny had given up his seat next to her so a family could sit together. At first, it seemed like a sweet gesture. As the flight went on, though, she'd grown resentful of watching him zoning out with his earbuds in while she spent the whole flight next to a fussy toddler. He hadn't even notice how miserable she had been.

After Trip slid her bag back into the bin and settled into his seat, the flight attendant appeared with their coffees. They both took the cups, put in their respective earbuds, and spent the rest of the flight in companionable silence, the steady tapping of their keyboards filling the space between them.

Chapter Eleven

When they hit the tarmac in Denver, they met up with Alex, who looked much better after a three-plus-hour nap on the plane. Jasmine chuckled as she pulled him aside to suggest he fix his hair before they left the airport. They grabbed an Uber to the hotel across from the convention center where the event was being held.

A crowd was already gathering outside, waiting to get in. Jasmine spotted a few signs immediately: "Cheaters shouldn't talk about elections" and "Playboy Princes Are Out of Touch with CO Voters." Her stomach dropped. She glanced at Trip—his jaw tight, face set.

He'd seen them.

"You okay?" she asked quietly as they walked inside.

"Let's get this over with."

They had booked rooms for the night even though they weren't staying—just needed a staging area before the event. Since taking the job, Jasmine had marveled at the amount of money the Ashworths threw at logistics to avoid a headache.

The real benefit of wealth, it seemed, wasn't the money itself but the time it saved.

She went to her room to change and freshen up. She had chosen a particularly casual outfit for this event, distressed jeans and Air Force 1s with a vintage "Rock the Vote" t-shirt she'd found at a thrift shop back in the district. The 90s baby tee was shorter than she realized, leaving a few inches of exposed skin above her low-rise jeans, but she'd brought an oversized blazer to throw on downstairs. She touched up her makeup, checked her curls in the mirror, and dropped her credential over her head. When she stepped into the hallway, she nearly collided into Trip. He'd changed too—black jeans and boots, a "Timlin for Senate" t-shirt from Alex, topped with a plaid flannel.

"Oh, hey." Trip smiled as he stopped short to avoid a collision. His eyes swept her up and down. "Oh, wow, you look—that outfit, it's super different."

She immediately felt self-conscious. Maybe she should've put the jacket on already. "It seemed like this was a dress-down kind of event, and even though the office tends to be pretty formal..."

"Oh, no, I didn't mean—you look great," he half-stammered. "It's just that even when we've gone out on the weekends, you dress pretty conservatively. Not in a bad way, obviously. I just—you look really great. It suits you. The whole vibe, I mean."

She didn't know what to make of Trip acting so flustered, but it left her feeling flustered, too.

"Thanks." She hoped her blush wasn't as obvious as the heat in her cheeks suggested. She'd never been the type of girl to get bashful about a compliment, least of all from a guy like Trip Ashworth. "The Timlin shirt is a nice touch."

"I mean, gotta play to the home crowd, right?" he joked. "We should probably..."

"Yeah." They turned to head down the hall.

The elevator arrived, and Trip, as he often did, placed his hand on her back to guide her into the elevator first. This time, though, his fingers brushed the bare skin exposed by her tiny t-shirt. The flutter that followed in Jasmine's chest was not something she'd been prepared for.

When they reached the lobby, Jasmine stepped out of the elevator before Trip had a chance to reach out again, slipping her blazer on to avoid more accidental skin-to-skin contact. They spotted Alex by the walkway over to the convention center, and the three of them headed in together.

There were still about two hours to go before the rally kicked off, but Trip had to be prepped by the event staff, mic-checked, and given a final walkthrough of the agreed-upon panel questions. The plan was straightforward: each panelist would give a two-minute intro about who they were, why they supported Dave Timlin for Senate, and a standard *get out the vote* message. Then, a local journalism student would moderate a roundtable discussion before opening the floor to questions.

The Q&A was the part that made Jasmine nervous. The organizers insisted all questions were vetted ahead of time, but there was no guarantee that someone wouldn't go rogue once there was a mic in hand.

She watched, shoulders taut, as Trip greeted the other panelists: a local climate change activist from an Indigenous community, a Black community organizer from Chicago, and a rapper who was looking to raise his social justice credentials. Jasmine quickly assessed that Trip was the second most famous person on the panel—a good spot, hopefully, since it meant most of the out-of-pocket questions would go to the rapper instead of him.

Prep went smoothly from start to finish, and Jasmine managed to catch up with Trip one more time in the green room before he headed out on stage.

"You feeling okay?" she asked, biting the inside of her lip.

"All good," Trip assured her, taking a swig from a bottle of water.

"You know you don't have to answer anything from the audience, right? Just in case someone comes out of left field and asks about, you know, Mariana? Or Tess?"

"Jasmine," he said with a laugh, using his free hand to shake her shoulder lightly. "I'm not a campaign event virgin. I've been trotted out for appearances since before I could talk. Trust me, I've got this."

She exhaled slowly. Why was she so nervous? "Sorry, this is my first time at an event like this, I just want to make sure..."

"I don't do anything to further embarrass the Senator, I get it."

But Jasmine shook her head. "No, I don't want you to be uncomfortable. We're kind of offering you up for potential slaughter, and I don't want you to get blindsided."

Trip seemed mildly shocked by her explanation. "Jasmine, I mean..."

He didn't get a chance to finish the thought before one of the event staff, wearing a headset and positively humorless expression, yelled for the panelists to make their way to the stage. Trip followed where he was told, with a glance back at Jasmine before he headed up the stairs. Once he had disappeared into the wings, Jasmine joined Alex to watch the event from the back of the room.

Things seemed to proceed smoothly enough. Trip's opening statement sent ripples of laughter in the right places, and no one interrupted it to heckle him. And as they moved through the panel questions, the ones Jasmine had entrusted Trip to prepare for, Trip gave strong, well-reasoned and researched responses to each one, without coming off as stiff or overly rehearsed. And that megawatt smile, slightly crooked as always, flashed enough times for Jasmine to know there would be great photos to leverage later.

Then came the Q&A. Jasmine held her breath. She glanced down at the pre-screened questions in her hand and waited to see if it matched what actually what came out of the audience's mouth.

A young woman with warm tan skin, long curls and a shirt that read *Eat the Rich* stood up to ask the first question. "As a Latina in Colorado, it's hard to look at our Congressional delegation and get excited about the same line up of old, white faces. Why should we even care enough to vote when there's no representation by people who look like us?" A cheer went up in the crowd. It was similar enough to one of the vetted questions that Jasmine assumed they'd allow it to go through.

A couple of the other panelists jumped in, giving short, thoughtful answers about how to increase female and BIPOC involvement in politics in the state through grassroots organizing. They'd filled enough airtime that Jasmine was satisfied they'd move on to the next—but instead, the moderator asked, "Trip, anything to add?"

Jasmine groaned internally. Of course they'd put Trip on the spot about a diversity-related topic. He was white, cis, straight, male, and rich—there was no way he could answer without sounding at least a little patronizing. But since he'd been called out specifically, there was no getting around it.

Trip, though, looked at ease as he leaned into his mic. "I mean, I'm probably in the best position to talk about the power of representation, right? Because no matter where I turn—whether it's a history book or the current halls of Congress—I can find examples of leaders who look like me. I've never had to question whether who I was would be 'enough' to take any path I wanted. We need to do better at clearing the way for the amazingly talented BIPOC, female and LGBTQIA candidates we *know* are out there—if we relied a little less on the 'good old boy' network to tell us who to vote for. And yeah, I appreciate the irony of that coming from me, since I might as well have 'good old boy' tattooed on my forehead."

The crowd laughed.

"And that means putting our literal money where our mouth is—getting the DNC and campaign donors to change how they do business. That's where I think a guy like me might actually be able to do some good.

"But," he said, shifting tone, "when it comes to *this* race? The choice on the ballot in Colorado next month is between Mike Demeter and Dave Timlin—two middle aged white guys. And I trust Dave Timlin to speak for those who don't look like he does a hell of a lot more than I do someone like Mike Demeter, who's been openly hostile to both the Black Lives Matter movement *and* a woman's right to choose. I don't need to tell a group of smart, engaged voters like yourselves just how much maintaining control of the Senate means. So, on November 8th, go out and cast your ballot for Dave Timlin. And on November 9th, I'm committed to coming to the table with you to fight for a future for the party that looks a lot less like me—and a lot more like you. You in?"

The crowd went wild.

Alex leaned into Jasmine's ear. "He's good."

"Better than I expected."

It wasn't the first time she'd underestimated Trip Ashworth, and she was quickly learning it likely wouldn't be the last.

The questions continued for a few more minutes before Jasmine's biggest fear came true.

A young woman in a zip-up hoodie took the mic, and instead of the expected question on climate change, she yanked down the zipper to reveal a Mariana DaSilva tour t-shirt.

"Trip, why should we trust anything you say when you're a *liar* and a *cheater*?!"

The crowd started buzzing instantly. The moderator jumped in, trying to restore order, but Trip held up his hand to wave him off.

"I know a lot of people are making a lot of assumptions right now based on a twenty-second snippet of a song they *think* is about me," he said evenly. "All I can say is Mariana DaSilva is a talented songwriter and an even better person. She deserves the chance to make whatever art she wants—without every single syllable being dissected as a way to invade her privacy. She doesn't owe us anything but great music, and that's something she consistently delivers. So maybe we should spend less time speculating about what might've inspired a line in a song, and more time appreciating the lines themselves."

He paused, then smiled. "I wish her nothing but success with the new album. I mean, if the twenty seconds we heard are any indication... as my cousin Addison said, it's not *not* a bop," he finished with a laugh.

The crowd laughed, then applauded—loud enough to drown out the handful of hecklers still shouting.

Jasmine exhaled slowly. It was the best possible answer he could have given. Sure, the online trolls would still rip him apart for not confirming or denying the song's inspiration, but he'd win over just as many new defenders with that response. Gwen was going to be thrilled.

And Jasmine couldn't help but feel a flicker of pride herself.

The rest of the event passed without incident, and Jasmine moved to intercept Trip as soon as he came offstage. There was a reception at the hotel, but if they wanted to make their flight back to Washington, they needed to leave *now*.

They raced upstairs to grab their bags, and the valet flagged them down a taxi. Ten minutes into the drive, both of their phones started blowing up at once.

She assumed it was the office—footage from the event must've already hit social media.

But no. Each notification carried the same message from United:

Flight canceled.

Not just delayed, not rescheduled.

Flat out canceled.

Their plane wasn't leaving Denver that afternoon at all.

Chapter Twelve

Jasmine let out a small, anguished cry as she read the text message lighting up her phone. "Uuuugh! Canceled? Are they serious? What happened? There's not even any weather!"

Trip was scrolling frantically, hunting for the customer service number. "If they canceled out a whole flight, we better jump in the queue to rebook now to have any hope of getting home by Monday."

Jasmine let Trip handle the rebooking while she asked the driver to turn back to the hotel. There was no chance of getting out tonight, so it wasn't worth going to the airport just to pay the fare to come back into town. At least they already had rooms booked. She tried to tune out Trip's conversation with the agent, not wanting to know just how long it might take, and swiped over to text Danny.

Jasmine: Flight got canceled, stuck in Denver for the night.
Jasmine: Will keep you posted on what we find out.
Jasmine: Sorry!

She wasn't sure why she felt the need to apologize—it wasn't like she'd done anything that made the flight get canceled.

And then Danny's reply came, and she realized why she had. Danny didn't take it well.

Danny: WTF? What happened?

She took a deep breath before replying.

Jasmine: No idea. Trip's on the phone trying to figure out our reservation.

Danny: OUR reservation?

Jasmine: Everything got booked together.

Jasmine: And it's a good thing—he's got status. They'll probably try to get us on something sooner with him calling.

Danny: Well, thank God for Trip

Jasmine felt her blood pressure rising, but there was little she could do. She just hoped Danny would keep any digs about traveling on taxpayer money to himself, because she wasn't about to admit that Trip had personally paid for her flight.

Jasmine: It's not his fault either.

Danny: You wouldn't be in fucking Denver at all if it weren't for him.

Jasmine: But I am, and there's nothing I can do to change that ATM, so...

The typing indicator flickered on and off, and Jasmine knew Danny was trying to shoot off some kind of pointed barb about the situation—but kept coming up empty.

Danny: Just tell me this isn't going to be some bullshit "oh no, only one hotel room" situation.

This wasn't about her at all. This was about his mom. So much of Danny's shit kept being about his mom.

Jasmine: I already have my own room... had to have a place to get ready for the event.

More typing, more stopping.

Danny: Sorry

Danny: You just know how I get about this shit.
Jasmine: I get it.
Jasmine: I wish I was coming home tonight.
Danny: Yeah, me too.
Danny: Love you.
Jasmine: Love you too.

She gave another sigh as she dropped her phone back into her bag, tuning back into Trip's conversation with the airline.

"And you're sure there's no airline partner that... No, I mean, I'm fine with... All oversold anyway?" He pinched the bridge of his nose with his free hand. "Okay, so then the earliest is still...yeah, go ahead and book. Thanks."

He hung up. "There's some kind of issue in Chicago that's fucking up pretty much everywhere for United. The earliest they can get us out is four p.m. tomorrow."

"Four? But that won't get us back to Dulles until—"

"Past ten, yeah. I tried, nothing available earlier. They said we could fly standby, but..."

"Don't really want to spend the day in the Denver airport?"

"I mean, I'd like to not end up splashed across an Instagram gossip account, and that seems likely if I'm spending hours at the airport with some mystery woman fresh off this whole scandal."

Jasmine laughed. "I didn't realize you followed that kind of thing."

"Doesn't everybody? I need my weekly celeb tea. And I'm certain you do, too."

"Occupational hazard. I need to make sure *someone's* not being referenced every two minutes. You were popping up a lot this summer." It seemed no matter when or where he and Mariana were out in public, someone was submitting it to the anonymous gossip account on Instagram.

"That's fair."

The cab pulled back in front of the hotel, and they got out to retrieve their bags from the trunk and head back up to their rooms. It was still early, not quite six local time. Jasmine expected to order in and hole up in her room to get some work done, but just when she'd changed into sweats and gotten all of her devices connected to the Wi-Fi, there was a knock on her door.

Trip stood in the doorway, in garishly orange Princeton basketball shorts and a black t-shirt, looking a little sheepish. "Hey, uh, this is probably weird to even ask, but do you wanna hang out for a while? I have an inbox worth of complaints from law journal staff to deal with and I just can't yet."

Jasmine laughed. "So, you're going to use me as an excuse? 'Sorry, one of my dad's staffers insisted on debriefing with me after the event, it was brutal.' Something like that?"

"I mean, now that you mention it... But seriously, I wasn't sure if you were also in need of a distraction after the disappointment of not getting home tonight."

Jasmine hesitated for a second—Danny's face flashed through her mind—then pushed it aside. "I definitely have some work to do, but it sounds like we're hanging around a chunk of the day tomorrow, too, so sure. But, uh, given the number of Mariana DaSilva fans we saw in the crowd today and your valid fear of the reach of the nosy cell phone cameras, maybe we don't go out to dinner or anything?"

"Good call. Order up to the room, then? I'm sure there's a mediocre club sandwich waiting for us."

"It is the room service staple. Come in." She stepped aside so he could pass.

They consulted the menu and decided on a few items to split, along with a six-pack of beer. As they waited for the food to be sent up, Jasmine flipped on the TV and started scrolling through the cable offerings.

"There's literally nothing good on TV on Saturday nights. You streaming anything lately you want to catch up on?"

Trip shook his head. "Since classes started back up, I feel like I haven't even had the TV on for background noise. My Spotify is getting a workout, but I can't remember the last thing I streamed. You working on anything?"

"Uh, well, Danny and I do a lot of the Star Wars and MCU stuff on Disney+, but he'll kill me if I get caught up without him. Otherwise—um..." She stopped, embarrassed.

"What?"

"I—Look, you can't make fun of me."

"I mean, until I know what you're going to say, I can't make that kind of promise."

"Okay, well..." She hesitated, twisting her hands together. "I read this whole thing about how when people are anxious, they gravitate towards comfort shows—stuff they've watched a million times—because the predictability makes them feel better in periods of uncertainty."

"Okay..." he said, clearly amused but curious.

"And starting this new job has definitely made me, you know, a little anxious. So, I started my favorite comfort show again, and I've been working my way through a complete rewatch."

"So what is it? Some *Real Housewives* thing?"

"Do you really think I'm that shallow?" Jasmine said, mock offended.

"Hey, more than one *Real Housewife of Potomac* has come to a fundraiser for my dad—no shade. I'm just trying to figure out what you'd find so embarrassing that your ears are turning red just mentioning it. Spill it, Lewis. What's the deal?"

"*The West Wing*," she admitted, half under her breath.

"What was that?"

"*The West Wing*, okay?!"

And of course, Trip immediately started laughing.

"You promised!" she protested.

"I actually explicitly did not," He sat on the edge of the bed. "And honestly, I'm laughing because I don't know why you're embarrassed! It's a good show. A little massively unrealistic, but still a good show!"

"Oh, my God, stop! It's such a cliche! A poli-sci grad obsessed with *The West Wing*? I could not possibly be more generic."

"Eh, it's endearing. But c'mon, there's got to be a story there. Why a show that stopped airing new episodes when you were in grade school?"

Jasmine's eyes widened, surprised he wanted to know.

"Well, I mean, it's just me and my mom," Jasmine began, and Trip nodded along. "And as a single mom, she worked a lot. When I was really young, I spent most of my time with my best friend Bailey and her mom at their shop. But by the time I was in middle school, Mama trusted me to look after myself in the afternoons. This was when Bravo was showing, like, twelve hours of *The West Wing* reruns at a time. I knew it was about the government, and that my mom worked for the government, so I thought it would help me understand it better, why she seemed to have to work so hard all the time." She paused. "Turns out it had nothing to do with my mom's job. No one would make a TV show about tax policy analysis."

Trip laughed.

"But..." she continued before trailing off.

"What?"

"It's cheesy."

"I highly doubt that, but even if it is, I won't laugh. I actually promise this time."

"It's just—it's what made me want to work in politics. The show made me want to understand how it all works, and now I want to help other people comprehend it, too. Politics are too important to write off as too complicated or distant from real life, you know? It matters."

Trip was quiet for a moment, carefully weighing what she'd said.

"You're right," he agreed, softly. "It matters. You matter." He glanced up and met her eye for just a second before quickly looking away. "Anyway, what episode are you on? I'm down."

Jasmine scrolled over to the SmartTV settings and logged into her streaming account.

"I'm in the middle of season three, 'Dead Irish Writers.'"

"Oooh, that's a great one. Lord John Marbury is basically my dad if the Ashworths were British."

Jasmine flopped down on the far side of the king-sized bed away from Trip. "He would offer to grasp a woman's magnificent breasts?"

"Pretty sure that was the line he used on my mom back in the day, and it seemed to work for him."

Jasmine laughed and hit play.

They watched two episodes in relative quiet, mostly just reciting their favorite lines and pausing to bring in their room service order. By the time they got to the end of "The US Poet Laureate," they were each two beers in.

"I love how Toby literally won't let Sam talk to the woman he's trying to get with." Trip reached out for the empty bottle in Jasmine's hand to drop in the recycling bin. "It's like they all know Sam is the only male senior staffer with anything approaching game."

"Hmm, you sure about that?" Jasmine twisted the tops off the last couple of beers and handed Trip his. "Josh pulls Donna and Amy Gardner."

"Josh is a self-insert for Aaron Sorkin if there ever was one. That's the only reason Josh gets laid at all."

"Bold of you to assume that I'm not a LemonLyman girl. I think Josh could get it."

"See, you think that, and you really want to believe it. But at the end of the day, you're all Sam Seaborn girlies at heart. The ageless, boyish charm... the eyes..."

"You sure you're not just saying that because you bear a more than passing resemblance to Rob Lowe?"

"Aw, Lewis, don't make me blush." He shook his head, grinning. "Calling me hot this morning, now you're telling me I look like a TV star. If I didn't know better, I'd think you were trying to flirt with me." He paused for a moment. "No wonder your boyfriend can't stand me. Lucky for him, though, you've never liked me that much."

Jasmine frowned. "C'mon, Trip, you know I like you. You know, as a friend." She wasn't quite sure why she felt the need to clarify, probably because her gaze kept wandering to his tanned, taut biceps under the edges of his t shirt.

He played with the label on his beer bottle, a nervous habit he frequently exhibited. "Well, I can get why you wouldn't have been my biggest fan, at least at first."

"Honestly? Yeah, I had a lot of preconceived notions about you, and they weren't all that flattering. I mean, I spent the whole summer sweltering in D.C. while stalking *US Weekly* to find out if they were running pics of you hanging out around NYC or down the Jersey Shore. At least some of that was straight up jealousy." She paused to take a sip before she continued. "But the more we've been forced to hang out, the more I realized I misjudged you...and I'm sorry about that."

"Nothing to be sorry about. That you were willing to give me a chance, despite my reputation, is a lot more than most people have done. I appreciate all the work you've done to try and make me seem like something other than the world's biggest jerk who cheated on a beloved pop icon. So...thanks." Trip took another swig from his beer. "It's past eight, did you want to try and get some work done, or..."

Jasmine picked up her phone. It was after ten East Coast time. Danny was at work, probably driving deliveries for a few more hours. He'd gone mostly radio silent since their exchange earlier, just noting when he'd headed into work and might be unavailable. And to be honest, she was having fun with Trip—not in a PR way, but in a friend way. After a long, high-pressure day, it was nice to unwind. They both seemed to need it.

She set her phone aside. "I mean, the next couple episodes are pretty great...I'm not in any rush to get to bed. Do you want to just hang out a little longer?"

Trip gave her a small smile. "Yeah, that sounds great."

Jasmine turned back to the TV and hit play on the episode "Stirred." As they watched, her thoughts drifted to Trip—wondering how he felt about his dad's presidential aspirations, and how the things on the screen might reflect his reality in a couple years. The enormity of it almost overwhelmed her. She wondered how it didn't affect him—or if it did, how he'd learned to conceal it so well.

She almost asked him. After all, she'd had more honest conversations with Trip than anyone else for the past month. But something made her hold back—a need to keep up a veneer of professionalism she couldn't quite explain. So, she just leaned back against the headboard, sipping her beer slowly as the show played on.

Chapter Thirteen

"C'mon, Bay, focus!" Jasmine cried as Bailey's text tone went off again.

"Sorry, sorry..." She tucked the phone into the back pocket of her jean skirt and tossing her long braids over her shoulder. She gave Jasmine a once-over. Jasmine wore a cropped top and paper-bag waist pants set she'd gotten on Shein. She'd been trying to quit fast fashion—too many climate activists had passed through Senator Ashworth's office for her conscience to ignore. But trying to build a wardrobe on a Capitol Hill staffer salary made a little disposable clothing hard to resist.

"What? Do you not like the outfit?"

"It's cute, but *cute* the vibe?"

"I mean, it's a party, what else would the vibe be?"

"A party crawling with the who's who of D.C. under twenty-five. Maybe make a little bit more of a statement?"

"I can't play in their league, Bay. Better to not even try."

"Then at least let me give you a fabulous beat to bring some edge. And tie up those curls—it's still way too hot out there."

The first week in October hadn't brought much relief. The heat still clung to the city, climbing past eighty again today. The night would cool eventually, but Jasmine figured the party at the Ashworths' brownstone would be like most she'd been to in D.C.—too many people, and enough smoking and drinking to keep the air thick.

She pulled off the white top to avoid staining it with makeup and sank into the seat in front of the makeshift vanity in her and Danny's bedroom, so Bailey could pull her hair back before dipping into the primer.

"What do you think—am I finally healthy enough for a new set of braids?" she asked as Bailey swiped the primer over her face.

"Girl, why are you always in a rush to cover your crown!? These curls are *thriving* with just a bit of TLC."

"Told you I'd deep condition."

Did she do it partly to spite Bailey? Yes. And maybe just a little because both Trip and Addison had complimented her hair since she'd been wearing it natural. Not that she'd ever admit that out loud.

"Well, that's gonna backfire," Bailey teased, brushing eye shadow across Jasmine's lid. "Because with cooler weather coming, I say we leave it out. Let it breathe—at least through Thanksgiving," Bailey said as she worked eye shadow onto Jasmine's lids.

Jasmine groaned. "But braid maintenance is so much easier."

"And the second I put those braids back in, you're going to stop giving a shit about taking care of it through election day. This is a defensive maneuver, honey."

Jasmine hated to admit it, but Bailey was right.

"Okay, fine. But if I look a mess in the background on C-SPAN at any point, I'm blaming you."

"I'm willing to take that risk." Bailey's phone buzzed again as she patted concealer onto the center of Jasmine's lids to make the shade pop.

"Who is blowing up your phone tonight?"

"Oh, it's just Hakeem." Bailey tried to sound casual.

"Wait, *Howard* Hakeem? The senior week guy?"

Bailey had spent the second semester of her senior year at Howard in a flirtationship with Hakeem—a smooth Kappa Alpha Psi brother who looked like a young Kobe: bald head and charming smile, effortless swagger. They'd finally hooked up during senior week, but Bailey had quickly shut it down when he was headed back to Atlanta after graduation, convinced that distance would only mess things up.

"Yeah, well, turns out he decided on Howard for his MBA, too," Bailey said. "So he's back in the district and looking to hang tonight."

"So, you're *definitely* not coming to this party with me."

"Honey, I told you that from the jump. If you let yourself believe different, that's between you and Jesus."

"Fine, but wait—what about Tyrese?" Jasmine asked. The guy Bailey had gone out with last month hadn't come up again, and she'd been so busy with work to ask.

"Girl, you would not believe it. He's got a whole live-in girlfriend he failed to mention. And I am *not* about to be somebody's side piece."

Jasmine laughed, shaking her head. She'd been living vicariously through Bailey's dating drama for the past couple of years since settling down with Danny, and it didn't look like Bailey was slowing down any time soon.

"Gotta hand it to you, Bay—you always find a way to keep it interesting."

"We can't all be old and boring by the time we're twenty-two."

Even though Jasmine did her best to hide it, Bailey caught a flicker of something in her expression. "Ooh, girl, I know that wasn't nothing. Trouble in paradise?"

Jasmine sighed. "I don't know. Things have been…weird with me and Danny lately."

"How so?" Bailey's tone softened.

"He's been pissed at me since I got back from Denver a day late," Jasmine said, exasperated. "Which, like—I get it. But at the same time, I need him to trust me, you know? I've never given him reason not to."

"Don't you think it's more the handsome tabloid fixture you work for that's the problem?"

"Oh, it definitely is. He keeps harping on the whole 'he's a cheater' thing, even though I've told him more than once, I don't think it's true. I believe Trip when he says that's not what happened."

"And you *know* why that's getting under Danny's skin."

Of course she did. His family had originally moved to D.C. for his mom to take a job as Chief of Staff for a newly minted House member from Illinois—only to find out months later that she was also having an affair with him. She'd left his dad for that guy. No wonder the late nights and hotel stays sent him into a spiral.

"Obviously, I do. I'm trying to be understanding. But he pretty much gave me the silent treatment over a flight delay I couldn't control. If he expects me to offer him reassurance, he needs to actually talk to me."

"I mean, he's always been a little immature."

Immature. That word cut through Jasmine like a cold wind off the Potomac. Was that what she'd been thinking about Danny lately? With his contentment with delivering pizza and smoking weed and dreaming about writing without actually writing much—was it starting to grate on her as she looked to expand her ambition?

It wasn't the first time Jasmine had to shove that thought aside.

"I mean, I invited him to come tonight. But he decided he'd rather work. He says it's because he didn't want to miss two Saturdays in a row, since he'll be in Illinois next weekend. But come on, he can't sacrifice a single shift to spend time with me and my co-workers? It would be a chance to get to know them and understand what's going on there. But he'd rather avoid the whole situation, I guess."

"Why are you even going tonight? The happy hours after work, I get, but you've been actively avoiding partying with these people since you started this job."

Jasmine shifted uneasily. The truth was complicated—her position on the type of relationship she wanted to have with the Ashworths changed since she'd started hanging out with Addison and Trip. The whole arrangement to clean up Trip's image meant they'd needed to be seen out together, making it almost inevitable that she'd grow closer to both the Ashworths. And the Denver trip had felt like a turning point. Jasmine had realized Trip wasn't just a work project—he was also someone she enjoyed spending time with, outside the confines of the office and the calculating watch of both Gwen and Ben.

She was actually looking forward to seeing their home and their life there.

But saying that out loud felt like a weird betrayal of Danny, on some level. So even though she didn't have a good reason to hide the truth from Bailey, she decided a small, well-intentioned fib wouldn't hurt while she worked out exactly where her feelings were coming from.

"Oh, well, Alex's starting to freak out a bit that Timlin may actually lose the election. He doesn't want to go back to Colorado—Nigel's here, and plus, he's from an intensely red area. So, he's trying to make sure he strikes up as many relationships as he can, in case Timlin heads home, and he needs another spot to land on the Hill. And tonight's party is going to be packed with well-connected, second-generation political types. But Nigel's in New York for some UN monetary policy thing, and Alex didn't want to go alone, so I told him I'd come with him."

Bailey raised of one of her perfectly sculpted eyebrows. "And you're sure this has nothing to do with your curiosity about this Tess girl?"

It was true that the main reason Trip and Addison had planned this party in the first place was because Tess was going to be in town—en route back to Massachusetts after hitting a campaign event for her dad in West Virginia earlier today. With Mariana's album dropping later this week, there was no way Trip could chance getting spotted anywhere near Tess in public. But both he and Addison were insistent that they see her for the brief amount of time she was in town, so house party it was.

Guests had already been warned that phones would be secured at the door by the private security firm—the only reason Ben had agreed, even reluctantly, to the party. Gwen, of course, had been in a state of apoplexy over it. But Ben had been around long enough to know Trip was going to do what he wanted, so it was better to go along with it and secure some semblance of discretion than push him to all-out "fuck it" territory before the night even began.

"I mean, yes," Jasmine eventually conceded. "Part of me wants to see for myself that Trip is telling the truth—that there's nothing between him and Tess. We've gotten to be friendly enough that it's going to piss me off if I've been lied to. I want to either have a clear conscience about defending him, or square with the fact that he sucks and I have to defend him anyway."

"I mean, I asked about Tess, not Trip, buuuuut..."

"Ugh, not you, too, Bailey. I get enough of that with Danny constantly dropping shady comments about Trip—it's getting old real fast."

"I mean, Lord knows I hate defending Danny," Bailey said. "But you do talk about him a lot."

"Because he literally *is* my job right now," Jasmine protested. "Seriously, if I had to define my work portfolio at the moment, I'm basically working on the messaging around reauthorizing the Violence Against Women Act and Trip Ashworth reputation repair. That's it."

"Which isn't why you got into politics."

"No, but honestly? I'm kind of enjoying it," Jasmine admitted. "Trying to expand Trip's network on the Hill has forced me to expand mine, and it's been great connecting with people in a campaign cycle. It's something I wouldn't have done otherwise. I'm picking up a lot of great intel."

"Turns out it really is still not what you know, but who you know in this town."

"And maybe that's the best reason of all to go to this thing tonight—to start to lock down some of those connections."

Bailey hummed thoughtfully as she blended a couple of shades together on the back of her hand to test out before she applied to Jasmine's lids.

"Care to share with the class, Ms. Reid?"

"You don't sound like someone looking to leave D.C., that's all."

"I know, Bay, I know...I'll talk to him. I promise."

"And your mama."

"...Eventually," was all Jasmine would commit to, before they had to stop talking so Bailey could do her lashes and lips.

"Okay," Bailey said. "Take a look and tell me what you think."

She stepped aside so that Jasmine could see her reflection in the mirror over the table. Jasmine was immediately taken with her look.

"Flawless, as per, Bay. Thank you!"

"You make it easy, doll."

Jasmine carefully slipped her top back on and gathered up the rest of her things, getting ready to head out. Alex lived just a couple blocks away, so they were meeting at his place to grab an Uber. There were no Metro stops near Trip and Addison's—they lived in the mysterious black hole of Georgetown on the train lines.

She texted him when she left her building. Alex was already waiting for her outside when she approached. He looked ready for a party with the kind of crowd they'd be hanging with tonight.

He'd managed to find time to get his haircut. Though he had already admitted defeat to exhaustion-related dry eye and opted for glasses, they were trendy clear acetate frames rather than his clunky backup pair.

"Hello hottie," she greeted him with a laugh and a hug.

"Are you sure I look okay?" he said, nervously running his fingers through the hair on the back of his neck and adjusting his glasses.

Alex was from rural Colorado, where his parents ran a small B&B in ski country, and he'd confessed to Jasmine he often felt out of his depth navigating certain circles in the city. She assured him that he was fitting in just fine, but he still had bouts of nerves with events like this.

"Amazing," she said. "You sure Nigel is okay with you going out looking like that without him?"

"Nigel is currently at some swanky reception at one of the best hotels in New York, drinking free champagne, so that man gets no opinions at the moment."

The ride Alex ordered glided up the curb.

"Come on, then," Jasmine said, grinning. "Let's go see how the D.C. elite does it."

Chapter Fourteen

They arrived at the Ashworth's residence—an imposing Federal-era semi-detached brick brownstone on P Street. Its symmetrical façade and stately black shutters gave it the kind of timeless authority that new money can buy but never quite replicate. Jasmine guessed this place must have gone for north of five million dollars when Jack purchased it, back when Trip moved to Washington for law school. It was sort of funny that they'd spent this much money on a place in Georgetown when the law center was clear across town. But as they approached the door, she understood. Privacy like this doesn't come cheap.

She shot one last "I love you" text to Danny before they headed up the stairs, remembering she'd have to surrender her phone as soon as they crossed the threshold.

Alex rang the bell, and they were greeted by a security guy in a dark t-shirt and jeans, complete with earpiece. He wordlessly handed them each a pouch to secure their phones.

"This is as bad as when we went to see Kevin Hart," Alex muttered as he got his pouch checked for a secure close.

"I mean, that's your fault for going to see Kevin Hart." Jasmine stashed the oversized gray bag in her crossbody.

"Nigel's idea. Maybe he's funnier if you're British? Okay, so my boyfriend has terrible taste in comics."

"But he does have excellent taste in blonds."

They found their way to the surprisingly cramped, blindingly white kitchen, where there were tubs of ice on the counters studded with drinks. Jasmine grabbed a couple cans of hard seltzer and was about to turn to give one to Alex when a hand landed on her mid-back—and immediately, without turning around, she sensed it was Trip.

"There's cider in the other one. That's what you usually get at Union, right?"

She spun around to face him. He was more put together for tonight's party than usual. His fashionably cuffed pants, impeccable white sneakers and a simple but expensive-looking button-up were magazine-cover worthy. "This is fine, thanks. And hi, by the way."

She was surprised when his long arms closed around her in a friendly hug, but it felt...weirdly normal. So, she returned the gesture, careful not to drip condensation from the cans of White Claw down the back of his linen shirt.

"Come on," he said in her ear before releasing her. "Grab Alex, and I'll take you to where the real party is."

Jasmine arched an eyebrow, but he just flashed that slightly crooked grin at her. She walked around the island to where Alex was bopping his head awkwardly to the anonymous lo-fi beat coming from the speakers.

"Trip said to follow him." She handed Alex a drink and they made their way over to Trip and followed him up the stairs.

"Why does it feel like I'm about to be peer-pressured into snorting coke? Because that's exactly why my mom warned against partying with guys like you," Jasmine joked as they got further away from the rattling bass of the party.

"Nope, sorry, my dealer is in Miami this weekend," Trip deadpanned.

Jasmine slid him a healthy amount of side-eye, unsure if she was supposed to take that seriously.

Trip burst out laughing. "C'mon, Jazz, you have to know I'm one hundred percent kidding."

"See, I *don't*! And that's why you make my job such a *fucking* nightmare sometimes!"

Trip just kept laughing. "I know. I'm literally the worst. Seriously, though, the most intense substance you'll see tonight is Addie's dab pen. I retired mine partway through undergrad."

They continued all the way up to the third floor, with Alex glancing questioningly at Jasmine as they did, but all she could do was shrug.

Once they reached the landing, Trip pushed open the door to reveal a cozy space with sloping ceilings and built-in bookshelves. Low couches and comfortable-looking chairs ringed a deeply hued rug.

One of the couches was occupied by Addison in an outrageously cute—and likely outrageously expensive—corset top. Next to her was a new but familiar face, looking effortlessly gorgeous with chin-length wavy white-blonde hair and wearing a nose ring that Jasmine was sure didn't score her dad any points in West Virginia polling. The paparazzi photos didn't do her any justice, but Jasmine still instantly recognized her as Tess Kensington.

"Jasmine, Alex—welcome to the inner sanctum!" Addison cried.

"The what now?" Jasmine laughed.

"You know, the holy of holies, *Devir*!" she offered. Jasmine was no less confused.

"This is what happens when Uncle Dennis marries a nice Jewish girl," Trip quipped. "We end up with Hebrew references."

"And a lot of pissed-off Episcopalians," Addison said. "Honestly, for my dad? Probably part of the appeal."

"He does enjoy being the black sheep," Trip agreed before plopping down on the other couch. "Have a seat. This is where we hang out during these things—once we've made the rounds."

"You hide out at your own party?" Alex asked.

Addison nodded. "There's a certain image to maintain in front of that crowd. We like to have a separate space to actually relax, just for the inner circle."

"So welcome to it," Trip said. "Jasmine, Alex, this is Tess Kensington. Tess, these are the two we told you about who've been helping me navigate the whole situation."

Tess smiled broadly at them. "Nice to finally meet you both. Trip can't shut up about either of you. And I mean, these are the first peeps you've let in here that we haven't known since Sidwell."

"They're real ones, Tess," Trip said. "You'll see."

"I intend to. Now, come on, tell me all about both of you so I can start my amateur psychoanalysis!"

Addison groaned. "Take a night off from the mental gymnastics, babe!"

"It's a reflex at this point. It's what I get from hanging around with headcases and narcissists—present company very much included," she said, casting a look at both Ashworths.

"You wound me, Teresa," Trip said sarcastically, holding his hand over his heart with a huge grin on his face.

"Seriously, though, I want to get to know you both. Where are you originally from?"

Tess's warm demeanor set Jasmine at ease quickly. She could see why Tess was studying to be a therapist—with the easy way she had of getting others to talk and being genuinely interested in what they had to say.

The topic eventually shifted from Alex's and Jasmine's stories to Trip's scheduled interview with *Teen Vogue* coming up on Friday.

"Better than *J-14*, right?" Addison teased. "Wait, is that even still a thing?"

"It was when I was at Princeton," Trip said. "They ran pics of me from the Eastern Sprints, the rest of the heavyweight boat gave me shit for weeks." He paused. "Did pretty well with the boat bunnies at the next regatta as a result, though."

Addison heaved a throw pillow at him that he easily batted down with a laugh.

"*Teen Vogue* actually does some seriously good journalism," Tess countered. "It was a smart move to go with them. Which I'm guessing means it was all Jasmine's idea."

"I had a feeling I was going to like you," Jasmine said with a chuckle.

"Listen to this one—she's good," Tess said to Trip, gesturing to Jasmine with Addie's dab pen.

"Believe me, I know," Trip replied, holding Jasmine's gaze.

As the night wore on, they stayed up in the private haven, removed from the chaos of other partygoers. Trip ducked down a couple times to grab some more drinks while Alex, Addison, and Tess passed around the pen, laughing and chatting in the haze of vapor.

"Trip," Addison eventually said. "We should go down and check to make sure our house isn't being destroyed—not just grab fresh drinks and dip."

Trip got to his feet. "You're right. But you stay here—I've got it. Jasmine, Alex, you wanna come with me and I'll introduce you to some people? There are a few guys clerking for the SJC who graduated from Georgetown last year. Might be good connections to have."

"Oh, that sounds great," Alex said, a note of relief in his voice. "I actually came tonight to kind of network, in case things go sideways for Timlin. I really should put in a little bit of effort on that front."

"Let's make sure we talk to Congressman Schuyler's son, then," Trip said. "He's been with the DNC for a couple years. He'll know any of the House members who might be staffing up after the election."

"I don't need to network, but I do need to find a bathroom," Jasmine announced, pushing to her feet herself.

"I'll show you where it is on the way," Trip said, and the three of them headed downstairs.

Jasmine used the restroom and went back upstairs to rejoin Tess and Addison—but stopped short outside the door when she heard voices inside.

"I'm not mad we got a few minutes alone," Tess's voice, laced with a flirtatious giggle and weed smoke.

"Yeah, that's Trip. He can be smooth when he wants to be."

"Too bad I'll never appreciate his moves."

"Well, I appreciate all of yours," Addison drawled softly.

Through the crack in the door, Jasmine saw the two of them kissing, Addison's body hovering over Tess's on the small couch.

Jasmine quickly spun around and headed back down the stairs, not wanting to interrupt. She'd known from the beginning that Addison was pansexual, she'd worn a pan-pride flag pin on her suit jackets all through June and kept one pinned to the cork board behind her desk. So it wasn't surprising to see her kissing a girl. But when that girl was Tess? She wasn't sure she was meant to know.

As she almost tripped down the stairs, keeping her head down, she ran straight into someone coming up. When she looked up, she met Trip's eye.

"Hey, I was just coming to look for you," he said. "Is something wrong? Why are you in such a hurry?"

"Oh, I, um…I think I saw something upstairs that maybe I don't think I was supposed to? With Addie and Tess?"

Trip rolled his eyes. "This always happens when they get even the tiniest bit high together. I give them five minutes alone and they can't keep their hands to themselves."

"Okay, so are they…" Jasmine started, but Trip glanced around quickly before closing his hand around her upper arm and pulling her down the hallway into one of the bedrooms.

He gestured for her to sit on the navy-blue duvet that covered the king-sized bed. She glanced around at the rich gray walls and dark wood furniture and swallowed. This was his bedroom.

It all happened so fast that Jasmine was just now registering that she—Jasmine Marie Lewis—was alone with John David Ashworth III in his bedroom. Well, *that* definitely hadn't been part of the plan for the evening. She tried to tell herself it wasn't a big deal, but her heart, thudding in her chest, told a different story.

"Trip," she began, determined to ignore that she was sitting on his bed. "Is there something going on between Addison and Tess?"

Trip snorted out a laugh. "There's been 'something going on' between Addison and Tess since prep school. Off and on, anyway."

"Wait, so Tess is…"

"Gay," Trip confirmed. "She's been out to us for years. She was Addison's first kiss. It's sorta sweet, in a completely nauseating kind of way."

Realization dawned. "Okay, so, then those paparazzi photos..."

"Tess did spend the night with an Ashworth that night, but it sure as hell wasn't me."

"I don't get it. Why doesn't Tess just come out? Is it really going to be that big a deal for a Senator's daughter to say that she's into women?"

"If her dad was any other Democrat, they'd print it on their campaign literature and try to parlay it into a Pride parade grand marshal gig. But Hank Kensington isn't just any Democrat. He's the only Democrat in the entire West Virginia Congressional delegation."

"How does that even happen in a statewide office?" Jasmine's political strategist side took over.

"The Kensington coal reputation is huge in West Virginia. Everyone's granddaddy worked for the family at some point, and that loyalty runs deep. Kensington Energy is still the biggest employer in almost half the counties in the state. He gets re-elected mostly on brand recognition, but even if they can't beat him, there's certain elements within the state Republican party would *love* to tarnish him in the eyes of 'values voters.'"

"His daughter's identity isn't a values issue."

"It shouldn't be, but polling data across the state disagrees. You know the huge tide of anti-LGBTQ sentiment and legislation coming out of the red states right now. With the balance of the Senate as tight as it is, Hank can't afford for anything to come out about Tess until after the election. The party is counting on him holding that seat through this cycle."

"So, Tess has to keep who she is a secret until her dad loses or retires?"

"Nope, we have a plan."

"We?"

"Dad and Hank go way back—they were roommates at Princeton, which is part of why we've always been close to the Kensingtons. Tess just came out to her dad last year, after he'd already announced he'd be seeking another term. Hank came to my dad, not knowing what to do about it. He wanted her to be able to live her life, but knew if the news came out during an active election cycle, she'd be a target for every Republican in the state. He couldn't do that to her. So, after he talked to Adds and me, Dad made Hank a promise: once he's President, he'll appoint Hank as Secretary of Energy. It'll get Hank the hell out of West Virginia electoral politics, but with his reputation intact back home, and let Tess come out safely."

"*Once* he's president?"

"You've seen the polling data same as I have. He's the front runner by a lot, both in the expected primary field and against a hypothetical Republican."

"We're more than two years out, that's not any kind of guarantee."

"Nope, but it's the best shot we've got right now. And if that doesn't happen, Hank's already promised Tess he won't run for reelection."

Jasmine exhaled slowly. She couldn't even imagine how Tess must feel, having to conceal who she was for the sake of her dad's career and her own protection.

"And that's why you didn't dare ask her to speak up about the whole Mariana situation..."

"Because she doesn't need a target on her back. She's careful who she trusts, but if anyone really started digging, they'd probably find someone willing to talk, even if it's just a rumor or wild speculation. Better for me to take the fall than have her outed against her will in front of the entire internet."

Jasmine stared at Trip for a long moment. "You're a really good guy."

Trip dismissed the comment with a wave. "It's what any friend should do. Unfortunately, I didn't feel right about outing her to Annie, either, so when she assumed the worst, I had to let her."

"I get that. But then why are you telling me?"

"I mean, you saw them." His eyes softened. "But we were going to tell you tonight anyway, so I get why Addison didn't feel the need to hide it. Because I trust you, Adds trusts you. And we know Tess can, too."

"She absolutely can. You all can." She paused. "Are you going to tell Alex, too?"

"Shit, I left Alex downstairs with Chris Schuyler. He's probably bored to death talking about redistricting. Come with me, we can grab refills and rescue him before we interrupt the girls up there."

"Sounds like a plan."

Before they headed into the hallway, Trip stuck his head out and quickly checked the hallway for any rogue partygoers. "Can't be too careful. Don't need to start any new rumors that you'll need to quash on my behalf."

"Yeah, good call." With the hallways empty, Trip's hand once again fell on her back to guide her into the hallway. A sensation she was growing used to.

How much she liked it wasn't something she'd admit.

Chapter Fifteen

Jasmine and Gwen sat off to the side of the conference room while Trip spoke with Lauren, the reporter that Jasmine had worked with from *Teen Vogue*. Lauren had attended the Denver event, and after Trip's stellar performance there, agreed to do an exclusive interview for the online version of the publication, maybe with a longer profile piece in a spring issue when Jack announced his candidacy.

But they had to get through this first. And as great as Trip was in a public appearance like a campaign rally, prepping him for a one-on-one sit down had been a completely different animal.

The problem with Trip was that he knew how to turn it on in front of a crowd, experience from a couple decades of being in the spotlight. But up close, that veneer could crack. Jasmine had come to understand it wasn't that Trip was disinterested or a jerk, just that his anxiety could overwhelm him easily, and what was charming when he felt at ease read as arrogance when the pressure was on. He'd resisted her attempts to talk about it, though, so the pre-interview coaching sessions she'd been putting him through all week hadn't been very productive, vacillating between tense and friendly. He went from charming to defensive in the blink of an eye, attempting to cover up his discomfort with dense policy analysis and a distinct lack of the humor that make him so likeable.

And unfortunately, that's exactly how the interview was going.

Lauren initially seemed charmed by Trip, his easy smile and an up-close glimpse of his movie star good looks winning her over. But under the veneer of girlish amusement, her intense dark eyes revealed a tough interviewer, and even though she'd cleared the topics with Jasmine and Gwen ahead of time, the exact wording of her questions seemed to get Trip's back up. He was leaning hard into his academic side, like he wanted to come off as serious and substantial rather than just another rich, entitled pretty boy playing the political game, but it wasn't working.

As he wrapped up a long and complicated answer about legal precedent in sentencing for drug crimes, Jasmine let out a silent sigh. She didn't want to interrupt, but Trip needed reassurance that he didn't have to convince Lauren of his intellect, he needed to look like a nice guy. The kind of guy who would never cheat on Mariana DaSilva.

The album had come out the day before, and it was, predictably, a shit show. The rest of the lyrics to "American Royalty" pointed the finger even more squarely at Trip, with the line about green eyes and jealousy. Addison had once again assumed custody of Trip's phone, and Gwen and Jasmine had turned off the Google alerts they had for Trip's name to stop the deluge. She had even deleted her personal email app from her phone, sick of going off every ten minutes with another email from someone she hadn't spoken to in years, looking for tea on the Trip and Mariana situation.

The drama with Trip would have been enough to send Jasmine into stress induced ulcer territory on its own, but to make it worse, things were still weird with Danny. It had been another series of late nights that week with interview prep and album anxiety, while Danny continued to quietly resent how much she was working, never addressing it directly but making barbed comments whenever he got the chance. He'd left Thursday morning to visit his mom and stepdad in Illinois for the weekend, and Jasmine was kind of glad they had some time away from each other.

Her relief at not seeing Danny again until Sunday night set off a whole lot of other questions in her mind that she was trying to ignore.

It was eating away at her while she listened to Trip talk about the difference between punishment and rehabilitation—ignoring Addison's texts asking how it was going and picking at her cuticles every time Trip strayed from something they'd explicitly prepared for him to talk about.

She must have tuned out while making notes about a bill Trip referenced that was stuck in committee, because she was startled when Gwen nudged her sharply. She immediately refocused on what Lauren was asking.

"It seems like substance use issues would strike close to home. Your dad very famously went to treatment for alcoholism a handful of years ago."

"And he's not alone. More than twenty million Americans will battle addiction this year. The biggest difference between my dad and others, though? He was able to access treatment when he needed it. Only about ten percent of people out there with a problem can say the same. And that's exactly what the bill that's currently held up in committee is aiming to fix—which is why it has my dad's full support."

"Though your father has been incredibly open about his experience in finding recovery, there are other personal topics he never touches. Neither of you have ever publicly discussed your mother's death. Did that contribute to your father's difficulties with alcohol? Is that why the Ashworths never talk about Francesca?"

Trip immediately looked to Gwen and Jasmine, his face etched with alarm.

"Didn't she get the no-fly list?"

Jasmine panicked.

"Of course she did. Lauren, do you remember the document I sent—"

"I mean, yeah, but I'm a reporter, it's my job to ask the hard questions, even when people don't want to answer them."

Lauren was looking at all three of them like they were fools to believe a journalist would respect the boundaries they'd set for this interview.

"We sent those for a reason," Gwen practically hissed. "One that was very clearly spelled out for you."

Lauren just laughed.

"I'm going after the story—and this *is* the story."

She turned back to Trip.

"Why on earth would you want to hide one of the things that makes people the most sympathetic towards you?"

But Trip was already on his feet.

"I'm not hiding anything, it's just—it's private. I don't—I can't..."

Trip's composure was cracking, his anxiety rolled into rage.

"You people are all the same, a story no matter the cost—you have no shame. I'm done with this interview."

And he walked out of the conference room.

"You follow Trip," Gwen said to Jasmine. "I'll handle her."

There was a flash of anger in Gwen's eyes that actually frightened Jasmine. Despite her small stature and sunny personality, Gwen could be *fierce*—and given Ben's protective instincts around Trip, she knew Lauren was about to feel Gwen's wrath.

Jasmine bolted out into the office suite and spotted Addison standing in the doorway of their shared office space. She had stuck around to be there for Trip when they wrapped up the interview.

"What the hell happened?" Addison asked. "He didn't even look at me when I called his name, just stormed out."

"The fucking reporter asked about his mom," Jasmine fumed.

Addison looked stricken.

"Oh, God, is he—"

"I have no idea. Did you see which way he went?"

"He's in Uncle Jack's office," Addison said, indicating the doorway at the back into the Senator's private office.

"Thanks."

Jasmine rushed over, but she stopped short in front of the door. She knocked, and got no response, so she knocked again.

"Fuck off, Adds," Trip barked through the closed door.

"It's not Addison, it's me," Jasmine said tentatively.

Trip yanked the door open and stared her down, fire in his eyes. "Why the hell do you think I'd want to talk to you right now?"

Jasmine was taken aback. "I just wanted to see if you were okay..."

"I'm not fucking okay, and it's your fault—you and your image-obsessed boss."

Jasmine felt her own anger start to flare.

"Trip, neither of us had any idea she was going to go off script. Both of us told her that the no-fly list was serious, to not even think about—"

"And a shit ton of good that did," Trip cut her off, punching the wall so hard that the picture frames shook. "*This* is why I hate the fucking media. They have no goddamn boundaries!" He turned away from her, and she could see his shoulders shaking as he attempted to catch his breath.

Watching him, her anger melted away. He may have unfairly lashed out at her because she was the most convenient target, but he was hurting.

She made an impulsive decision and took a step forward and rested her hand on his back, like he'd done for her countless times. She half expected him to jerk away, to put up a wall between the two of them. But instead, he stiffened ever so slightly for a second before relaxing under her touch.

"Trip, just breathe," she coached him. "I'm right here, just breathe."

His angry heaves evened out into longer, smoother breaths, until it started to hitch again. But this time, it was because he was crying.

"You don't know...what it was like," he half gasped. "These fucking vultures, they didn't let her have a moment's peace, not even when she was..."

Jasmine said nothing, just began to move her hand in slow, reassuring circles on his back.

He took a quivering breath. "The day we were bringing Mom home from Sloan-Kettering in the city, taking her down to the house in Stone Harbor, to...to die." He stopped, squeezing his eyes shut as if to try and prevent the memory from overtaking him. "Somebody who worked for the hospital wanted to make a quick buck, tipped off some photographers that we were leaving. They took her picture through the goddamn windshield, splashed it all over the *New York Post*. She barely wanted *us* to see her like that, never mind the whole world. So frail, so weak. So far from who she was, from how she wanted to be remembered, but the fucking cancer…" His voice cracked on the last word, and he was reduced to slightly ragged sobs. "They couldn't even let her fucking die without a telephoto lens invading her privacy, taking her dignity. And there was nothing we could do. It's the price we pay for the power and privilege."

Jasmine's heart broke, listening to Trip cry. She put her hand more firmly on his back and guided him to the couch against the wall, gently pushing him to sit while he buried his head in his hands. She sat down next to him and wrapped her arm around his shoulders, clinging to his upper arm with the other hand.

"I'm so sorry, Trip," she murmured softly in his ear, tears in her own eyes. "It's so unfair. All of it."

He didn't reply, just sat there trying to regain control. Gwen appeared in the doorway, concern lining her features. Jasmine shook her head slightly.

"She's gone, and I told her the feature is off," Gwen said. "I'll be in my office if you need me."

"Can you ask Addie to come in?" Trip said without looking up.

"Of course." Gwen disappeared back into the office hallway.

With Addison on her way, Jasmine figured that was her cue to leave, so she quietly unwound her arm from Trip's shoulders and stood up, but his hand closed over hers that lingered on his arm as he looked up at her with watery eyes.

"Please, can you—*will* you—stay with us for a while?" Trip asked softly, almost pleading. "I'm sorry I…"

"Shh, no," Jasmine quickly reassured him. "I get it. And yeah, I'll stay as long as you need me." She settled back down onto the couch and once again began to rub small, soothing circles on his back, the way her mom had always done for her when she was upset. He finally let himself lean into her touch, the tension in his shoulders giving way under her hand.

The office door opened carefully, and Addison stepped in. "Hey, Trip, you gonna be okay?"

He glanced over at Jasmine. "I think I will be."

Addison came over and sank down on his other side, the three of them crammed onto the small two-seater couch. But none of them seemed to mind, as Addison leaned her head onto his shoulder. Jasmine wasn't entirely certain how long the three of them sat there in silence, just focused on keeping Trip anchored through the moment.

Eventually, Addison broke the spell when she rose to her feet. "Come on, it's getting late. Jazz, I know Danny's out of town, you wanna come hang out at our place tonight? We'll order delivery and watch stupid rom-coms."

"Rom-coms?"

"Our guilty pleasure," Addison said with a smile. "Trip prefers *Legally Blonde*, but my favorite is *Clueless*. It's your first time, so you get to choose."

If Trip wanted his comfort movie, she was more than happy to hand the choice off to him, but he gave her a small smile and encouraging nod.

"Okay, then, if I'm picking...we're doing *Ten Things I Hate About You*."

"Excellent choice!" Addison crowed as Trip smiled a bit wider. Addison extended her hand and pulled Trip to his feet while Jasmine stood.

"I should run home and change first," she said, looking down at her suit and fancy shoes. "I've got a sports bra and sneakers in my desk, but nothing to really just hang out in."

"Oh, no need, you can borrow something from us," Addison assured her. "Well, probably from Trip. You're way too tall for most of my stuff!"

"I've got plenty of hoodies and sweatpants," Trip offered. "They'll be baggy, but cozy. And the drawstrings should help."

"Perfect, thanks."

Trip held her gaze for a beat too long, and she found herself thinking about how much she she'd enjoy curling up in an oversized hoodie of his. She'd always loved stealing them from friends and boyfriends—they were somehow always more comfortable than anything she purchased for herself.

Addison paused in the doorway and held out her hand. "Keys?"

"Adds, I'm fine to drive," Trip tried to protest, but Addison shook her head.

"In case that reporter decided to tip off a photographer out of spite, you're riding in the back." Jasmine was impressed by Addison's evasion techniques. Clearly, this wasn't their first press evasion.

Jasmine ducked into her office to retrieve her things. She checked her phone quickly and there were a couple texts from Danny—she hesitated, thumb hovering over the screen before turning it off and dropped it back in her bag. Tonight wasn't about Danny—it was about Trip.

"Ready to go?" Addison called from the waiting room, and Jasmine shouldered her bag, ready make sure Trip was going to be okay.

Chapter Sixteen

What was supposed to be dinner and a movie with Addison and Trip at their place, somehow turned into Jasmine spending the whole weekend there. Danny wasn't due back until Sunday anyway, so she had no reason to rush back to an empty apartment. As promised, Trip lent her some sweats, including an oversized Princeton hoodie that she changed into right away, and the three spent Friday night watching movies and eating their way through Addison's junk food stash before Jasmine crashed in one of the guest rooms. The next morning, Ben and Gwen both texted the staff group chat to tell them to take the weekend off, so they decided to hang out for the day. Trip invited Jasmine to join her for his run, and she found herself enjoying the silent companionship as they looped their way around the Mall. By the time they returned, Addison had invited Alex and Nigel over for takeout, wine and game night.

Unsurprisingly, Nigel, Jasmine and Trip were all absurdly competitive, and their ill-conceived Monopoly game got cutthroat while Alex and Addison just laughed at their ridiculousness. After too much boxed wine and too little sleep, they decided to venture out for an early, casual brunch. A couple mimosas took the edge of her wine-induced headache. Jasmine said her goodbyes and caught an Uber home, still wrapped in Trip's Princeton sweatshirt that she half-heartedly promised to return.

As he hugged her goodbye, Trip spoke quietly into her ear. "Truly, thank you for being here. Keep the hoodie, if you want."

He had a shy smile on his face when they parted, and Jasmine was grateful he looked so much better than he had Friday night. She hoped he was really feeling better—not just pretending for her sake.

She got home and took a long shower before combing deep conditioner through her hair so it could set for a while—hopefully, keeping Bailey off her back. She settled on the couch with her laptop and began browsing through some of the online chatter about Trip in the wake of Mariana's album release. There were a handful of items on Buzzfeed analyzing the lyrics off the album and theorizing which exes inspired which ones. But it seemed the steady stream of misguided "think pieces" about Trip's life seemed to be fading. Some had actually shown up defending Trip—at least in the abstract. It looked like their preemptive strike to shore up his image had made an impact, with each one referencing his standout appearance at the Timlin event. Jasmine breathed a small sigh of relief, hoping Gwen would be pleased.

She scrolled through videos tagged with Trip's name on TikTok. Nothing was gaining any kind of traction—no clips with lots of views or comments. That's when a key turned in the lock. She smiled, eager to see Danny and hoping the weekend apart meant they would be able to reset.

"Hey babe," she said, rising to wrap him in a hug. "Welcome home."

Danny smiled and kissed her. "I missed you."

"Missed you, too. How was Springfield?"

"Same as always. Scott's kids weren't around this time, so it was just me, Mom, and the Governor being awkward as fuck for the entire weekend. But with the Governor's mansion being all the way out there, it's not like I could even go see my friends in Chicago." He paused, shrugged. "What are you going to do?"

Jasmine nodded sympathetically.

After four terms in the House, Danny's stepdad had been elected Governor of Illinois two years ago, and his mom moved to Springfield with him. It had been a huge scandal initially—Scott announced he was divorcing his wife because he'd fallen for his married Chief of Staff, who was also getting divorced. But Illinois politics had never much cared about scandals, and Scott won the state's highest office easily. Danny had to learn to live with it, doing his best to survive those awkward visits every few months.

"At least you'll have a six-week reprieve, right? Until Thanksgiving? Six whole weeks Scott-free."

"Thank fuck for that." He dropped his bag on the floor. "But hey, how'd it go?"

"It was kind of a shit show, honestly. I didn't expect it would go so poorly, but, yeah."

"I'm sorry, baby. But hey, you can register to take it again next month, right? One more shot before you have to get your applications in."

For a moment she was confused, thinking he'd been talking about Trip's interview, since that was what had consumed her thoughts for weeks. Then it hit her.

The LSAT.

She'd completely forgotten.

Jasmine had registered for the October LSAT months ago, knowing she needed to boost her scores before she applied to law schools. It was the reason she didn't go to Illinois with Danny for the weekend—she was supposed to take the test.

But with everything going on at Senator Ashworth's office, it slipped her mind. She'd turned off her email notifications, which meant she missed the reminders. She missed the test entirely.

Danny raised an eyebrow when he saw her expression change.

"What's wrong? Can you not—is it too late to register for the November date?"

"No, I mean, I..."

"Jasmine, what's going on?"

She drew a slow breath. "I didn't take it, Danny. I—I forgot."

"What? You—Jasmine, how the fuck do you just forget?"

"Friday was Trip's interview with *Teen Vogue*, and it was a disaster. The reporter really, like, went after something he didn't want to talk about, and he was really shaken up. I stayed with the Ashworths to help him through it, and—"

"So you spent the weekend with *Trip* instead of taking the test you need to get into law school? The one that *our entire future* hinges on?"

"It's not what you're think. He needed Addison and me. You don't understand what it was like for him, when she—"

"I don't give a shit, Jasmine! This fucks with our plans. How the fuck do you expect me to react?! Why are you throwing away your future for this fucking prick?"

Her pulse pounded in her temples. "First of all, you've made absolutely no effort to actually get to know him, so you have literally no idea what he's really like. Second of all, I'm not throwing away anything, I—I don't even want to go to law school, Danny!"

"Wh—what? Jasmine, of course you do, it's all you've talked about since I've known you."

"It's what I thought I had to do. I didn't stop to ask if it's what I *wanted* to do. But now that I'm out there, doing the media and messaging work—I'm good at this. And I don't need another two hundred grand in debt to prove it. Plus, I enjoy it, more than I thought that I would. So I don't—I just don't think that's the path for me anymore."

"Okay..." Danny said, slowly. She could almost see the gears turn behind his eyes.

"A little out of left field," he said at last, "but we can deal with it. Since there's no timeline now—we don't have to worry about starting school—we can move now, right? Why wait another year to escape this town?"

A tight knot formed in the pit of her stomach. This was it.

"Danny, I—I don't want to leave my job. I don't want to leave D.C. If anything, I want to do more. I'm working for someone who could very well be the next President of the United States. I'd be crazy to walk away from this right now."

Danny's face was blank. "I'm sorry, what?"

"I—I'm staying in D.C."

"This wasn't part of the plan. You said if I gave you a year, you would—"

"I know," she cut in. "And I had every intention of doing that. But that's before I knew—"

"Before you knew *him*," Danny snapped. "This is about Trip, isn't it?"

"This has nothing to do with him—at all. I've been thinking about this since the beginning of the summer. I just didn't know how to tell you, especially when I knew..."

"You knew it'd be over."

She tried to avoid that thought for weeks. She kept telling herself that Danny would come around—that if he really loved her—he could figure out how to be happy if they stayed.

Besides, he could write from anywhere. He didn't need to be *somewhere* the way that she needed to be on Capitol Hill.

But deep down, she knew that he wouldn't. Couldn't. The sense of stagnation that frustrated her so much had always been partly he was still here—stuck, at least in his own mind.

Some part of her knew once she said it out loud, it was over. And now it was.

"I'm sorry, Danny, I am. I just—this is where my life is. Where I want it to be."

Danny's eyes filled with tears. "But you promised me..."

"I did. And I'm so sorry I'm breaking that promise." Her throat tightened, vision blurring. "I love you."

"Not enough," he said bitterly.

He turned and walked out of the apartment, leaving Jasmine alone with her tears.

She let herself cry for a while, until she could breathe again. The idea that this was really the end slowly set in. She regained a little of her composure, and stepped into the shower to rinse the conditioning treatment from her hair.

She had no idea where Danny had gone or when he'd be back, but she needed a plan for what to say to him when he did return. When she got out of the shower and threw on some clothes, there was a text waiting for her.

Danny: At Ed's for the afternoon. Need you out tonight.

Panic hit hard, and tears choked her throat again.

The apartment was Danny's. He'd rented it after he graduated from GW while Jasmine still lived in the dorms her senior year. When he renewed that summer, they hadn't bothered to add her name—there hadn't seemed to be a reason to giving they weren't planning on staying.

She didn't have a choice. She had to go.

Her mind raced through her options. A hotel was possible—off-season rates wouldn't be terrible—but the thought of sitting alone in a cheap, anonymous room made her chest hurt. Her mom wasn't an option. She would want to know what had happened between her and Danny. Jasmine wasn't ready to have two soul crushing conversations in a single day.

Bailey was out, too. She lived with her mom, and there's no universe where Mama Reid wouldn't call Mama Lewis the second Jasmine showed up. Alex and Nigel came to mind, but they already had three other roommates. Squeezing in one more would be tight.

But there was another option. She scrolled through her phone and Facetimed Addison.

"Hey Jazz, what's up?" Addison said smiling brightly. She immediately noticed Jasmine's puffy eyes and tear-streaked cheeks. "Oh, babe, what's wrong?"

"Danny and I—we just broke up."

"Oh, my God, I'm so sorry. Are you okay?"

"Not really," she said honestly. "But the biggest issue right now is he's throwing me out of the apartment, and I don't know where I'm supposed to go—"

"You're supposed to come here," Addison replied immediately. "We didn't even change the sheets in the guest room yet—just come. Pack a bag for a few days, and we'll figure out how to get the rest of your stuff over here this week."

"Addison, thank you, but I just need somewhere to stay for a night or two until I figure out—"

"Jasmine, respectfully, shush. If you don't want to stay here long-term, we'll help you find something else, sure. But we've more than got the room. This is an open invitation to live with us—for as long as you need or want it."

Jasmine could cry all over again. Addison had every reason—every privilege—to keep her distance. That she would open her heart and her home to her as a genuine friend was something Jasmine hadn't expected when she took this job.

"Thank you, truly."

"Okay, pack what you need for the week. Trip'll be there in half an hour. I'm running out for emergency wine and dinner—what do you want?"

"Anything but pizza."

Addison snickered. "Let's do Shake Shack, then. Text me your order. I already know Trip's."

"Will do, and thank you, again."

"Anything for the inner circle. See you in a bit, babe."

Jasmine hung up and started packing—suits separates, workout clothes, and pajamas, just essentials for now. She tucked Trip's Princeton sweatshirt deep into her bag. Leaving it behind for Danny to discover would have been an unmitigated disaster, confirmation of an untruth he was already convinced of.

She picked up her phone to text Danny and let him know that she was leaving. She had a flurry of missed texts that she scrolled over smiling for the first time all night at Trip's messages lighting up her screen.

Trip: OMW

Trip: Oh, make sure you bring your travel mug.

Trip: We have a stupid-expensive espresso machine. Bet we can make those chai things you like.

Her shoulders finally dropped. Trip remembered small things about her—details that made her feel seen. Comforting, and sort of exciting.

Maybe she'd known that when she called Addison—that Trip would be there, too. But after what Danny accused her of, she couldn't admit that. Not yet.

She slipped her tumbler into her bag, and texted Danny.

Jasmine: Leaving in ten. I'll text later this week to grab the rest of my things.

He left her on read.

She sighed, gathered her bags, and headed downstairs to wait for Trip.

Trip's black SUV rolled up to the curb. He popped the hatch, grabbed her bags from her and loaded them without a word. Jasmine circled around to the passenger side and climbed in.

When he'd gotten back in and closed the door, he looked over at her. "You okay?"

"Better now," she said honestly, a tired smile on her face. "Thank you, truly."

"Of course." He shifted into drive and turned up the radio without another word.

They both saw him—Danny, turning the corner as they pulled away. He'd seen who'd come to get her.

Chapter Seventeen

Living with Addison and Trip was easier than Jasmine had expected. As an only child, she had a hard time adjusting to new roommates in college. She'd even struggled getting used to living with Danny, worried the whole first month that he was judging something about her, like how long she showered or the fact that she shed hair everywhere. But the Ashworths had welcomed her from the moment Trip carried her bags into the living room and Addison enveloped her in a tight hug. From that first night, neither of them pushed her to talk—just kept her wine glass filled and a steady stream of *The West Wing* episodes playing on the TV. Trip and Addison showed that they cared about her, in ways she didn't expect.

She couldn't live in a cocoon of *West Wing* reruns forever. She had to start telling other people what happened. Bailey seemed wholly unsurprised when she filled her in on how things ended with Danny. She'd known she was living in a fantasy to believe Danny would magically accept that she didn't want to leave D.C. But the harsh reality of Bailey basically expecting them to break up stung. Jasmine hated that she had allowed her denial to sink in that deep. Bailey had seemed a little upset that Jasmine had reached out to Addison first. Once Jasmine explained the impact that it all had on her living situation, though, Bailey said she understood.

To Bailey's credit, she stopped bringing up her relationship with Trip. She seemed to understand that Jasmine needed time to process the breakup before pressing her about whether her feelings for Trip might have evolved from professional to personal.

Jasmine didn't have the energy for any more complications right now—not after her conversation with her mom went worse than she expected. Mary Lewis was a serious woman and had been all of Jasmine's life. Her "keep your head down and grind" work ethic had guided her rise at the Treasury. Over her long career, she'd reached a position of real importance. But she always wanted more for her daughter. She didn't want her to have to spend decades proving herself. The "right" presentation, the "right" opportunities. It all mattered.

So, when Jasmine approached her with the news of the breakup and her decision to forgo law school, Mary didn't react well. She wasn't especially bothered by the breakup—she was never Danny's biggest fan—but she hit the roof over Jasmine passing on law school to stay working for Senator Ashworth.

"Jasmine Marie, you're going to throw your lot in with some rich old white man and pray *he* gets a better job? And what if he loses? Where does that leave you?"

"With a great resume builder. I can find another job on the Hill, I'm sure."

"Just to be at the mercy of whatever happens the election cycle after that? There's no stability, no certainty in that kind of life."

"Maybe I'm not focused on stability right now, Mama."

"You can't afford not to be, Jasmine. Don't expect that someone's going to come in and take care of you. Women like us can't count on anyone's loyalty. You've got to make your own way."

"Senator Ashworth has a great reputation for taking care of his staffers. It's one of the reasons I decided to work for him in the first place."

Mary just snorted. "That will only last as long as he's winning. Don't think they won't forget you the second that they have to pack up and head home. I've been around government types a lot longer than you. Politicians are opportunists—every one of them. That's why you're your own credentials, something no one can take away from you if an election doesn't go their way."

They argued for another hour, but Mary was no closer to accepting that Jasmine could make a way that didn't include a prestigious law degree and a crushing amount of debt. Jasmine returned to the brownstone much later than she intended. She went into the kitchen to make a cup of tea to calm herself down before she tried to get some sleep, but she was so wound up—with tears blurring her vision—she dropped the mug before the water had boiled.

"Shit," she mumbled, stooping to pick up the chards of ceramic scattered on the tile.

"Jazz?" Trip's voice, thick with sleep, called from the back stairs. "You okay?"

Jasmine glanced over as he wandered into the kitchen. He looked half asleep, his hair a bed-headed mess and wearing a low-slung pair of gym shorts.

It wasn't the first time she had seen him shirtless—she'd spent plenty of time scrolling through his beach pictures online all summer. And it wasn't like his physique had been a mystery under his workout clothes when he let her tag along to his fancy gym by Dupont Circle. But it was the first time she'd seen him up close—really seen him—and heat rose in her cheeks as she tried to ignore a very different heat coursing through her at the sight of all Trip had to offer.

Because now was definitely not the time for that.

"Crap, did I wake you being such a klutz?" Guilt washed over her as she remembered him saying he'd been up until three a.m. last night, racing to meet a tight *Law Journal* deadline.

"I'm sorry, you must be—"

"Jazz, stop. What's wrong?"

"I told my mom I'm not going to law school, and it didn't go well."

"Shit, I'm sorry," he said, taking the broken pieces from her hands and tossing them in the trash. He immediately turned to pull down two other mugs and dropped tea bags in them.

"Do you wanna talk about it?"

"You should go back to bed..." she weakly protested.

"I'm fine," he assured her. "Let's have some tea, and you can talk about it—or not. Whatever you need." Trip glanced down, realizing he was half-naked. "But uh, I should probably put a shirt on for a serious conversation, huh?"

Jasmine nodded, and Trip retreated to the hall closet to grab a hoodie while she poured the water into the mugs and sat at the island. When he returned, she filled him in on the disastrous conversation with her mom.

"She just sounded so disappointed in me. Like—*how could I possibly be so stupid*, you know?"

"I do, believe me. You're looking at the most prolific parental disappointment in the greater D.C. area."

She had to admit, he was probably one of the best people to relate to at least that part of what she was going through.

"How do you handle it? That feeling you're never going to do anything but let him down?"

"I mean...not well," he said with a small laugh. "I guess I've started to care a little less, when I know I have other people who see me for more than he does. People like Adds, and Tess. And you," he added, almost under his breath.

Jasmine stared down into her tea, smiling. It stirred something in her—something she wasn't ready to name—that Trip cared what she thought of him.

They ended up talking for hours, the conversation meandering from disappointing their parents to stories from their childhoods to comparing their Spotify playlists. Jasmine had been deeply delighted to find out that Taylor Swift was his most-listened-to artist, though Trip insisted that Taylor was his comfort music, and it kept him calm and focused while he was studying. Jasmine still gave him endless shit for being so white and basic, but secretly found it just as endearing as he had found her *The West Wing* habit.

By the time they finally went to bed, it was one a.m., and Jasmine felt significantly better than she had when she'd arrived home.

But the conversation with her mom was ringing in her head the morning of election day. Gwen informed her that the DCCC had invited all the in-town staffers for sitting senators who weren't up for reelection to a watch party at some huge hotel ballroom. When she confessed her anxiety to Addison on the way to work, Addison just laughed.

"Oh, babe, the D-triple-C isn't worth getting your panties in a twist."

In the month that she'd been living with the Ashworths, Jasmine had grown used to commuting into the office with them. Addison and Trip shared his SUV, since their brownstone only had one off-street parking spot, so the three of them would generally drive over to the Russell Office building together and then Trip would make the ten-minute walk to Georgetown Law Center. He insisted he didn't mind being stuck near the Capitol after his class, getting his work done in the law library while Jasmine and Addison worked late. He could take the bus or an Uber back if he didn't want to stick around that part of town, but he rarely did, preferring to ride back with Addison and Jasmine, no matter how long it took.

Jasmine looked forward to their carpool far more than she had her solo train rides. It carved out time each day just for the three of them—to debrief office gossip with Addison and debate policy points with Trip. That ritual had become a small but vital anchor in her new routine.

But this morning, even Addison's friendly reassurances did little to calm Jasmine's nerves. This kind of event was business as usual for the Ashworths. Photos of various family members with presidents and princes lined the walls of the Senator's office the way most families casually display wedding or graduation photos. For them, this kind of thing was as familiar as a family dinner where they would of course have a seat at the table. For Jasmine, it still felt like something she needed to earn, to prove she belonged there. That pressure sat with her all day—right up until Trip arrived at their office to walk over to the event together. She pasted on her Gwen-approved networking smile, ready to watch the election returns with a few hundred other young staffers.

The ballroom hummed with a nervous energy from the moment they arrived, and it only intensified as the polls began to close across the country. By little before nine p.m., Jasmine was on her third glass of wine, watching the early blowouts roll in Massachusetts and Vermont.

The night was shaping up better for Democrats than expected. Usually, midterms had been unkind to the party in power, but they weren't losing nearly as much ground as strategists feared they might. They were going to lose the House—a foregone conclusion—but the Senate was tilting blue so far.

Her eyes scanned the room in search of the Ashworths. West Virginia had already been called for Senator Kensington, so the cousins had slipped out to Facetime Tess before she had to go on stage with her dad at their campaign headquarters back home. Addison had invited her to join them, but she declined, wanting Tess to have some privacy to react however she needed with just her closest friends.

When she gave up looking for them in the throng, she inched closer to one of the giant video screens, watching the countdown to the polls closing in Colorado. Jasmine, along with the rest of their friends, had been sending encouragement to Alex in their group chat all day. He'd either been too busy or too nervous to respond, which had Nigel on edge, so Jasmine and Addison had spent the day coaching him through his nerves, trying to keep him from spiraling and piling that energy onto Alex, too. Nigel had no context for what an American election night looks like, and they had advised him to pop a gummy and chase it with a glass of wine. Alex probably wouldn't be answering until morning.

As the Colorado poll closure clock ticked down to zero, Jasmine took a deep breath. She hadn't realized just how anxious she was about this race until that moment. It had been her idea for Trip to make an appearance at Senator Timlin's Denver event and follow-up online posts—something that now felt more personal than she expected. A creeping guilt tried to convince her that if Timlin lost, it would somehow be her fault for pushing Trip to get involved. Who knew how many Mariana

DaSilva fans there were in Colorado? It wasn't like the polling data asked that question.

Though, if Gwen was doing the polling, they sure as shit would have.

Gwen and Ben had begged out of the party that evening with equally flimsy excuses. Addison guessed they were watching the returns naked from Ben's bed—a mental image Jasmine could have gone her whole life without.

There was nothing to be done now. Whatever was going to happen with Senator Timlin—and by extension, with Alex—had already been decided. The only thing left to do was count. Jasmine drained the last of her wine and clutched the glass, trying to steady herself.

Minutes later, Addison came bounding up to Jasmine, Trip a few paces behind her. "One down, one to go," she said cheerily before taking a deep drag from her beer.

"Don't say that too loudly, Adds," Trip fake admonished. "The D-triple-C cares about every race tonight."

"Oh, please, don't pretend you give a fuck about any of them other than the ones that affect our friends."

"Us holding the Senate affects all our friends—and *your* job."

"I liked you better before you gave a shit," Addison mumbled.

Trip ignored that, motioning for them to follow him to the bar for another round.

It was close to two a.m. when the 'Breaking Results' banner flashed on the screen. The talking heads droning on about where vote counts were being reported had Jasmine expecting Michigan House races, but the map of Colorado appeared instead. This was it—Timlin's race.

Jasmine squeezed Addison's hand tightly. The outline of the state filled in blue.

Colorado had gone for Timlin.

The room erupted. Addison pulled out her phone to record the moment for Alex in Denver. With Addie preoccupied, Jasmine turned to Trip. "Can you believe it?" she yelled.

Trip lifted her off her feet in a hug, spinning her around despite the crowd pressing in around them.

When he set her back on her feet, still laughing, she unwound her arms from Trip's neck. Their eyes met.

Suddenly, the noise dimmed. All Jasmine could see was Trip—his green eyes alight, that signature smile on full display.

She couldn't make herself look away. And it seemed he couldn't either, as his face settled out of raucous joy and into something that looked almost like a realization, as if something he'd been trying to make sense of had finally clicked into place.

They held each other's gaze, long past polite. Eventually, Addison broke the spell when she waved her hand between them. "Selfie for Alex," she shouted.

"Right, of course," Trip said, looking down, flustered. As they crowded together for the picture, his arm snake around Jasmine's waist, landing on her hip. It wasn't his usual friendly touch—Jasmine's stomach fluttered.

And she might have liked it a little too much.

Chapter Eighteen

With the election behind them, an unusual calm settled over the Ashworth Senate office for the rest of November. Jasmine knew from her internship with the House Appropriations Committee last year that the holiday season was unproductive in Congress—even more true in an election year where lots of offices were packing up and preparing to head home.

Ben and Gwen spent most of their time holed up with consultants, narrowing down who they wanted to take the lead on Senator Ashworth's presidential campaign announcement in the spring. That left Jasmine and Addison managing the day-to-day. The Friday before the Thanksgiving recess consisted of navigating the last batch of constituent complaints and weeding through holiday party invites to determine which ones the Senator and his wife needed to attend, and which ones they could politely decline without igniting a controversy.

Jasmine set aside the stack of expensive-looking paper invites she'd gone through that day to send on which ones to prioritize back to the home office in Philadelphia before picking up her phone and groaning at seeing another message from her mom.

Did you take a look at the email I sent with some additional flight options?

They're all a bit out of the way but will get you there.

After she and Danny broke up, it took Jasmine over a month to realize she wouldn't be going to Illinois for Thanksgiving like she planned. She'd had enough time to cancel her flight, but she didn't have a backup plan. Her mom was going to Alabama to see her family, and wanted Jasmine to come along, but by the time she thought to look, flights were outrageously expensive and enormously inconvenient. Between the flight issues and her dread of answering her extended family's well-meaning but meddlesome questions about what happened with her boyfriend and where she was going to law school, she couldn't make herself commit to going.

Dealing with constituent complaints and party invites was easier than dealing with her family.

Addison looked up from her laptop across the room. "You okay over there, Jazz? I didn't realize my uncle's social calendar was such a nightmare."

"It's not *his* that's the problem, it's mine. My mom wants me to go to Alabama next week, and I can't make myself say yes."

"Family shit can be a lot. You want to see a group that puts the F U in dysfunctional? Come to an Ashworth family gathering." She paused for a second, before she sat up a bit straighter in her desk chair. "Actually, you *should* come to an Ashworth family gathering. Come with us to Stone Harbor."

The entire Ashworth clan descended on the cluster of family beach houses in a picturesque Jersey Shore town for the long weekend. Addison and Trip had been telling her stories of the more ridiculous family shenanigans that had taken place over the years. It sounded kind of wonderful to Jasmine, who'd grown up far from her extended family that all still lived further south.

With Addison's invitation extended, Jasmine wasn't sure she should accept.

"I don't know, Addison. Isn't it weird to have, like, an employee crashing on your family Thanksgiving?"

"Ben will be there—he's been coming for years. Auntie Chess always insisted." Ben's family was in Oregon, and the holiday weekend wasn't long enough for him to fly all the way to the west coast. He took a full two weeks off over the Christmas recess in exchange. So, it made sense that the Ashworth hospitality had taken him in, too.

"Is Gwen coming with him this year?"

"I'm not sure, but she's originally from Arizona, right? I can't imagine she's flying back there just for a couple days, either, so it wouldn't surprise me."

"Think they'll finally own their relationship if they show up for Thanksgiving together?"

"Who knows? People have a way of stretching the boundaries of plausible deniability around here."

Jasmine could feel the tips of her ears turn red, and she was glad that Bailey had convinced her to leave her hair natural, because the volume of her curls concealed it. She was sure Addison wasn't talking about just Ben and Gwen, but also her and Trip.

And Jasmine didn't know *what* was going on with her and Trip. They had definitely shared a moment on election night. She replayed the shift in his face over and over, unsure how to make sense of the way he reacted when she was in his arms. But she noticed that both of them found any excuse to be close to each other.

It wasn't uncommon for Trip to drape his arm around the back of the booth at the diner they often went to for breakfast on Saturdays, not really around her but resting against her shoulders if she leaned all the way back. Jasmine may have taken to asking for his help stretching after they worked out together. She told herself it was just convenient—he was an athlete, he would know what was best—but it didn't explain why her pulse spiked more from his hand on her knee than from their entire run. It was assumed by their friends that the two of them would be next to each other on the couch for movie nights, their shoulders touching while they annoyed everyone else by whispering back and forth about the spoilers they'd both looked up online before it started. It all felt easy and light and playful.

Even though, on some level, Jasmine knew it was none of those things. They were roommates, he was her boss's son—and above all else, he was Trip Ashworth. None of that boded well for any kind of romantic connection between them.

But they kept flirting with it anyway. Whatever "it" would turn out to be.

Jasmine was certain Addison had asked Trip what was up with the two of them, but had yet to broach the subject with her. So maybe she really didn't mean anything by her remark, and it really was just Gwen and Ben she was referring to. But Jasmine couldn't rule it out, that she was trying to get something out of her, too.

She sidestepped it entirely by returning to the topic of Thanksgiving.

"I mean, if you don't think anyone would mind if I tagged along…"

"Not at all," Addison chirped brightly. "I'll tell my mom we need another seat at the kids' table."

"Kids' table?"

"In the Ashworth family, you're pretty much stuck at the kids' table until you get elected to public office, it is what it is," she laughed. "And fair warning, the houses fill up, so you're going to be stuck sharing a room, and possibly a bed, with me, if all the air mattresses have already been claimed."

Jasmine laughed. "I can manage that. Not like you take up much room anyway."

"Again with the height jokes," Addison said with a roll of her eyes. "Just because I live with two freakishly tall humans doesn't mean I'm some kind of hobbit. I'm 5'3!"

"You keep telling yourself that's something worth mentioning, boo," Jasmine shot back, laughing.

The next day, Jasmine called her mom to break the news that she wasn't going to be traveling to Alabama for Thanksgiving.

"I'm sorry, Mama, it's just so expensive to get there, and I'd have to turn right around and come home for work anyway. I'll see everyone at the reunion in June, though. Promise."

"I don't know. I don't like the idea of you sitting in D.C. all alone, especially not when you were supposed to be with your ex-boyfriend and now..."

"Well, the Ashworths invited me up to New Jersey to have dinner with them."

Jasmine's mom grew silent on the other end of the phone.

"You think louder than anyone else I've ever met," Jasmine complained. "Just say it."

"Baby girl, are you getting a little *too* familiar with these folks? What's their game?"

"There's no game, Mama. They're just genuinely good people, willing to open their home up to me. I'm not the only one—I think the whole staff is going. They really do just want to include us, since the job makes it hard for us to travel."

Hearing that others from outside the family would be there did the trick to bring her mother's disapproval down a notch. "If it's the norm for the office, I suppose it makes sense for you to go—could help your career. But I'm surprised you didn't ask Bailey if you could visit with the Reids that day."

Jasmine shifted the phone to her other ear and stared at the half-empty mug in her hand. She hadn't even thought to talk to Bailey about plans for Thanksgiving.

"Oh, I know how many Mama Reid has to cook for that day, no need to add to her burden by showing up with another empty plate," she murmured, tracing the lip of the mug. Mary seemed to accept that answer, but Jasmine knew Bailey never would.

Once she hung up with her mom, Jasmine let out a slow breath and opened her chat with Bailey.

Jasmine: Hey girl. You busy rn?

A text bubble popped up almost immediately.

Bailey: Just closing up the shop, What's good for tonight?

Jasmine hesitated, thumb hovering over the keyboard before typing.

Jasmine: You wanna just grab some dinner and catch up?
Bailey: I'm down.
Bailey: Feel like I've barely seen you these last few weeks.

Jasmine's guilt deepened. Work had been relatively calm the last couple weeks, it wasn't really a good excuse. She'd been spending time with Addison and Trip, even outside of work, and she hadn't been putting in the effort with Bailey that she should. Which was going to make telling her where she was spending Thanksgiving even harder.

Jasmine arrived at the restaurant, ordering two sweet teas. Bailey blew in about ten minutes later, already talking a million miles an hour.

"Jazz, you would not believe the conversation I had with Hakeem today..."

Jasmine smiled as Bay launched into the rundown. They'd moved from flirting into a situationship, but Hakeem wouldn't define it—except now he was asking her to come meet his family on Thanksgiving.

"Can you even believe that? Won't call me his girlfriend in front of his boys, but wants to act like I'm his wifey to his grandma? A little consistency would be nice, that's all I'm saying."

"I hear that," Jasmine laughed. "So, are you going to go?"

"Of course not, you know I'm not missing a Reid family meal. I am not driving all the way to Atlanta to risk having to choke down some dry-ass turkey when you know Mama Reid throws down in the kitchen."

"Is it just about the food, though?"

"That's my story and I'm sticking to it." Bailey took a sip of tea. "Speaking of Thanksgiving plans, though..." she said. "Mama told me you're not going to Alabama?"

Jasmine shook her head. "Too far. Too expensive."

"Then come through. We'll fix you a plate."

"Oh, I'm actually—I'm going to New Jersey. With Addison." She left Trip's name out of it.

"You really want to spend the holiday with your boss's family?"

"It's not like that. We're friends. They've been great to me since the breakup."

"But at the end of the day, they are still Ashworths, and you are not. You'd do well to remember that."

Jasmine blinked. "What the hell, Bay?"

"They seem nice enough, I guess. But I don't know. I'm not down with them treating you like some kind of pet project—a Black girl from the district to trot out to prove they're woke."

"That's not fair."

"And the worst part? You let them. Because you sprung for some man who's never going to give a girl in your position the time of day."

"I'm sorry, what did you say to me?"

"You heard me. The way you talk about him? It's giving freshman crushing on the hot senior. But honey—you're the help."

Jasmine couldn't have been more shocked if Bailey had physically slapped her. "*Excuse* me?"

"You work for them. You're not in their league, and they won't let you be, not with treating you like you need a handout all the time."

Jasmine couldn't remember the last time she'd been this angry at Bay. In their many years of friendship, they'd fought like sisters over things like clothes and boys, but they'd had to tell each other some hard truths, too. This was the first time Jasmine felt like Bailey was dead wrong.

"I'm not a fucking housemaid—I'm a communications professional working in the goddamn U.S. Senate. I didn't realize you thought I was so fucking unworthy that the only reason they'd have for being decent to me is because I've been wearing my hair natural. You don't get it. Neither you nor my mom."

"Or maybe if the two women who know you best are both trying to tell you what's up, you're the one who doesn't get it."

"*Or maybe* both of you just don't want to see me getting close to someone who's not y'all. There's a reason neither of you liked Danny all that much, either."

"Because we don't want to see you get used and discarded—like what happened to your mama."

"I am *not* my mama." Jasmine rose to her feet. "I can handle myself, thank you very much." She reached into her bag and pulled out some cash, tossing it on the table to cover the drinks. "Let me know when you're ready to stop being a bitch about the people I care about and we'll talk." And she stormed out of the restaurant and back to the train.

Normally, it was a pain in the ass that there was no Metro stop in Georgetown, but tonight Jasmine was grateful for the mile-long walk from Foggy Bottom to the Ashworths'. Her fight with Bailey was buzzing in her head. Was Bailey right? Was Jasmine setting herself up to be in a similar position as her mom— raising a baby on her own after the white man she thought loved her had up and left? Jasmine's upbringing had been focused on avoiding her mother's mistakes. Was she walking straight into one now, blinded by charm and money and the illusion of being taken care of?

She slowed as she approached P Street, needing to pull herself together before walking into the house. A nagging sensation in her gut told her Bailey could be right—that she needed to protect herself and her heart and not get in too deep with the Ashworths, Trip especially, before she couldn't find her way back out.

She had nearly made up her mind to tell them she wasn't going to New Jersey after all. She couldn't go to Bailey's either—not after that blowout—but she'd be just fine here on her own for a few days.

When she walked in, Addison's laughter floated out from the kitchen, underscored by Trip's lower voice rumbling in what she knew was a spot-on impersonation of Ben. She paused in the doorway for a moment, just watching them.

Addison noticed her out of the corner of her eye. "Jazz, you're back early! I thought you were going out to dinner."

Jasmine opened her mouth, ready to spill a half-truth—that Bailey had to reschedule and that she was going to stick around D.C. after all to get a chance to see her since they had to cancel tonight.

But then she glanced over at Trip, and the moment they locked eyes, concern creased his face. He knew something was wrong. And she couldn't bring herself to not be honest about it.

"Bailey and I got into a huge fight. I don't really want to talk about it."

"Then we won't," Addison said immediately. "But since you're back early, we can get a head start on these pies I stupidly promised to bring! I got everything on the list you emailed me, but there was no way I was attempting this pecan pie recipe with only Trip for backup."

Jasmine smiled. Just like that, all the careful logic she'd constructed on the way home—about why it would be best to put distance between her and the Ashworths—fell apart.

She wanted to spend Thanksgiving with people who cared about her. They did. So she would.

"Sounds like a plan. Adds, can you grab my tablet from my desk while I get washed up? I want to see the recipe on something bigger than my phone."

Addison nodded and headed up the back stairs. Jasmine went over to the sink to wash her hands—but before she could, Trip's hand landed on top of hers.

"Hey, are you really okay?"

"I mean, only kind of. But it'll be fine. We've been friends for ages. We'll work it out."

"If you want to talk about it, I'm here," he assured her, giving her hand a squeeze before stepping back.

Even though Trip was probably the one person she shouldn't talk to about it, she felt a familiar thudding in her chest—the way her heart always seemed to react these days when Trip showed her, once again, who he really was, at least to her.

For a moment, she let herself believe that whatever was happening between them was more real than imagined.

Chapter Nineteen

The three of them left D.C. mid-afternoon the Monday before Thanksgiving, hoping to dodge the majority of the traffic. The Senate was technically in a State Work Period the week, so Jasmine had gotten Gwen's blessing to work from New Jersey—reviewing position statements and pre-drafting press releases for the votes they already knew the Senator's position on.

They spent most of the four-hour drive gossiping about just how obvious their bosses would be about their "secret" relationship.

"Ben always stays in the pool house," Addison said. "We'll have to see if Gwen gets a bedroom elsewhere, or if they deem that unnecessary."

"Does he stay the whole weekend?" Jasmine asked. "If he heads back earlier, and you want time with just your family, I can probably catch a ride with him." Four hours in the car with Ben didn't exactly sound like her idea of a good time, but she couldn't shake the slight edge of feeling like an imposition.

"Not sure what he's planning to do this year, but you can't leave early," Addison said. "This is your first time. You need to experience the full Ashworth Thanksgiving."

"It's more than just a turkey dinner?"

"Are you kidding?" Trip half-laughed from the driver's seat. "There's beach bonfires, cutthroat Monopoly games, and a Christmas movie marathon."

"Movie marathon?"

"*A Christmas Story*, *Home Alone*, and *Christmas Vacation*," Addison explained. "It's the only way."

"We used to watch *It's a Wonderful Life*, but it started to feel a bit on the nose," Trip snorted, referencing the very public struggles of several of his family members with mental health and substance use issues.

"Yeah, maybe best to steer clear of those issues on a holiday," Jasmine agreed.

"As best we can, anyway," Trip said, a look Jasmine couldn't decipher on his face, but she didn't press, and the conversation moved on to what horrible boyfriend their cousin Amanda was going to bring home this year.

By early evening, they'd reached Stone Harbor. The Ashworth family owned a cluster of beach houses right on the sand. The rambling "old house," as Addison and Trip called it, had been in the family for four generations now. As the oldest, the Senator had inherited it after his mom passed away—but the will stipulated that the whole family still be able to use it. Addison's dad claimed to the third floor, so they would all be staying together, while other cousins, aunts, and uncles filled the other properties along the same stretch of beach.

By Wednesday night, a bonfire blazed on the sand where the sprawling Ashworth clan gathered to kick off the holiday. Jasmine stuck close to Addison and Trip as they sipped beers around the fire. She was once again wrapped in Trip's Princeton sweatshirt, letting it soak up the smell of the woodsmoke like a memory.

Thanksgiving passed in a blur of food and laughter. Jasmine tried her best to keep up with all the inside jokes that flew around the tables, but even when she was lost, she felt welcomed. Even Ben, ever stoic, had raved about her pecan pie, saying it was as good as the one his Georgia-bred grandmother's.

By the time night had fallen, Jasmine was slipping on that woodsmoke-tinged sweatshirt and heading out to the sand where another bonfire was being lit. The Senator left right after dinner with his wife, heading to New York to visit with her family for the weekend. Jasmine caught a flash of disappointment on Trip's face—one he was determined not to let anyone else see—before he shook his dad's hand goodbye.

She knew, even though Trip would never admit it, that he needed someone to be there for him since it was clear his dad wouldn't be.

And she was grateful it got to be her. She told herself it was only empathy—that she understood what it felt like to be left behind—but the way her heart accelerated watching him stare into the fire said otherwise.

She grabbed a couple of beers from the overflowing coolers on the wraparound porch along with a blanket from one of the Adirondack chairs before heading down to the bonfire. Trip was sitting near the flames, half-listening to one of his cousins playing guitar. The music almost drowned out the argument his cousin Amanda was having with the useless boyfriend she'd brought with her this year.

Jasmine stood over Trip, holding out one of the bottles. "You in a turkey coma?"

He looked up, startled. "Oh, sorry, I didn't see you. Uh, yeah, something like that." He took the beer and pulled a long draw from it before his unfocused eyes fell back on the fire, his fingers anxiously peeling at the label.

She reached out her hand. "Come on, let's take a walk."

"You don't have to—" he began, but she cut him off.

"Come on, let's go."

He smiled, setting the bottle in the sand, and grabbing her hand to let her pull him to his feet. She dropped it as soon as he was steady, but stayed close enough that their fingers brushed together every few steps as they walked toward where the waves crashed against the shore.

Jasmine stopped to spread out the blanket she'd brought and sat down, motioning for Trip to join her. He wordlessly settled next to her, eyes fixed on the dark sea.

"So..." Jasmine began. "Wanna tell me what's wrong? You've been kind of distant since your dad left."

Trip sighed. "Sorry, I don't mean to be an asshole about it."

"No, not at all, Trip. I just want to make sure you're okay."

"I should have warned you when Addie invited you in the first place—I can get kinda, I don't even know, about Thanksgiving. Not exactly my favorite holiday."

"How come?"

"It *used* to be my favorite," Trip said. "Most of my family is still in Pennsylvania full-time, but we spent almost the whole year in D.C., since I was enrolled in school there. Even when my dad went back every couple of weeks, Mom and I stayed in the District. And we usually spent Christmas in Italy with Mom's parents. In the summer, everyone was always coming and going on different weeks down here, so the only time we got to see all the Ashworths together was Thanksgiving weekend.

Plus, it was just all about food and family—no pressure of gifts or decorating or anything. It was the happiest I remember my parents being. The least stressed."

Jasmine smiled softly, picturing what Trip's parents must have been like when they were younger. She'd seen photos—his dad, the dashingly handsome junior senator from Pennsylvania, and his gorgeous Italian wife.

"But," Trip said heavily, his gaze dropping to the sand, "that all changed when I was fifteen. When I came home for Thanksgiving break my sophomore year, that was when my parents sat me down and told me Mom was dying."

The breath caught in Jasmine's throat.

"She'd been diagnosed about six months before," Trip continued. "The odds are never good with pancreatic cancer, but Dad had convinced himself they could beat it. He pulled every string he could to get her any and every available treatment—experimental meds, acupuncture, even stuff like energy healers, which did *not* go over well with my deeply Catholic Italian grandmother," He gave a humorless laugh. "By November, they knew nothing was working, and it was just a matter of time. She held on for a few more months—Addison's mom always says that Mom wanted to watch spring come one more time, to make sure we had hope. But that Thanksgiving was the point of no return. She wasn't going to get better, and we were already on borrowed time."

"Trip..." Jasmine breathed. There was nothing else she could think of to say, so instead she just reached for his hand again. He seemed to be waiting for her to do that, immediately lacing his fingers through hers, holding tightly.

"And would you believe that's only the *second* worst Thanksgiving of my life? The worst was two years later."

Jasmine didn't say anything, but she knew Senator Ashworth's bio well enough to do the math—and knew exactly which year Trip was referring to. That was the year that Jack spent Christmas in rehab.

"The first whole year without my mom was kind of a blur," Trip admitted. "I smoked a ton of weed just to stumble through it, but everyone was content to let me be pissed at the world for a while. Dad had his own way of escaping. He was either working or drinking. Sometimes both. By the fall of senior year, we were both too deep in our own shit to figure out how to talk about it. But I *needed* him to talk about it, you know? And he just shut me out. Made it go away every time I got caught smoking weed at Lawrenceville—or the time I had sex with and then ghosted a girl who turned out to be a Congressional page and the granddaughter of a major DNC donor. But he wasn't actually there for me—just had Ben and the rest of his staff clean up my messes."

Jasmine swept her thumb soothingly across the back of Trip's hand as he spoke, pressing in closer so he could feel her solid warmth against him.

"It all came to a head here, over Thanksgiving. He was already drunk. I should have known better than to confront him like that—but when he disappeared into the library, I followed him. I asked him what the fuck his problem was. Could he not stand to be around his own flesh and blood? That's when he yelled—no, he couldn't stand the fucking sight of me, because I look just like Mom. It was a constant reminder the love of his life was gone and all he had left was her fuck-up of a son."

Jasmine literally gasped, but Trip just gave a tired sigh. "I called him an asshole and stormed out. Uncle Dennis caught me in the hall—he'd followed me, expecting something bad to happen, and he'd overheard the whole thing. He charged into the library and told Dad that was it—they were done coddling him. If something in him was so broken that he would speak to his own son that way, he needed help. Dennis told Dad if he didn't get on a plane with him to check into rehab the next day, he'd go on record with the *Philadelphia Enquirer* telling everyone in Pennsylvania what he just said to me. Didn't seem to care much if he lost his son, but cared if he lost his seat, so off he went."

"Has he...is it any better now?"

"He apologized eventually—part of one of the steps he worked in AA. But sometimes I think he still feels so guilty he convinces himself that I am some kind of fuck-up, just to ease his conscience. And even though he's said he's sorry, I don't know if I've forgiven him for it yet. Or if I will." He gave another mirthless laugh. "Bet you're regretting asking now."

Jasmine fixed her own eyes on the sand, knowing this was the moment. If she really trusted him, it was time to tell him her story, too.

"No, Trip, I—I get it, truly." She took a deep breath. "You know how I told you my dad died in a car wreck?" He nodded. "Well, what I didn't tell you is he was drunk when it happened."

There was a flash of surprise in Trip's eyes, but he just tightened his grip on her hand.

"Mom always said he didn't have a real problem, but I'm not sure she knew for certain. He'd all but ghosted us right after I was born. When he came around again, asking to see me, my mom told him he needed to show up in other ways first, before I got old enough to be disappointed when he ran off again. He got mad and left, and the next morning, she got word that he'd wrapped his car around a tree on his way home from a bar." Tears filled her eyes. "I barely even remember him, never even had the chance to know him. And I don't think I'll ever forgive him for that. So, yeah. I get it."

Trip's eyes were teary now, too, breaking through the numbness that had sheltered him all night. He reached over to brush away the tear that had escaped from the corner of her eye, his hand lingering on her cheek.

"For what it's worth," he said softly, "he's the one who missed out. Not having a chance to know you. You're the best person I know."

They held each other's gaze for one, two, three long moments before Trip slowly leaned towards her—stopping when their lips were just a breath apart. Jasmine closed her eyes and the distance between them.

The first kiss was tentative, testing. When she pulled back, afraid she'd just made a terrible mistake, Trip's hand slipped from her face to the back of her neck and he kissed again. This time was different—urgent, unguarded. The vulnerability they had shared had broken something open, and neither could deny what had been simmering between them since election night.

Without breaking the kiss, Trip guided her back down onto the blanket, his weight shifting over her. Her hands tangled in his hair while his slid under his sweatshirt she was wearing, tracing over the smooth skin he found there. Every brush of his fingers, every taste of his tongue, every slip of his skin on hers just made her feel like it would never be enough.

The spell was broken when Jasmine felt her phone vibrating in the pocket of Trip's sweatshirt, pressed between them. Trip's phone buzzed, too, and they both groaned.

"Cock-blocked via group chat," he mumbled. "But if that's Adds..."

Jasmine nodded as he rolled off of her and she sat up, pulling out her phone. Sure enough, Addison had texted them both, wondering where they were.

"Guess that means we should get back," Jasmine said, reluctant.

"Yeah, but before we do..." Trip leaned in for another kiss. "Thank you. For being here tonight. I know we need to talk about this—what this is—but I hope it means... something."

"It does," she said quickly.

He smiled, relief flickering across his face.

"But more than anything, seriously, just... thank you."

She gave him one more kiss before standing, shaking sand from the blanket. Together, they started back toward the old house, the cold night wind carrying the faintest trace of woodsmoke and salt.

Chapter Twenty

Jasmine was awake entirely too early the next morning, still trying to make sense of last night. Addison was sound asleep in the queen bed next to her, curled up on a tight ball, looking smaller than usual. It made Jasmine smile, seeing her sophisticated friend look so innocent and sweet. She slipped out quietly, grabbing Trip's hoodie to pull on over her pajamas before she made her way down to the back deck.

She and Trip hadn't said another word about what happened out on the beach when they rejoined Addison up at the bonfire. But as the night wore on, emboldened by a couple more bottles of beer and the hope that everyone was too intoxicated to notice, Jasmine settled down on the sand between Trip's knees. He pulled her back against his chest, his hands once again finding their way under his sweatshirt she was wearing to trace along her bare torso, his freezing fingertips leaving trails fire on her skin.

Eventually, a very drunk Addison pulled on Jasmine's hand to head to bed, and they parted for the night with nothing more than a tight hug.

Now, the next morning, Jasmine leaned over the railing and watched the ocean, trying to figure out what the day would bring. Getting involved with Trip romantically had so many layers of complications, she could barely think straight.

But her heart didn't seem to want to listen to anything her head had to say.

A mug of coffee was suddenly set down on the railing by a familiar hand. Before she could even turn to acknowledge Trip's presence, his arm came around her waist as he pressed himself into her back, speaking low in her ear. "Couldn't sleep either, then? You thinking about last night too?"

His breath on her neck was near enough to send a shiver down her spine. She closed her eyes, trying to steel herself to do the responsible thing.

"Trip, about last night, we really should…" She turned to face him. But before she could finish, he pulled her into him, kissing her. And just like that, the idea that she should say no evaporated.

When he broke apart from her, he took a deep breath. "There are a million reasons we shouldn't do this, I know. And Gwen will probably have a million more we haven't even thought about yet." Jasmine couldn't help but chuckle. "So," he continued, "I get it completely if you want to tell me to fuck off and leave you alone. And I'll do it. We can forget it ever happened, go back to being roommates. But…" He paused. "But I can't stop thinking about you, not just this morning, but for weeks now. I've wanted to kiss you, for so long. I—I have real feelings for you, ones that make the complications worth it to me. I'm just hoping you feel the same way." He looked away as he said it, like he was part shy and part fearful of how she'd respond.

When she couldn't find the words, she kissed him.

The deck rail creaked against Jasmine's back as Trip pressed his hips flush to hers. Jasmine's hands ran over him, trying to feel every line of his shoulders through his own sweatshirt. She gasped when his hands brushed across the top edge of her pajama bottoms, and he smiled against her lips.

"Well, this is a sexual harassment seminar waiting to happen if I ever saw one," Addison's voice deadpanned from the French doors leading out onto the deck.

Jasmine instantly broke away from Trip, heat quickly rising up her face. Trip didn't look guilty at all—he wore the smile of a cat who'd caught the canary.

"Addison!" Jasmine squeaked. "You were sound asleep, I didn't think..."

But Addison dismissed her concerns with a laugh and a wave of her hand. "I've been expecting to walk in on this scene since election day. Gotta hand it to you, Trip, waiting until you have the whole family as an audience is a choice."

"Not the whole family," Trip said pointedly. "The Senator already left."

"Which buys you a little time to figure out how to disclose," Addison, sliding her gaze between the two of them. "Assuming this is, you know, an actual thing."

Trip glanced at Jasmine. She'd yet to actually confirm that, though the eagerness with which she'd let him slip his tongue past her lips probably should have been a good indication.

"Yeah, this is a thing. We're like...together?" Jasmine asked, a question in her tone.

Trip chuckled. "Yeah." He pulled her back to him and kissed her forehead. "We're together."

"Ugh, this is too adorable for this early in the morning, I might be sick," Addison said with a look of faux disgust. "I'm going to get a cup of coffee, please figure out how to detach yourselves before I come back."

Trip turned to Jasmine. "Well, now that that's settled...we do probably need to figure out what to tell Ben and Gwen. I don't know enough about Senate ethics rules to know what exactly we need to share, but as a soon-to-be attorney, I can tell you disclosures work best before they're compelled."

"It's completely embarrassing to admit—but watching you go all lawyer on me is incredibly sexy," she teased, thrilled to actually be able to openly flirt with him the way she'd held back from doing for weeks.

"Oh, really?" He pushed his hips back against her. "Well, play your cards right and maybe I'll let you call me counselor. I doubt I'll have any objections to raise. Though there will be other things raised..."

Jasmine's giggle barely escaped before it was silenced by Trip's lips once again finding hers. And as badly as she wanted to see where things could go, she had another idea that might be almost as fun.

"We should go tell Ben and Gwen. Right now," she said with a mischievous grin.

"So, you wanna go wake up your boss, hoping to catch him in bed with your other boss, to distract them both from the fact that you're there to admit you're dating *their* boss's son?"

"Precisely."

"That's evil...I love it." He grabbed her hand and pulled her towards where the one-room pool house sat off to the side of the old house. Trip marched them right up to the French doors with the blinds drawn and knocked obnoxiously loudly, trying to contain his laughter.

And they were immediately rewarded for their boldness, when it was Gwen who opened the door, clad in a robe she was still hastily tying.

"Debbie, I'm so sorry. Is my car..." And when she looked up and saw that it wasn't Addison's mom but her assistant and her boss's son standing in front of her, she froze in stunned silence.

"Morning, Gwen. Is Ben awake yet? Jasmine and I need to talk to him."

"Jasmine, Trip! What a nice surprise! I just popped over before breakfast to look at some headlines with Benjamin, and..."

Her terrible attempt at a cover was blown just seconds later, when a shirtless Ben who had clearly just rolled out of bed and definitely had not been looking at headlines appeared over her shoulder. "Baby, who's here—" And just as Gwen had, Ben immediately froze when he saw them at the door.

"You are so busted, dude," Trip managed to get out before bursting into laughter.

Ben didn't look as amused. "John David, you'd do well to remember that I do not work for you, but your father, who is already well aware of my relationship with Gwendolyn. That, and I know where all your bodies are buried."

"Oh, relax, Ben," Trip said, his laughter fading but a smile remaining on his face. "It's not like we haven't all known for months. Neither of you are any good at hiding it."

Gwen had finally recovered enough to say, "Speaking of not hiding anything, I can't help but notice that the two of you are looking a bit cozy this morning." She gestured between Jasmine and Trip whose hands were still firmly wound together.

"Yeah, that's the actual reason we're here. But, uh, Ben? Can you put on a shirt before we come in? I know this is the beach house, but it's a little early for all that."

"I'll remember how much you're enjoying this, Mr. Ashworth," Ben noted threateningly, turning to grab a shirt.

"Well, come on in, then," Gwen said, and Trip and Jasmine sat down on the small couch in the sitting area to the left of the bed.

"Now, to what do we owe the honor of this far too early morning visit?" Ben asked, all business.

"Well, we wanted to tell you both right away, in case there's some kind of formal disclosure we need to make," Trip began, before glancing over at Jasmine.

"There's been a change in the, uh, nature of my relationship with Trip." God, she sounded awkward.

"And when did this change come about?" Ben asked.

"Uh, last night?" Trip said, like it was a guess. "Officially this morning, I guess, but last night was the first time we…"

Gwen held up her hand. "Stop right there. We do not need to know the particulars of what happened between last night and this morning."

Heat flooded Jasmine's face as Trip shook his head and jumped in to clarify. "No, that's not what I'm implying. We didn't spend the night together. In any capacity. We just—we kissed, and then this morning we did the whole DTR thing."

Ben looked confused.

"Oh, for God's sake, Ben, it means 'define the relationship,'" Gwen said, shaking her head. "How on earth did you survive the dating pool before me?"

"He didn't," Trip deadpanned. "He just tried to time his coffee runs at the office to 'accidentally' bump into women he was simping over from other offices. It didn't work, by the way." Ben glared at Trip, but turned to Jasmine.

"And Miss Lewis, the definition is…"

"Trip's my boyfriend," she said, testing it out loud for the first time, and finding she liked the way that sounded. Trip apparently agreed. His hand slipped protectively around her hip.

Ben sighed in relief. "Thank you for informing us, though I'm not strictly certain you had to."

"Are you sure?" Trip asked skeptically. "I feel like there are rules for everything."

"I'll run it by counsel. They'll know best," Gwen said, walking over to the bed to retrieve her phone and fire off an email. "But technically, Trip doesn't work for the Senator in any official capacity, and there's been no complaint of sexual harassment or favoritism as a result. We may just need to make a note of it in Jasmine's file and move along."

Jasmine gave her own sigh of relief. This had gone much smoother than she anticipated. Maybe that was a good omen for their relationship as a whole.

"From a PR perspective, I'd advise you to keep a low profile for a few more weeks, until we figure out a strategy to go public. After the Mariana situation, Trip's next relationship is bound to catch some attention, whether with someone famous or not," Gwen said, not looking up from her phone. "We need to be prepared for them calling out Trip for taking advantage, and Jasmine being a gold digger. Neither will stick, but it's better to know it's coming." Ben nudged her gently. Her face softened into a smile. "And for what it's worth, we're both very happy for you. We've been hoping this would happen."

"So, wait..." Jasmine said, glancing between Ben and Gwen. "Do you two...gossip...about us?"

Ben let out a small chuckle. "We can't let the junior staffers have all the fun, now can we?" Jasmine wasn't sure which was more surprising, that Ben actually deigned to give a shit about the romantic misadventures of his staff, or that he'd just laughed about it.

Gwen's phone pinged. "Oh, looks like Mitch Bolton is up early this morning, too," she said, referencing the attorney Senator Ashworth kept on retainer. "He said we'll have you sign affidavits on Monday affirming the dates and details, just in case there's a lawsuit later, and then you're in the clear!" Another ping. "And he's charging us four hundred dollars for that."

"Pocket change," Trip scoffed. "So...we're good here?"

"For the moment," Ben said. He paused for a moment, before he added. "Be good to each other, okay? You both deserve that."

They got up to head back to the main house.

"Oh, by the way, we're totally telling Addison!" Trip called as the door was closing—just before the strait-laced Ben dropped the first f-bomb Jasmine ever heard from him. Trip and Jasmine laughed the whole way across the pool deck back to the old house.

With the approval of Ben and Gwen, Jasmine and Trip settled into the annual Ashworth Christmas movie marathon that afternoon, openly cuddling up on the couch under a blanket as *A Christmas Story* played. None of the cousins watching the traditional triple feature even batted an eyelash at their sudden closeness—proof, Jasmine thought, that their chemistry had probably been obvious to everyone.

As the day wore on, they abandoned all pretense. By the time *Christmas Vacation* was playing, Trip took advantage of the blanket covering them, one of his hands dipping below the waistband of her joggers and toying with the top edge of her panties. The other skimmed the side of her breast over the skintight material of the thin cami she wore underneath the Princeton sweatshirt.

She turned toward him, catching his smirk and a raised eyebrow. She retaliated, inching her hand ever further up his thigh, lightly fingering the seam on the inside of his sweatpants. His hands froze for a second as he registered what she was doing—proof she was getting to him just as much as he was getting to her.

Addison, next to them on the couch, kept glancing their way between handfuls of popcorn and laughter at the ridiculous movie. When it ended, she leaned over and whispered, "I won't be expecting you to come to bed with me, then," nodding towards Trip with a conspiratorial grin before she rounded up their empties to take into the kitchen.

"I think Addison just kicked me out of our room," Jasmine said to Trip, feigning a pout.

"I think I have room for you with me," Trip said, his voice low and warm in a way she hadn't heard before. "If you want to, of course."

"I can't remember a time I've wanted anything more," she said, as he leaned in to kiss her.

"Then don't let me keep you waiting," he murmured against her lips. Hand in hand, they headed upstairs.

Chapter Twenty-One

It had been a while since Jasmine had slept with someone new. She didn't know if that was where it was headed, but she knew Trip's reputation—a bit of a womanizer, no stranger to casual sex. But she also knew his reputation was only half-true, at best.

Still, she was surprised when he seemed nervous.

He'd been so confident—almost brazen—when they were downstairs. As she shut the door to the small bedroom Trip stayed in, with its nautical-themed décor and crisp white walls, *nervous* was the only word for the look on his face.

"You okay?"

"I hope I wasn't too forward down there. We don't have to do anything—we can go at whatever pace you—"

"Trip," Jasmine gently interrupted. "I know." Her voice faltered. "Are *you*—I mean, do you want to slow down?"

"Not at all. Which probably means I should," he admitted.

"What do you mean?"

"Look, I know what my reputation is, and I know *you* know what my reputation is. You could probably write a thesis on my hookups at this point." He blew out a breath. "I just don't want you to think this is about sex for me."

"Of course I don't think that." She paused, a small smile tugged at her lips. "If it was, this would have happened already."

The anxiety on his face shifted to surprise. "What?"

She smiled and closed the distance between them, looping her arms around his neck. "Trip, I don't know if anyone has ever told you this, but you're an incredibly attractive man."

His hands found her waist almost instinctively. "I seem to remember someone mentioning I was hot, yes..."

"And I've been sleeping in a bedroom twenty feet down the hall for weeks."

"Okay..."

"So if this was just about sex, I figure a very attractive man like you would've knocked on my door long before now."

"I never would've—"

"I know," she cut him off with a small smile. "You've been nothing but kind." She kissed his jaw. "And respectful." A kiss nearer his ear. "Truly a gentleman. But..." Her teeth grazed his earlobe as she leaned in. "If you had, I'd have said yes."

Trip exhaled a low laugh. "If you knew what I was thinking most of those nights, I don't think 'respectful' is the word you'd choose."

His fingertips traced her spine while the other hand slipped lower, cupping her ass.

"Well, why don't you tell me? Then I'll decide the best word for it."

"I'd rather show you," he murmured against her ear.

She nodded. His hand slid up her back and cradled her neck before his mouth crashed into hers.

After a few breathless seconds, Jasmine decided she was wearing far too many clothes. She pulled off his Princeton hoodie and tossed it aside. Trip followed suit, his near-threadbare Philadelphia Eagles T-shirt joining it in a pile.

Even when she'd seen him shirtless, she never let herself look for long. Now she could. Her palms slid across the taut muscles of his chest, nails tracing the line of his abs. Her gaze followed, lingering on the impressive bulge his sweatpants barely contained. She bit her lip, anticipation curling low in her stomach.

Trip's mouth followed the line of her throat, ending down at her collar bone. His hands caressed her breasts, tracing lazy circles over her nipples, stiffening under his touch beneath the fabric. A moan escaped her lips, and she felt his mouth curve into a smile against her skin.

"Fuck, I want to make you do that again," he murmured as his hands moved to the bottom of her camisole and skimmed underneath it. Jasmine responded by reaching down and pulling it off herself.

Trip guided them toward the bed, his hands gliding over her bare back. He sat her down on the edge of the bed but didn't join her as she anticipated. Instead, he sank to his knees in front of her. He took her right nipple between his lips, gently swirling his tongue over it before moving to the other side. His fingers quickly replaced his tongue to leave neither side neglected. They'd barely gotten started, and Jasmine could already feel the heat building inside her. She knew she'd be begging for release soon.

Trip's hands traveled down her body, stopping at the waistband of her joggers and glancing up at her, awaiting her approval. She nodded as she lifted up enough so he could ease them off her hips—but he left her panties on. Of course, this would be the night she went for practical instead of pretty. She almost apologized for the plain black fabric, but the look on his face stole the words from her.

He looked like he'd won the lottery—she forgot all about her wardrobe.

Wouldn't matter in a few minutes, anyway.

Trip leaned in again, eager to reclaim the taste of her skin, exploring the curve of her breast with his tongue—as if relearning her by touch. His hand slipped lower, the damp material dragging softly beneath his fingers as he circled over her clit. A sound slipped from Jasmine's lips—half whine, half moan—the anticipation a delicious kind of torture.

His kisses drifted lower, his warm breath ghosting over her stomach, and Jasmine's breath caught—not just from anticipation, but from the startling awareness of what he intended.

He noticed the change and sat back on his heels, concern flickering across his face. "Do you...not want me to?"

She shook her head quickly. "No, I didn't expect you to want to."

She and Danny had been together for a long time, and while their sex life had been fine, it had fallen into a routine. Jasmine didn't remember the last time he'd gone down on her—though he'd never turn down a blow job. But with Trip, that was his first instinct: to focus on her.

He looked straight at her, his green eyes dark with lust. "I've been fantasizing about how you'll taste for weeks." The words sent a rush of heat straight to her core, stronger than she expected.

"It's just—my ex, he didn't..." she stammered, not even sure why she was bringing it up now, when this gorgeous guy was literally on his knees for her.

"Then he's an idiot," Trip said flatly. Jasmine couldn't help it—she laughed.

"So can I..." he asked, hooking his fingers into the waistband of her panties, and waiting for her okay.

She nodded, and he slipped them down her legs, adding them to the pile of discarded clothing on the floor.

Trip began part way down her thigh, tracing kisses to the crease before just lightly brushing his lips—barely—over her mound, then continuing down her other thigh. When he moved further from her center, Jasmine groaned in frustration.

"Patience," Trip smirked, repeating the pattern, this time adding small nips, licks and sucks between the kisses, keeping her guessing which sensation would come next. It took everything she had not to beg him to stop teasing, but she wanted to see exactly what he could do.

When he made his way back to where he started, his hands joined in, lightly stroking over her outer lips. She pushed her hips into his touch and one of her hands threaded through his hair and he took that as his cue to dip into her center. His fingertips quickly found the right spot, teasing her with feather-light touches before building in speed and pressure. Jasmine already felt like she was seeing stars—and that was before his mouth replaced his fingers, mimicking the same slow, deliberate rhythm before he gradually went harder and faster.

He paused long enough to rasp out "You taste fucking incredible" before diving back in.

Jasmine had felt self-conscious when Danny had done this, afraid the way she smelled or tasted would be off putting. The way he would quickly abandoned the task led her to believe that must be the case. But Trip worshipped her—unhurried, intent, lost in her. And as the vibrations of his sounds of enjoyment rumbled through her, Jasmine decided she didn't care if it was real or performance. Either way, it worked.

When he found what made her unravel, he kept his tongue steadily working while he slipped one, then two fingers inside her. When he curled them up to stroke just the right spot, she shattered. She'd had plenty of orgasms before, but nothing quite like this, as her whole body seemed to quake under Trip's touch. He didn't relent until she stilled underneath him, and he gently withdrew himself from her, his tongue passing over his lips as if to savor the ghost of the taste of her.

"Holy shit, Ashworth," was all that she could say as she came back to her senses.

"And that's how it's done," he said with a self-satisfied smirk curving his lips.

Jasmine laughed. "You're a cocky bastard."

"Thanks for noticing."

She sat up, caught him around the waist, and pulled him onto her on the bed with her.

"Your turn." She pressed her lips to his throat.

"You don't have to—" he began, but his words broke off in a hiss as she palmed through his sweatpants.

"Hmm, but you see, I want to," she practically purred into his ear, rolling him onto his back and straddling his hips, her eyes bright with desire despite being thoroughly satisfied.

"I'm going to wake up now, right?" Trip's hands roamed over her bare body. "This is just a dream?"

"Oh, you're not sleeping," she murmured, grinning. "And I hope you weren't planning on doing much of that tonight."

He didn't answer. He just pulled her down and kissed her like she was a drink of water and he'd been dying of thirst.

And Jasmine wanted him just as badly.

Chapter Twenty-Two

The most interesting thing about being in a relationship with Trip is how it changed nothing—and everything. They kept the familiar rhythm of the last couple of months: riding to work in the same car, having dinner together on the nights they got home early enough, spending weekends with Nigel and Alex. Their tight-knit friendship remained intact.

It was a convenient way to mask the truth: Jasmine was falling for Trip in a way that was exhilarating and terrifying. The first night back from New Jersey, she'd pretended she was going to her own room, but after a few minutes of tossing and turning, she slipped down the hallway to Trip's room. Half-asleep, he simply lifted the corner of the covers and invited her in. That had been it. She'd spent every night since with his body curled around hers, his heartbeat against her back centering and soothing in a way she couldn't describe.

Their intimacy threaded through their day, too: the cup of tea that appeared at her elbow as she scrolled through polling data late into the night, the protein bar she tucked into his backpack when he had marathon editing sessions, the sweet kiss pressed to his cheek when he was on the phone with his dad, and the way his hand found hers under every table—constant but discreet, a protection of their privacy.

As the days slipped into weeks, she couldn't hide this from the other important people in her life. She didn't want to deal with Bailey's judgment or her mom's disapproval. But she knew, deep down, that this with Trip was real. And it hurt to imagine them not knowing how much he was changing her life.

Maybe a small part of her still worried that they were right. Trip hadn't given her any reason to doubt him, but they had been careful not to take their relationship public. Jasmine wasn't naive about the vitriol they both might have to face.

With all in mind, she decided to approach Bailey first.

The Saturday before Christmas, Jasmine turned up at the beauty shop about fifteen minutes before closing, a pecan pie in hand. She'd spent the morning baking with Alex and Addison while Trip went on a top-secret holiday gift related mission that she was absolutely forbidden to join. He'd promised to be back by dinner, so she hoped if things went well with Bailey, she could spend the evening with them.

Jasmine drew a deep breath and pushed open the door, the familiar jingle of Mama Reid's bells announcing her arrival as it had for more than fifteen years.

Bailey's back was to the door, finishing up her last client of the day while working a cloud of mousse down through the long braids.

"We're closing up for the night, but if you want to holla at me for an appointment, my card's on the counter."

"I'm overdue for a fresh set," Jasmine said. "I was told I could schedule an appointment after Thanksgiving."

Bailey whipped around. "Jasmine?"

"I come bearing pie," Jasmine said tentatively. "I know you're going to your grandma's house for Christmas Eve, and she thinks you make this every year. Can't have her calling you out."

Bailey's eyes flicked between the pie and Jasmine's face, clearly weighing forgiveness against necessity. After what felt like an eternity, she held out her hand. "Gimme the pie, girl."

"Nuh uh." Jasmine hid it behind her back. "If you want the goods, we need to work this out first."

Bailey laughed. "You drive a hard bargain, ma'am. Lemme finish this up and we can talk."

Jasmine took a seat by the door while Bailey closed up the shop after her customer left.

"You wanna go upstairs?" Bailey and her mom owned the building and lived on the two floors above the street-level salon.

"Depends. You got coffee up there?"

"Auntie Lou sent Mama some fresh chicory blend from Louisiana. You good?"

"That'll work." The scent of chicory always set Jasmine at ease, reminding her of cozy nights spent at the Reids while her mom worked late.

Jasmine followed Bailey up the backstairs to the kitchen and set the pie down on the counter before hanging her coat over the back of one of the familiar kitchen chairs. She listened with a smile as Bailey hummed a tune while she brewed a pot of coffee and began warming milk on the stove, making a café au lait just like her mom always did.

A few minutes later, Bailey dropped two steaming mugs on the table and sat across from her.

"Been wondering when you would come around…no matter how pissed you are at me, I know you ain't about to let someone else braid your hair."

Jasmine laughed. "Believe it or not, I'm not here to talk about my hair." She paused, growing serious. "I'm here because I want to fix this, Bay. A lot has happened in the last month, and every time I couldn't call you, it kinda killed me."

"So why didn't you pick up the damn phone then?"

Jasmine sighed. "Because it's the reason we had the fight in the first place."

"Did something happen with the Ashworths? Is that why you're back here—you need a place to stay?"

"No, Bay, it's actually…the opposite. Trip and I are together. Officially."

Bailey fell silent. "Since when?"

"Since Thanksgiving. The day after, technically. That's the date on the disclosure paperwork at the office, anyway."

Bailey's eyebrows shot up. "Oh, you told your boss? You're all in then?"

"It seemed better to be honest upfront. It turned out not to be a big deal, but we wanted to make sure it was all good."

"And Trip was okay with that?"

"He insisted. He said that a voluntary disclosure was better for me."

Surprise flashed across Bailey's face before she reverted to her vaguely reproachful look. "So it's been almost a month, and not a whisper anywhere about Trip Ashworth's new mystery girl?"

"We're keeping it low. Whoever Trip dates after Mariana is going to be scrutinized. Even juicier if it's a member of his dad's staff. And he knows that it's going to be a hundred times worse because he's white and I'm not. He's trying to protect me."

"You think he's doing this to protect *you*?"

"I know he is. He gets that it'll be hard to have people saying shit about me, and he doesn't want me dealing with that until I'm ready—or as ready as I can be."

"Aren't you worried your career? People talking about your love life on the internet?"

"A little," Jasmine admitted. "But not enough to stop."

"You told your mama yet?"

"Of course not." She shook her head vigorously. "She's going to hate this. That's why I'm telling you first—so I can practice by dealing with your disapproval."

"Why do you think I would disapprove?"

"Come on, Bay." Jasmine gave her some serious side eye. "You've made it clear exactly where you stand on the Ashworths."

"Look, am I genuinely concerned they don't have your back as much as you think? Yes. I'll always worry about you playing in a world where people care more about *what* you are than *who* you are."

"And I get that, and I appreciate it—Mama, too. But this... Trip is different."

"You can see why that's hard to believe about a guy like him, right?"

"I didn't get him at first, either. But he's been through it. He's slow to open up, but once you're in, he gives everything. And I feel so lucky I'm one of those people. If you came around more, you'd see it, too."

"Yeah, well, I guess part of the issue is that I'm jealous," Bailey admitted, staring into her coffee. "All of a sudden, you're spending all your time with *both* of them, not just Trip. It's like you got this fancy job up on the Hill and forgot about your lowly beauty shop girl bestie."

"I know, and I'm sorry. I let myself get caught up. I need to make sure I still make time for the people who matter." She reached out for Bailey's hand. "You're my day one, girl. That'll never change, no matter who I work for."

"Or sleep with? 'Cause girl, you got a glow, and I know that ain't some new highlighter poppin'."

Jasmine smiled, "Oh my God, thank goodness I can finally talk to someone about this. I can't say anything to Addie—it would be too weird since they're related."

"Well...?" Bailey leaned in.

"Hands down, best ride of my *life*."

They talked for more than an hour, dissecting how good Trip was in bed, and then catching up on the salon gossip. Bailey had finished a particularly juicy story about their pastor's wife when Jasmine glanced n at her phone. Trip had texted he'd be home around seven. It was already quarter of, so Jasmine decided to ask.

"So, you wanna give the Ashworths a shot tonight? Trip's almost home. We can order in and watch a movie or something."

"You sure they want me there?" Bailey said, avoiding her eyes. "I'm guessing you told them about the fight."

"They both knew I was coming over to try and work it out. I'm sure you're more than welcome."

To prove her point, Jasmine tapped out a text to Trip quickly.

Jasmine: Okay if Bay comes through tonight?

Trip immediately replied.

Trip: Everything okay there?

She smiled at his concern.

Jasmine: Yeah, we're good.

Trip: Then of course.

Trip: First time she's here for movie night—you know the drill.

Jasmine smiled as she tipped her phone to show Bailey the phone screen.

"The drill?" Bailey asked.

"Newbie picks the movie and the takeout spot."

"Well alright then. I'll grab my coat."

Jasmine dropped a quick text to Addison and ordered an Uber. When Jasmine let them into the brownstone Addison was waiting for them by the door.

"Bailey, welcome!" she cried. "Alex and I opened the wine about an hour ago and should probably stop attempting to decorate cookies as a result. Can I get you a glass? Or a frosting spoon to lick?"

Bailey laughed at Addison's enthusiasm. "I'll take both. I'm sure you fancy people know how to pair wine and desserts properly."

She followed Addison into the kitchen while Jasmine hung their coats.

Trip returned a few minutes later, pulling Jasmine into his arms and kissing her soundly in the middle of the kitchen while their friends booed.

"Bold of you to think that would stop me," Trip said when he came up for air—and just to prove his point, kissed her again.

"Okay, I get it," Bailey said approvingly as Trip laughed against Jasmine's lips.

"Did you all decide on dinner yet?" Trip asked, pulling out his phone. "When's Nigel getting here?"

Nigel rolled in before dinner arrived. After they'd demolished their Thai food and settled into the living room, Bailey scrolled through the streaming options.

"*New Year's Eve*," she declared. "I don't even care that Christmas isn't until the end of the week—I've watched every Christmas movie there is. I'm ready to move on."

"Oh, speaking of New Year's," Trip said to Jasmine. "Did you ask her?"

"Ask me what?" Bailey said.

"Well, there's a big New Year's Eve charity gala that Trip co-chairs," Jasmine explained.

"It's for cancer research," Addison said. "It's overpriced and overhyped, but at least it's for a good cause—an especially close one around here."

"And it means we bought a table," Trip said.

"Gwen's also treating it as the 'soft launch' for my relationship with Trip. You know—don't walk in together, but get our photo taken being cozy. Let it get out that way. So, two favors: one, will you come?"

"Is it an open bar?"

Jasmine nodded in confirmation.

"Well, it *is* for a good cause..." They all laughed.

"And," Jasmine said with a dramatic pause, "I need you to dress me."

"You want to wear one of my designs to a fancy gala where the goal is to get your picture taken?"

"I'm probably going to be a nervous wreck. I'll feel more confident if I'm wearing something you made."

Bailey's face melted into tears. "Girl, you know I'm there for you!" Jasmine teared up too as they hugged.

"Nothing a little fashion can't fix!" Addison sighed happily, and Nigel nodded in agreement.

"Imagine how she'll react when you ask her to make your wedding dress," Trip whispered into Jasmine's ear, as she sat back. She whipped her head toward him, but all he only smiled.

"Am I allowed to invite Hakeem?" Bailey asked.

"Depends, has he asked you to be his girlfriend or is he trash?" Jasmine shot back.

"Nah, we all good."

"The table seats up to ten and with you five and Tess, we're already out of people who like me, so sure!" Trip joked. "Jasmine can send you the details, dress code, hotel info, flight time—"

"Hold up, flight time?"

"Oh, did we not mention it's in New York? It's for Sloan-Kettering up there," Addison said. "And since it's impossible to travel that week, we're flying private."

"Oh, Lord, are you serious? Girl, what kinda come-up are you working here?"

"Please," Trip scoffed. "If anyone's dating *up* in this situation, it's me."

"He's smooth, too," Bailey said approvingly. "Okay, I know I said we said movie night, but we've got less than two weeks to make fashion magic happen. Jasmine, get your iPad so we can go through what I've got on hand. I'm calling Hakeem."

Trip looked at Jasmine, eyes wide, as she stood. "What kind of monster have you created here?"

"The most fashionable one in the District, trust," she laughed, disappearing to grab her tablet.

Chapter Twenty-Three

Three nights before Christmas, Jasmine helped Trip and Addison organize their stuff for their trip to Pennsylvania the next day. Trip didn't spend his holidays in Italy anymore—he preferred visiting in the summer when the weather was better and travel was less insane.

Maybe that was why Jasmine caught herself daydream about next year, imagining a week under the Tuscan sun. Just a little.

For now, though, they were preparing to spend Christmas apart. Addison and Trip went up to Jack's house in the Philadelphia suburbs, while Jasmine planned to spend the holiday with her mom—and, hopefully, break the news about her and Trip. The plan had "high disaster potential," but at least they were staying in D.C., so if things got heated, Jasmine could retreat to the brownstone.

The front foyer looked like a holiday ad—suitcases, bags of brightly wrapped gifts, and a neatly packaged pie Jasmine baked to send along after its Thanksgiving success. Christmas at the Ashworths' was much smaller than Thanksgiving at the shore, just Jack and Dennis's families and occasional cousin or two that skipped the family ski trip out west.

Trip had joked about betting how long his father would actually stay at the Gladwyne house, but Jasmine heard the sadness beneath the humor. That house had been Trip's home, the one his mother had filled with Mediterranean touches that made her feel closer to Italy. Even after Jack's second wife remodeled it, wiping away almost every trace of Francesca, Trip could still feel her there. That was why Trip and Addison refused to celebrate Christmas anywhere else—and probably why Jack never stuck around for very long.

Jasmine, wearing another of Trip's hoodies that she'd commandeered from his dresser, was straightening one of the gift bags when Addison came bustling past, already in her coat.

"Going out with Nigel to finish his Christmas shopping. See you in the morning!" she called, hurrying the door.

Trip appeared in the doorway, leaning against it with a smirk. His hair was still damp from showering after his workout, and he'd thrown on joggers and a worn Lawrenceville t-shirt. "Looks like we've got the place to ourselves."

"I'm onto you both, Ashworth. This is a set up. Nigel told me the other day he finished his shopping early because he needed to have everything shipped back to the U.K."

"Yeah, the Ashworth 'smooth' gene seems to skip Addison," he said with a chuckle. "But she tell me she wanted us to have some time alone tonight before we head out."

"I think we'll survive five whole days apart."

"Maybe. But one of those days is Christmas, and I wanted to give you your gift before we left." He reached for her hand. "Come on—it's under the tree."

Even though none of them would be home for Christmas itself, Addison had insisted they decorate anyway. Trip loved pointing out the irony that the one who was raised Jewish was the one who was obsessed with Christmas.

The artificial tree in the corner glowed with garishly bright multicolored lights and a mismatched collection of ornaments that Trip and Addison had collected over the years, and others they grabbed together on a chaotic Target run the week after Thanksgiving. Nigel brought them a Waterford crystal ornament like his mum had back home, and Alex insisted they string it with popcorn and berries "for character."

Jasmine had tucked Trip's gift under the tree, near the back behind presents bound for Pennsylvania, so he wouldn't be tempted to peek.

"Now, just remember, I'm a girl on a budget, here," Jasmine joked as she handed Trip his gift.

"You didn't have to get me anything," Trip protested. "Just getting to be with you is gift enough."

"You can't say those kinda things to a girl..." Jasmine rubbed her hands over her warmed cheeks.

"Try and stop me." He leaned in to kiss her lips before opening the package.

Inside was a DVD case *Legally Blonde*.

"Jazz, we don't even own a DVD player," he said, turning it over in his hands.

"Then maybe you should look inside," she teased him.

He popped it open, and found two folded sheets of paper inside—printouts of the tickets she'd bought online.

"They're doing a production of the musical version of *Legally Blonde* at Arena Stage this spring," she said. "I know how much you love the movie, so I thought it'd be fun!"

Trip broke into a smile. "I love this so much, thank you."

Warmth bloomed in her chest. She knew she could never compete with what the Ashworths could buy materially, but she could still give him something that showed how well she knew him—and this one, she thought, she'd gotten exactly right.

Trip reached under the tree and produced a somewhat clumsily wrapped parcel. "Sorry for the shitty wrapping job. This is why I bribe Adds to do most of mine. But I wanted to put in the effort for this one. Open it!"

Jasmine smiled at his enthusiasm, more excited to *give* her something than he'd been to open his own. She tore away the paper and immediately recognized the Kate Spade logo on the box.

Inside was a wristlet wallet in the same matching purple leather as her work tote.

"I hope this is the right one to go with your bag," he said. "I refused to let Addison help me, so I had to make my best guess."

"It's exactly right." Jasmine turned it over in her hands. "I can't believe you chose this—of all things."

"What? Is it the wrong thing? I saved the receipt, we can always—"

"No, no, not all," she interrupted quickly. "It's perfect." She lowered her head, then asked softly, "Have I told you why I love that bag so much?"

Trip shook his head.

"When my mom got her first really big promotion at the Treasury, she went out and bought herself her first designer bag—a Prada one she carried for years. She told me it was the first nice thing she felt she could invest in, and it gave her the confidence to walk into the Treasury and feel like she belonged there. So, when I got the job in your dad's office, I did the same thing. I took a chunk of my savings and bought *my* very first designer bag, that purple Kate Spade tote I carry every day. I couldn't justify spending that kind of money before, even when I was at Georgetown. And I know it's not, like, a Birkin or anything," she added with a laugh. "But walking into that building with that bag felt like armor. Like proof I belonged there. It's totally impractical, there's a reason everyone who works on the Hill uses a backpack," she said smiling. "But I'll carry it until it wears out, because of what it means to me. So, for you to give me something that matches it..." Her voice caught. "It feels like—like you're handing me the keys to the kingdom. Like you think I belong, too—enough for you to think this is something I should have."

She looked down at the simple leather wallet, emotion tightening her throat.

"You should have everything." He took it from her and pulled the zipped open. "There's something else inside."

He handed her a small, square box.

"Trip, what is—" She stopped abruptly when she lifted the lid. Inside were gold fringe earrings with a ring of tiny diamonds in the center. "Trip," she breathed, touching one lightly. "They're beautiful, but they're too much—they must have been so expensive..."

"They didn't cost a thing," Trip said, softly. His eyes met hers before dropping away, a small, wistful smile tugging at his lips as tears filled his eyes. "They were my mom's."

Jasmine's breath caught as he quietly continued. "One of the best things about my mom was that she didn't care at all about having money. She lived for simple things—good *cacio e pepe*, cheap red wine she bought by the jug, fresh-cut sunflowers wrapped in grocery store cellophane. But the one bit of luxury she loved was jewelry. My dad bought her all kinds—rings, bracelets, you name it—but especially earrings. Gold earrings were her signature. She was never without them."

His voice grew steady. "Before she died, she picked out a few pieces she specifically wanted Addie to have. But she was very clear that the rest of it was mine—to give to a woman who was special to me. She wanted to be a part of it, even after she was gone. That's where I went on Saturday—out to the Gladwyne house—to pick these out for you."

"Trip, I can't accept these." Her voice cracked. "It's only been a few weeks. Are you sure you're ready to..."

"I'm done pretending she didn't exist," he said. "Letting the memory of who she was collect dust in an empty house in Pennsylvania. She would have loved you, Jasmine—who you are and who you let me be." His tears spilled freely now. "And no matter what happens between us, I want you to have a part of her, too. Please. You don't know what it means to me for you to have these."

Jasmine was crying now, mascara running down her cheeks. Words failed her, so she kissed him instead, hoping that would could say what she couldn't. And with the way he pulled her close, arms wrapped tight around her like he couldn't let her go, she knew he understood.

When they finally parted, Jasmine reached for her phone and snapped a photo of the earrings still in the box before typing out a message.

"What are you doing?" Trip asked.

"Sending a pic to Bay—letting her know we'll need to plan my look for New Year's Eve around these earrings. I'm wearing them to the gala." Her smile turned sly as she swiped over to another photo she'd snapped earlier.

"Why don't we go upstairs for you to unwrap the rest of your gift?" she teased, biting her bottom lip as she hit send and walked away. "Preview in your texts," she called over her shoulder.

Trip groaned when he opened the photo—a shot of Jasmine in red lingerie, the bra little more than a bow stretched across her breasts for him to untie.

Laughing, she pulled off the sweatshirt as she entered their room, tossing it aside. She could already hear Trip's footsteps pounding up the stairs behind her—by the rhythm, she guessed he was taking them two at a time.

Chapter Twenty-Four

When Jasmine told her mom about Trip, it went better than expected—if "better" meant Mom hadn't launched into a full lecture. She'd listened quietly, asked careful questions about his family and work, then said only, "You know this will make things harder for you, right?"

Jasmine knew exactly what she meant. Not about him. Not about them together. About the noise that came with being a biracial woman dating a man like Trip Ashworth—wealthy, white, already a public figure. Her mom worried about the headlines, the online comments, the racism that would inevitably follow.

Though she stopped short of forbidding it, she still hadn't agreed to meet him. That part stung more than Jasmine wanted to admit.

That conversation lingered in Jasmine's mind as she boarded the small plane bound for New York three days later. The New Year's trip promised to be epic from the start: seven of them aboard a private plane bound for JFK, taking enough selfies to fill the group chat for months—though, officially, the photos were embargoed from social media to avoid environmental backlash.

Once they landed and reached the hotel, they met up with Tess who'd taken the train down from Boston. Dinner a tapas restaurant doubled as both a group outing, and the careful rollout of Trip and Jasmine's relationship, seating Tess as far away from them as possible and acting as loved up as was appropriate in a large group dinner, at least as appropriate as possible for the amount of sangria they consumed.

The next morning, when Trip was still asleep, Jasmine crept into the sitting area of the suite that connected with Addison's room. Tess was already up, curled up on one of the couches and scrolling through her phone. Though she had her own room on a different floor, Tess had slipped into their suite with them last night without a word and followed Addison into her room. It was obvious how much that bothered them both, to be surrounded by other happy couples but unable to be anything other than friends in public. She and Trip had exchanged a knowing glance as they closed themselves off in Addison's room and said nothing else.

"Morning," Jasmine said softly. "You want coffee? I was going to call some up."

"Sure, thanks."

Jasmine called room service to get breakfast sent up, and Tess set her phone down. "You ready for tonight?"

"As I'll ever be," Jasmine said. "I don't know why I'm nervous, we're just going to a party. We don't even plan to walk in together—no big 'reveal.' But I still feel...exposed, I guess."

Tess smiled knowingly. "It's weird, people talking about you online. That never really goes away."

"How do you handle it?"

"Better than Trip," she said with a snort of laughter. "But I also know it's a whole other level for him."

"And what I'm about to sign up for. We've been so careful, but we almost blew it last week. Trip came by the office, and we went down to grab a coffee at Cups & Co. He leaned in to kiss me goodbye, and Addison had to fake a coughing fit to remind us to we were in public."

Tess looked down. "Yeah, Addison knows a thing or two about having to keep a relationship under wraps," she mumbled. "That'll be over tonight, though, right? No more hiding."

"Which also means that after tonight, it's out of our hands. There'll be plenty of people with something to say about Trip dating someone biracial. My mom's having a hard time with that part—the racist shit that's bound to show up online. I'm pretty sure she still thinks this whole thing is a mistake."

"Yeah, it's hard when your parents can't accept your choices."

"Are your parents, you know, supportive?" She hated to be so vague about it, but she didn't want to put Tess on the spot.

"Personally? Yes—one hundred percent. They know that I'm gay and are totally fine with it. The public side's more complicated. It's not that they don't want me to come out. They're afraid of how people will treat me when I do. It comes from a protective place, and I appreciate that—but sometimes it's hard not to feel like they wish I wasn't gay even if only to make my life easier, you know?"

"But that makes it hard on you and, you know, anyone you date."

Tess shook her head, looking away. "I don't, really. Date, I mean. Not when..." She exhaled slowly. "I've been in love with Addison for years. We probably look totally toxic to an outsider—all the back and forth, all the secrets. I keep breaking promises to her about when we can finally actually be together, and it...it's hard. I tell her to move on, find someone who can be with her unapologetically because that's what she deserves. But we keep finding our way back to each other."

Jasmine was quiet for a moment, turning Tess's words over. There was something about that phrase—*unapologetic*... Tess wanted to love Addison without apology. Jasmine wanted the same thing with Trip. She was done hiding, done feeling like she had to justify her happiness to anyone—not the internet, and not even her mom. So that was the energy that she needed to carry into tonight.

"I think it probably means something that you do keep ending up together," Jasmine said softly. "And hey, we just need to win a presidential election, and it'll all work out, right?"

"Minor detail," Tess said with a slight chuckle. "Hey, can I see what you're wearing tonight? Addison told me it's to die for—and that you're going to look *fire* in it."

They spent the day in the hotel, getting ready for the nine p.m. event. Nigel unpacked an alarming amount of imported skincare, which everyone dove into like a competitive sport. Hakeem immediately scored major points for being effortlessly stylish and unapologetically into self-care. Bailey unraveled Jasmine's twist-out, shaping her curls into perfection, while Addison coaxed Tess's platinum blonde hair into soft beach waves.

Even though they were just casually hanging out, Trip seemed to find excuses to touch Jasmine—helping her smooth a face mask across her skin, massaging her shoulders, and massaging her shoulders as she was touching up her pedicure that has gotten dinged inside her winter boots. It was all very innocent, but had Jasmine's heart racing just the same.

Trip had to head down to help handle event logistics starting at seven, so around five, everyone scattered back to their respective rooms to get ready, with Bailey handing out strict time slots for when she'd be coming by to do their makeup.

The door had barely closed when Jasmine pinned Trip back against it, a mischievous smile on her face.

"What's this about?" he asked with a smirk.

"We've got thirty minutes before Bailey comes to do my makeup—make them count," she said, crashing her mouth against his.

Trip didn't need much encouragement. His hands quickly found the zipper on Jasmine's sweatshirt, tugging it down, and letting it fall to the floor before following the path with his mouth, nipping at her shoulder until Jasmine shuddered. She pressed her hips into his, feeling his hard on already growing in response.

"Watch the hair," Jasmine warned, breathless. "If Bailey sees I flattened out curls, she'll know exactly what we were up to."

"Babe," Trip murmured against her skin. "If I do this right, half this hotel is gonna know exactly what we're up to."

Her attempt at a response dissolved into a low moan as his hand had moved between her thighs, rubbing his thumb over her clit through her leggings. Her knees almost gave out. Trip must have sensed it, because in the next moment, she was now against the wall, breath catching. He reached over to his overnight bag for a condom. His joggers and boxer briefs were gone in a blur, and Jasmine pulled his t-shirt over his head, tossing it aside he rolled the condom on. He left her bra in place, slipping off her leggings and panties off with ease. In one motion, he lifted her against the wall, slowly lowering her down until they were fully joined. He easily supported her weight with his muscled arms, holding her there a moment as she adjusted to the incredible fullness, a shiver and a soft gasp escaped her lips before he began to thrust up into her.

It felt incredible, but Jasmine knew she wasn't going to come like that. After a few minutes, Trip sensed it, too. A man of determination, he never considered it acceptable to finish if she didn't, so he shifted tactics. Gently, he lowered her from the wall and guided her toward the bed. He sat down and drew her onto his lap, his hands roaming her curves.

"Ride me," he requested, letting her take control. She slowly lowered herself onto him, taking her time, savoring the delicious stretch and way he filled her completely. She pushed his shoulders to get him to lie flat on his back before she began to rock her hips, keeping him deep. Trip groaned beneath her, his hands gliding over the curve of her thigh. With a wet fingertip, he found her clit, teasing it with slow, deliberate strokes. A loud moan escaping her lips as she began to pick up speed. It didn't take long for her climax to hit, radiating through her as she clenched around him as she cried out his name. She was sure Tess and Addison could hear, and for the first time, she didn't care.

Trip was still hard beneath her, so she leaned forward, gripping the headboard as she began to ride him, bobbing slowly at first before picking up speed. The pleasant aftershocks continued to ripple through her each time her clit brushed against his pelvis as she worked to bring him along. With her breasts now hovering over him, he yanked the cups of her bra aside to thumb over her nipples as he watched them bounce with her rhythm. The effect was immediate—his eyes shut face contorting, and a loud, guttural "Oh, fuck!" spilling from his lips as he reached his peak.

She slowed and stilled, then pushed herself off him. With a lingering kiss, Trip got up and headed for the shower. By the time Bailey arrived, he was dressed in his tux, frantically scrolling through his phone.

"Everything okay?" Jasmine asked, coming up behind him and placing a reassuring hand on his shoulder.

"The musical act for tonight is stuck in Michigan, snowed in. Their label is working on getting someone else in, but it's New Year's Eve, everyone's booked."

"Do you need to—"

"Yeah, sorry, I should get down there to see what we can do. You okay coming down with the others?"

"That was the plan all along." Jasmine gave him a quick kiss goodbye before he took off, apologizing to Bailey as he left.

They chattered animatedly while Bailey did Jasmine's makeup and helped her into the outfit she'd made for her for that evening. Once Bailey saw the gold earrings that Trip had given her, she pulled out a high-necked halter jumpsuit she'd been working on—solid gold sequined with wide legs and a cutout that showed Jasmine's toned midsection. Jasmine fell in love with it. It had the exact party vibe she wanted for this event and was constructed so the inevitable photos wouldn't risk a wardrobe malfunction. With gold strappy heels and her hair full, Jasmine felt like a disco goddess, and it felt exactly right.

"Girl, you are gonna break necks tonight," Bailey cried excitedly as she stepped back after helping Jasmine slide up the zipper.

"I'm really only interested in one person's reaction. Do you think Trip will like it?"

"I think Trip's going to be speechless. But I think you could show up in a sack and those earrings and that would still be true. That man is in *love*."

Heat rose in Jasmine's cheeks. "I mean, we haven't—not yet, anyway."

"Don't need to say it out loud for it to be true. And that goes for you, too, miss ma'am. And once your mama sees that, she's going to come around. Now come on, let's go get your boo."

The whole crew met up in the lobby. Adds and Tess were both clearly a little high already, and Alex and Nigel looked like they might have pre-gamed with some champagne in the room. This night was promising to be epically messy, and a whole lot of fun.

They stepped inside the glittering ballroom, navy blue fabric draped over the tables with twinkle lights everywhere. It looked like fields of stars—breathtaking.

Jasmine spotted Trip talking intently with a woman in a headset. He looked up and saw her, and did a double take. She shot him a smile, and the look of wonder on his face was something she didn't think she'd ever forget.

She made her way over to him. He excused himself from the conversation to greet her with a kiss, his arms slipping around her waist.

Trip tucked her curls behind her ear to admire the earrings. "They look perfect on you." He leaned down and placed a lingering kiss right below her ear.

Heat crept up her neck. Trip's idea of a "soft launch" felt pretty firm to her.

"Did they work it out?" she asked with a firm press on his shoulder, needing him to back off before she took this soft launch straight back upstairs.

"I think so? The label hasn't talked to anyone on the event staff, but a band just arrived to load in, so they found someone. You want to take a walk with me backstage and see if we can find someone who knows what's happening?"

Jasmine nodded, and Trip guided her to the back set of doors, arm still draped around her hip. Trip went to open the door to the smaller ballroom being used as a staging area for the talent, when it opened from the other side.

And the two of them came face to face with Mariana DaSilva.

"Trip!" she cried. "I was just coming to find you. Hi!" She opened her arms, and Trip dropped his arm from Jasmine's waist to hug her awkwardly.

"Hi, Annie," he said, slipping back into her nickname instantly. "What—what are you doing here?"

"I'm the replacement act for tonight. I didn't book any New Year's Eve gigs this year, I needed a break. But when one of the label execs heard your act got stuck in the Midwest, he asked if I'd come as a favor. And when I found out it was you, and what it was for, of course I said yes right away!"

"Wait, you knew I was involved and came anyway?"

"You're the reason I wanted to come," Mariana clarified. "I figured I owed you one, after, you know, everything with the song."

"Annie, you don't..."

"I shouldn't have just dropped it on TikTok like that. I was in the studio, and was upset about the breakup. So my producer suggested I write about it. The song just kinda happened. He loved it, the label loved it, not to mention the buzz it would generate, and all of a sudden, it was on the album in less than two days. I should have let it cool off a little, but it all moved so fast. You ended up getting a lot of hate you didn't deserve. I'm sorry."

Jasmine stood there, watching Trip's face soften. It was hard to believe he could be *this* forgiving after everything. She remembered how much the situation had weighed on him, how it had consumed him for weeks.

Trip looked conflicted. "I'm grateful for the apology, really, Annie. It's just..."

"I saw the video of you at the rally for that senator," she interrupted him. "What you said was really cool."

"Well, I meant it," Trip said softly.

Jasmine felt an uncomfortable knot tightening in her chest about his reaction. Was he still hung up on Mariana? Did seeing her change things?

But the uncertainty didn't last long, because when Trip looked at Jasmine, a brilliant smile came over his face. He pulled her flush to his side.

"And if you hadn't, maybe I wouldn't have this amazing woman with me now. Annie, this is my girlfriend, Jasmine Lewis. We met when she had the unfortunate task of cleaning up my image in the aftermath of your viral TikTok," he said with a laugh. "So, in a way, we have you to thank for that."

"It's nice to meet you, Jasmine," Mariana said, smiling sincerely before she turned to Trip. "You seem really happy, and I'm happy about that."

"I am," he confirmed softly, almost as if he was finally letting himself believe that, too.

"So should I leave 'American Royalty' off the setlist tonight, then?"

But Trip glanced at Jasmine with a conspiratorial smile. "No, you should play it. Call me up when you do."

Jasmine started laughing. "Gwen's going to kill you."

"Then I'm taking you down with me, Lewis," he warned her. "I'm going to tell her you allowed it."

"You sure about this?" Mariana asked.

"Definitely," Jasmine said. "I'm a media staffer for his dad's senate office, and this is better publicity than money can buy. Plus, it'll get people interested in the event itself, maybe raise a few extra bucks in the process."

"Then let's do it," Mariana agreed. "I've gotta go get ready, but it was really great to see you, Trip. And to meet you, Jasmine. I hope tonight is a huge success."

"Thanks." He turned and guided Jasmine back towards the main ballroom.

"You okay?" she asked softly before they opened the doors.

Trip stopped and turned to face her fully. "Literally never better." He cupped her face in his hands. "That's my past. You're my present. And if I'm lucky, my future, too.

Jasmine's breath caught. She kissed him, not caring who might see.

When they pulled apart, Trip grinned. "Ready to ring in the New Year?"

"With you? Always."

Chapter Twenty-Five

It was only the 3rd of January, and Alex had already won their bet about Gwen's first epic meltdown of the New Year.

"I can't believe none of you thought this was a terrible idea!" Gwen shrieked. Addison and Jasmine sat silently at the conference table, trying to balance their amusement at Gwen's over-the-top reaction with their desire to keep their jobs.

"It's really not that big a deal," Trip said. "Sure, it went viral, but doesn't that help put the controversy behind us? Now it seems like I'm in on the joke."

"Except it set off an avalanche of 'are they getting back together' speculation!" Gwen leaned over and clicking on a new article that popped up while she was ranting. "And look—now that the pictures of you and Jasmine have started getting out, the love-triangle nonsense is starting. Just look at this one. 'Pop Princess Spurned for Senate Staffer.'"

She began reading. "Breaking news: We reported Mariana DaSilva was reunited with former flame and chart-topping inspo Trip Ashworth at NYC NYE cancer benefit. But now we've learned he wasn't alone. He had another girl on his arm—and his lips—at midnight. It looks like there might be more heartbreak ballads to come from the unlucky-in-love pop icon. Rumor has it the mystery dime piece is a staffer in his dad's senate office.'"

Gwen huffed. "And we're not even going to touch the comment section."

"I mean, at least they're right about how hot you are," Trip murmured to Jasmine. "See, Gwen? They figured out I'm not with Annie and we didn't have to say anything."

"And now the deep dives into Jasmine start. Who is she? How'd she steal Trip away from an international pop star?"

"Uh, Annie broke up with me. Months ago."

"You say that like it matters," Gwen said witheringly.

Trip glanced over at Jasmine, uncertain. She jumped in to try and calm Gwen down.

"Look, Gwen, this has changed the narrative around the Annie and Trip break up entirely. Nothing about him cheating, nothing about Tess at all, and she was there. From that perspective, it was a huge success."

"We don't work for Senator Kensington," Gwen said.

"But Teresa is important to me as well," Jack said from the doorway. They all looked up as he strode into the conference room with Ben following closely behind. "And if this protects her, I trust that Trip and Jasmine made the right decision."

Trip looked a bit shocked but quickly recovered. "Thanks, Dad."

"Of course, Senator," Gwen said.

"Speaking of which," Ben broke in. "We need to get to the chamber if we want to see Senator Kensington get sworn in again. He's asked Jack to serve as his escort. Trip, Addison, are you going to watch from the gallery?"

Trip nodded. "Tess invited Jasmine as well, if that's okay."

Gwen waved her hand. "Go."

Trip rose from the table and reached for Jasmine's hand, which she immediately took. Jack glanced at their joined hands. Jasmine started to pull away, but Trip's grip tightened. She held on, giving his hand a reassuring squeeze.

Jack looked at Trip for a moment, before simply nodding and walking out.

"Well, that's officially the most enthusiastic reaction I've gotten to a relationship since prep school," Trip half joked. But Jasmine got the sense it was also the truth.

Ben glanced at Trip. "Your father has already expressed his approval of this relationship to me. I believe his exact words were 'about time he found a woman with a brain in her head' and left it at that."

"Be nice if he told me that," Trip sighed, and Ben gave him a sympathetic nod before they left the office.

As they waited for the underground train that would take them from the Russell Building to the Capitol, Ben pulled Jasmine aside for a moment.

"How you holding up, kid?" His tone was as close to affection as Jasmine had ever heard from him.

"I'm doing okay," she said carefully, unsure exactly what he was asking.

"I know it's probably a lot—everything people are saying online…"

Jasmine understood what Ben was really asking. "Oh, I mean—yeah, people suck. But we knew that was going to happen."

"Racists have been here even longer than politicians," he said with a grimace. "Coming up, I heard it all—been called everything from a Stokely Carmichael radical to an Uncle Tom. Black folks never seem to be able to get it right in this town."

"We've both gone private on our personal social media accounts and turned on comment moderation on the others. I feel bad for the intern back in Philly that has to weed through it all, but Trip's doing everything he can to shield me from it."

"He knows that's basically impossible, right?"

"Yeah. But it means something to me that he's trying."

"I'm sure it does." The train car pulled up, and they stepped forward. "And you can come to me with anything that's bothering you, okay?"

"Thanks, Ben," Jasmine said, a little surprised by his kindness. He just gave her a nod and a small smile.

The rest of the day passed in a blur of photo ops, interviews, and the kind of small talk Jasmine was quickly learning came with the job.

Later that night, after a long celebratory dinner with the Kensingtons in a private room at Old Ebbitt Grill, Jasmine was getting ready for bed. Trip, already stretched out in bed, scrolled through the hashtag of his name on Instagram to laugh at wildly inaccurate stories about New Year's Eve.

"Oh, this one is fun. Apparently, I got you hired at my dad's office to keep you close enough to fuck around. Like—does anyone check their timelines?"

"Please tell me that's not in anything reputable."

"I mean, if we're calling *People* and *US Weekly* reputable, we're in trouble. But no—that's some random Annie stan account."

"Her fans are a *lot*. Are we worried about any of them doing something if they see us at the show this weekend?"

After her performance at the gala, Annie had stuck around and spent a surprising portion of the night with Jasmine, Trip and their friends. It had been a lot of fun, and it was easy for

Jasmine to see why Annie—who'd told them to call her by her nickname—was someone Trip had fallen for. Still, she couldn't help being grateful it hadn't worked out between them.

At the end of the night, Annie had invited them to her first tour stop in Boston. Gwen had been against it, Ben had been for it, and Trip didn't give a damn what either of them thought—he left the decision up to Jasmine. She hadn't wanted to make Addison pass up the chance to see Tess, so she agreed they should go. But now she was second-guessing that choice, wondering if there would be any crazed fans who would target them at the show.

"Honestly, I think it'll go a long way to smoothing things over with some of the fans if they see that she asked us to be at her thing—not the other way around," Trip said. Then he added, "But don't wear your favorite shoes, just in case."

Jasmine laughed. "Yeah, I could see a drink getting *accidentally* dropped on me."

"The price you pay for getting with all of this." He flexed his arms comically behind his head, showing off the sculpted muscles he'd work hard to maintain on the rowing machine.

Jasmine took advantage of his position, sliding to straddle his hips, pinning his wrists against the headboard. "A bargain," she teased, before she leaned down and gently bit his earlobe, earning a string of profanities falling from his lips before he pushed back against her, easily taking control the way she liked.

The rest of the week flew by in a blur of getting the new Congress up and running. There were endless meetings with new staff who didn't know how the phones worked, much less how the Senate does business. Jasmine was exhausted by the time they headed to Dulles on Friday night for their quick flight to Boston. She fell asleep on Trip's shoulder not long after takeoff, cozy in his Princeton sweatshirt. Unfortunately, the brief flight wasn't a long enough for a real nap, and she passed out again the moment they reached the hotel.

Saturday was spent exploring Cambridge with Tess, hitting all her favorite spots. Trip had to talk Tess and Addison out of getting matching tattoos at one of the places in Harvard Square after realizing they'd been recognized. Jasmine didn't miss the flash of disappointment on Addison's face when Tess agreed, but she knew Adds wouldn't want to make a big deal of it. She simply slipped her arm through Addison's and gave her hand a tight squeeze.

Late in the afternoon, they returned to the hotel to get ready for the main event: the opening night of Mariana's tour. She was playing mostly smaller venues this time, and the Boston show was at a five-thousand-seat music hall in the shadow of Fenway Park. The line to get in already stretched down the block by the time they finished dinner and headed to the private back entrance. They were recognized immediately as they were ushered through the VIP line, phones flashing as fans snapped pictures and posted them online.

Inside, Jasmine could almost see the press pool down the hallway from the VIP entrance, covering the launch of Annie's highly anticipated tour. She swore she spotted Lauren Wong from *Teen Vogue* among them, though it was too far away to be sure.

The four of them joined about two dozen guests in the green room and grabbed another round of drinks while they waited for Annie to finish her soundcheck. Despite the crowd, Annie came straight to them when she walked in—warm and friendly as she greeted everyone, before Tess pulled her aside and gestured for Addison to follow.

Jasmine watched as Tess started talking rapidly. Addison blushed. Tess hesitated for a moment before hooking her pinkie around Addison's, a small smile on her face.

Annie's eyes widened. Her head swiveled, landing on Trip. She bit her lip as her gaze latched on him.

Jasmine held her breath. She wanted Annie to know the truth, but she was worried about Tess and Addison. She liked Annie, but she didn't trust her to keep other people's business private. She wished it didn't have to be so complicated for them.

Trip appeared behind Jasmine with a drink in hand, passing it over. Jasmine nodded over to the rest of the group. "Looks like Tess decided to tell Annie the whole story."

Annie walked over to him and slapped him on the arm. She was never going to make an impact on Trip's solid muscle, but he played along anyway.

"Ow," he said playfully. "What was that for?"

"For being an incredibly kind human and a huge jerk at the same time!" Annie cried, laughing.

"Accurate," Jasmine agreed with a laugh of her own.

"What, you're ganging up on me now?" Trip asked, feigning indignation before his expression softened. "Annie, I hope now you understand why—"

"I do," she jumped in quickly. "And I'm sorry I didn't believe you."

"It is okay. Not going to lie, I was pretty pissed about it for a while—especially when I was trying to protect Tess, too. But it all seems to have worked out how it was supposed to."

Annie glanced between them—Trip's arm wound around Jasmine's hip while her fingertips were tucked in the back pocket of his jeans—and smiled.

"Yeah," she said softly. "I guess it did."

A stage manager appeared to tell Annie to finish getting ready and to escort the Ashworth group out to their seats. The next couple hours were ridiculously fun. Watching Annie command the stage in front of her wild, devoted fans was an adrenaline rush.

As the first chords of "American Royalty" began, Annie stepped to the mic. "So everyone thinks they know what—or more precisely *who*—this next song is about. He's here tonight, so I'm just gonna give him his flowers. Trip, thank you for the inspiration for this one. I'm sorry I got it wrong, and I'm grateful for your forgiveness."

A buzz went up in the crowd. "Trip is a great guy," Annie added. "Don't let anyone, including me, tell you differently."

Phones went up everywhere, capturing Trip's reaction to Annie's public apology. He gave Annie a slight wave of acknowledgement and pulled Jasmine protectively into his side. Whether he was trying to protect *her* or himself from the glare of attention, she wasn't sure.

After the show, they were escorted back to the green room to hang out with Annie, her band and a few other VIPs. Trip was the buzz of the party—subject of far too many whispered comments and obvious glances—but he took it in stride, nursing a beer and staying close to Jasmine.

Around eleven, he glanced at his Apple Watch, his expression tightening.

"Everything okay?" Jasmine asked.

"Uh, yeah. Or...um, no, actually," Trip frowned harder as he scrolled through his messages. "I need to head back to the hotel. *Law Journal* emergency."

"Okay..." Jasmine blinked, trying to imagine what could constitute a *Law Journal* emergency on a Saturday night. "I'll come with you." She lifted her cup to finish what she could so they could go.

"No!" Trip said quickly—too quickly, with enough force that it made Jasmine freeze. "I mean, I don't trust Tess and Addison to get back by themselves. Will you keep them from doing anything stupid? They're a little cross-faded after they heard the drummer had good kush. If you stay with them, I'll deal with this and see you back there in a bit."

Trip kissed her before he went over to say goodbye to Annie before he slipped out.

Jasmine stayed with Addison and Tess for another hour, before convincing them to call it a night. Her long week had caught up with her, and honestly, she was fine being a little lame going to bed this early in the night.

She made sure that Addison and Tess got safely into their room, and then turned down the hall toward her's and Trip's—three doors away.

Just in time to see Lauren Wong exiting from their doorway.

Chapter Twenty-Six

Jasmine stood frozen in the hallway as Lauren walked in the other direction. She couldn't make sense of what she was seeing. The last time she'd seen them together, Trip had stormed out of the room and sworn he'd never speak to Lauren again. So, why was Lauren Wong—of all people—leaving their hotel room after midnight?

Her head was still swimming as she fumbled for her key card. The door finally clicked open, but she stopped short. Trip was sitting on the edge of the bed, head in his hands. He looked guilty about something—*and that was the thing that finally broke her.*

"Trip, what the fuck is going on?"

"Jazz!" he blurted, jumping to his feet. "I didn't expect to see you for at least another couple of hours."

"Thought you had plenty of time for Lauren to get out of here without me seeing her, you mean."

His eyes widened. "You saw Lauren leave?"

"I was right there in the hallway." Her voice rose. "So...I repeat, Trip, what the *fuck*?!"

"It's not what it looks like, Jasmine, you have to believe me. We didn't—she wasn't—nothing happened."

"Oh, come on...a random reporter was in your room in the middle of the goddamn night, and you want me to believe everything is fine?"

"Jasmine, you know me. I would never cheat on you!"

She shook her head, blinking rapidly. "I'm sorry, what? Trip, I don't—" She let out a bitter laugh. "It never occurred to me that you were cheating on me. I *know* you wouldn't do that."

He faltered. "If you don't think I slept with her, what are you so mad about?"

"Are you fucking kidding me?!" she shouted. "You met with a *reporter*. Alone. One who's had absolutely zero respect for your boundaries? How do you expect me to react?"

"Jasmine, I'm not—"

"Trip, you can't do shit like that! You need Gwen or me there anytime you talk to the press. I can't defend you if you don't let me in!"

"That's not what it was about, Jazz, I just—"

"Then what was it about? What was so important that you couldn't give me a heads-up before sneaking off to meet with a shady reporter with no sense of decency?"

Trip looked at the carpet. "I can't tell you that."

Jasmine nearly exploded. "Trip, what the fuck are you hiding from me?"

"Look, babe, I want to tell you, I do. I just—you have to trust me. I'm handling this, but I can't tell you about it yet. It's for your own good. I'm protecting you."

Her jaw dropped. "It's not your job to protect me from the media, Trip. It's *my* job to protect *you*."

"Bullshit." His voice raw now, a fire in his eyes. "You wouldn't be under a microscope if it weren't for me, fucking Instagram detectives and racist trolls saying vile shit about you in the comment section. And now it's—" He stopped short. "I won't let that happen, not again," he said, shaking his head and breathing heavily.

And that's when Jasmine knew. This wasn't just about her—it was about his mom, too, and how he couldn't protect her.

She understood. But she was too angry to let it go.

"You don't trust me?" she asked, voice breaking. "You really think *you're* in a better position to handle whatever this is? With a *reporter*, Trip?"

"Jasmine, I promise, when I can explain, I will, but it's just—"

"No." She grabbed her purse. "I'm done. You don't think I'm capable enough to manage mess you've made, so you know what? You can handle it yourself. I'm going to Addie's room."

She stormed into the hallway. She half expected Trip to follow her, but other than shouting her name as the door slammed, he didn't come.

Her chest heaved as she stalked down the hall, fury crackling just beneath her skin. The muffled sounds of laughter spilling from their room felt like it belonged in another universe.

She banged on their door. "Addie, Tess, are you still awake?"

A few seconds later, the door flew open to a giggling girls—until they saw her face. The laughter died instantly.

"Jazz, is everything okay?" Addison asked, trying to sober up quickly.

"No, everything is *not* fucking okay." Tears were already building in her eyes. "Trip—there was a woman leaving our room when I got back."

Tess's eyes grew wide. "Jasmine, you can't think that he—"

"No, I don't think he slept with her or anything. It was a reporter. The one from *Teen Vogue*."

"Oh, shit," Addison said, grabbing her sweatshirt and yanking it over her head. "I saw she was at the thing tonight." She pushed to her feet. "I'll go talk to him. I might not be back."

She leaned in to kiss Tess on the lips before she held out her hand to Jasmine. "Key card."

Jasmine handing it over without a word, and Addison took off down the hall.

Jasmine brushed past Tess into the room and sank down on the bed. The tears she'd been holding back finally spilled over, tracking silently down her cheeks. Tess sat beside her, wrapping an arm around her shoulders. Jasmine let herself collapse into the comfort, her quiet tears turning into full sobs that wracked her chest.

"It's okay, Jazz," Tess said soothingly. "Addison will talk some sense into him. She almost always can."

"But why couldn't I, Tess?" Jasmine's voice cracked. "He's never going to trust me the way he does you guys. He's never going to let his walls down with me."

"He *does*," Tess said gently. "I see it. He's different with you. And I've known Trip my whole life—I know he must have a reason for doing this, as stupid as I'm sure it is." She gave a fond roll of her eyes. "He doesn't always do the right thing, but it's always for the right reasons."

Jasmine shook her head, tears slipping down her cheeks. "How can they be the right reasons when it makes me feel like *this*?"

Tess just hugged her tighter, not saying a word but letting her cry.

When she was cried out, Tess eased her down on the bed, continuing to hold her until she drifted into a restless sleep.

Jasmine tossed and turned fitfully through the night, but Tess stayed with her, steady and warm, and Jasmine was grateful she didn't have to be alone.

By the next morning, Addison had slipped back in and crawled into bed on Jasmine's other side. Jasmine stirred first and shook her awake.

"Addie," she whispered urgently. "Did you talk to him? What did he say?"

Addison blinked blearily. "What?"

"Trip, Addison." Jasmine's voice sharp with exhaustion. "Did he tell you what's going on?"

Addison sat up, rubbing her eyes "No. He...Jazz, he took off."

Jasmine froze. "He did *what?*"

"I don't even know the details," Addison said, guilt heavy in her voice. "He wouldn't tell me much—just that he wasn't going to let anyone hurt you. Then he changed his flight. Caught the six a.m. back to D.C. before I could stop him. Said he needed to talk to some people."

"So he just *left?*" Jasmine asked, her voice hollow. The words barely made it past her lips.

"I told him he was being an idiot, but..."

"Wrong thing, right reason," Tess filled in, and all Addison could only nod.

"So what's going to happen when we get home?"

"I don't know. Depends on if he can fix whatever this is."

"If him "fixing" anything means that he's talking to a reporter, we're fucked," Jasmine said flatly.

"Probably," Addie said. "Come on, we've got to get to the airport."

Jasmine got dressed and they bid goodbye to Tess, who gave Jasmine a long, tight hug. She and Addison were mostly quiet for the entire trip home, only speaking when necessary. Jasmine hoped that Addison would understand that she wasn't mad at her—she just couldn't bring herself talk yet.

By the time their plane landed in D.C. and Jasmine took her phone off airplane mode, she half-hoped there'd at least be a text from Trip with when he'd be home. There wasn't.

But there *was* a message from a number she hadn't used in a few months, not since the disastrous interview blew up in Senator Ashworth's conference room.

Lauren Wong.

Lauren: Trip told me you saw me leaving last night
Lauren: It's not what it looks like
Lauren: Come to the Starbucks at Penn and 13th at 2
Lauren: I'll tell you everything

Jasmine stared at her phone, unsure what to do.

If she told Addison that Lauren had reached out to her, she could tip Trip off—and Jasmine might not get the answers she needed.

"Hey, Addie," she said finally. "Do you mind taking my things back to the house? I told Bailey what was going on, and she wants to meet up for coffee, make sure I'm okay."

She hated lying, but she didn't know where Addison's loyalties would land in this kind of mess.

"Of course, babe, whatever you need," she said immediately. Her earnestness only added to Jasmine's guilt.

But she knew what she had to do.

She texted Lauren back.

Jasmine: I'll be there.

When they deplaned, Jasmine handed Addison her overnight bag and headed to the Metro. The ride took about an hour—plenty of time to turn over the events of the last day in her mind. She'd been so happy just the night before. Could everything really collapse this fast? Had Bailey and her mom been right all along—was she naïve to think a relationship like theirs could ever survive public scrutiny?

Still, beneath the hurt and the exhaustion, a stubborn voice whispered: *Hear her out.*

At least she'd know.

Jasmine arrived at the Starbucks just before two, ordered her usual dirty chai and found a table in the corner. She considered asking Lauren if she wanted anything, but decided she wasn't ready to play nice just yet.

She was scrolling absently through her phone when she felt someone standing beside her.

"Jasmine," Lauren said briskly, sliding into the opposite chair. "Thanks for coming. When Trip told me you saw me last night, I wanted to set the record straight in person."

"I appreciate you covering for him, Lauren, but this is really between—"

"I'm not covering for anyone," Lauren interrupted. "Trip didn't do anything wrong. I'm the one who reached out to him. I asked to meet somewhere private."

"And he still agreed—and still kept it from me."

"He had his reasons. Just like I did, bringing this to him."

"Bringing *what* to him, Lauren? What are you talking about?"

"I guess I was trying to make it up to him. For going off-script and asking about his mom—it clearly rattled him. For the record, I still think that talking about Francesca is a good look for him *and* for Jack. As one of their media people, you should work on that angle before he announces."

Jasmine's tone iced over. "Thanks, but you can leave the media strategy to Gwen and me."

"Anyway," Lauren continued. "I've been trying to get back in his good graces so I could reschedule the feature—especially now that the Mariana DaSilva stuff is front-page news again.

When I picked up a tip from our features editor about a pitch that would be of interest to him, I offered to tell him what I knew in exchange for resuming the feature. He agreed."

"Wait, he *booked* an entire feature with you without running it by me or Gwen?" Jasmine's anger flared hot and fast.

"He knew one of you would shut him down if he tried to tell you, especially once he heard what it was about. He's determined to kill it."

"What the hell does someone have on him that he's so desperate to keep out of the press?"

Lauren's face shifted instantly. "Oh, sweetie," she said softly. "You really don't know, do you?"

Jasmine's stomach dropped. "Don't know what, Lauren?"

"The story...it's not about *him*. It's about *you*."

Chapter Twenty-Seven

"A story about me?" Jasmine couldn't have been more confused. "Who the hell is writing a story about *me*?"

Lauren scrolled through her texts. "Do you know someone named Dan Wakefield?"

Jasmine's stomach sank. "He's my ex. Why?"

"Well, apparently he's shopping a story, a long-form, first-person account of how politics breeds infidelity in the women in his life—first his mom with the Governor, and then you with Trip."

Jasmine's eyes widened. "I didn't cheat with Trip. My relationship with Danny had been done for weeks before we started dating."

"He's more saying you had sex with him," Lauren said bluntly. "Though he does mention that you're together now."

"Wait. You've seen this piece?"

"Just the pitch." She tapped on her phone. "Here, check it out for yourself." Lauren handed Jasmine her phone with a PDF pulled up on the screen.

She skimmed the pitch letter, honing in on the paragraph that compared his mom's affair that began on a business trip with the Governor to when she went to Denver with Trip—all but saying she'd slept with him while they were there.

"None of this is true." She looked up at Lauren in panic. "We didn't—this isn't what happened!"

"And you know as well as I do that it won't matter. That's why Trip is so desperate to kill it. He can't stand to see you get accused of something you didn't do."

Jasmine was once again quaking with anger, but it was now aimed squarely where it belonged: at Danny, for making up lies about her and for using Trip to do it. "Lauren, why are you telling me this? The real reason, not the 'I felt bad' crap, I know you don't."

She glanced around before leaning in further. "Listen, we both know that if Trip gets anywhere near this, that becomes the story. I didn't actually expect him to say he wanted to stop it—I more hoped it would get him further on board with talking to me on the record. I thought I'd give him the chance to correct anything Danny got wrong. But as soon as he started asking who he needed to talk to in order to make sure no one picked this up, I knew I had to bring you in to stop him."

Jasmine handed Lauren back her phone before pulling hers out of her bag.

She needed to find Trip.

"Thanks for this, Lauren," she said as she furiously tapped out a text. "I won't forget we owe you one."

Lauren got up from the table.

"Yeah, just keep that in mind when you're issuing campaign press credentials." And with that, she headed out the door.

Jamine texted Addison.

Jasmine: You must know where Trip went.
Jasmine: I need to talk to him right now.

Addison didn't immediately reply, although Jasmine knew she would be glued to her phone waiting for word from one of them. Jasmine wondered if Addison was asking Trip if he even wanted to see her.

But moments later, a screenshot of Addison's Uber app popped up in the thread. A description of what car to look for outside, sent to an address Jasmine didn't recognize.

Addison: That will take you straight to him.
Addison: That's Ben's condo at the Watergate, he's with Uncle Jack in Scranton this weekend.

Jasmine nearly laughed at the irony of going to the Watergate in hopes of *stopping* a scandal from erupting rather than creating one.

Even with her lingering guilt about lying, her heart swelled at Addison immediately getting her where she needed to go.

Jasmine: Thank you.
Addison: Anything for you babe.
Addison: Find him and make him fix this. And smack him upside the head for me.

Jasmine ducked outside to wait for the car, replaying the conversation with Lauren over and over again in her mind, trying to figure out what to say to Trip.

She slipped into the building behind someone else, heading up to the number Addison had texted her. She banged on the door, waiting for Trip to answer.

When he opened the door and his green eyes landed on hers, her carefully rehearsed questions left her mind completely.

"You're an idiot."

"Excuse me?!" Trip shot back.

"I said you're an idiot," she repeated. "Trying to kill a story like this? Have you learned nothing from Gwen and me over the last six months?"

Trip grabbed her wrist and pulled her into the apartment. "I learned maybe we don't talk about it in the middle of the hallway in a building crawling with people who work on Capitol Hill?" Trip hissed once they were inside.

"I'm sorry, Trip, I'm still in shock at how absolutely stupid you're being about this."

"How did you even find out—"

"Lauren texted me, told me how you were about to go rogue and try to bury a story about me—which will never work. *If* this gets published, it looks like whining from a jilted lover, and I look bad for a week. Maybe. But if you get caught, and you *will* get caught, it's an example of the son of someone rich and powerful killing the career of a poor writer before he even gets started. Not to mention it makes it look like it's true. People don't go out of their way to bury lies."

"Jasmine, I can't let him do this to you. I only wanted to—"

"I know what you wanted to do," she cut in, slowly exhaling. "And I love you for that."

She closed the distance between them, wrapping her arms around his neck and kissing him with an urgency even she didn't expect.

It wasn't how Jasmine expected to tell Trip that she loved him for the first time, despite knowing for weeks it was true. But it was important to her in that moment that he knew.

Trip met her kiss with the same aching desperation. They moved together toward the bedroom, nothing left between them but the sound of Jasmine whimpering his name as she came undone.

Jasmine melted against Trip's chest, still catching her breath when it dawned on her. "Oh, my god," she groaned. "Please tell me we didn't just have sex on Ben's bed!"

Trip burst out laughing. "No. This is a two-bedroom, we're in the guest room. It's basically my room. I used to crash here a lot before I moved to D.C. for law school. I preferred staying with Ben to staying with my dad and Elizabeth." He paused. "But I can't guarantee that he and Gwen haven't..."

"Stop! I can't!" Jasmine cried, dissolving into laughter. "And um, if we could maybe not tell Ben about this, that'd be great."

"My lips are sealed," he assured her, before putting those lips on hers.

When they broke apart, he caressed her cheek and looked in her eyes. "I love you, too, you know. I have for a while. I just couldn't figure out how to say it, when—"

"You didn't need to. You've shown me, over and over. Which is why I was so bothered last night when you shut me out. It's not who you are, it's not what we do.

"And that's all I was trying to do now, show you that I love you and want to protect you."

"And you can't, Trip, we both know that. We've seen it already, the shit people say online."

"And it pisses me off because Danny has to know what's going to happen if that piece gets published. It's bad enough that he's willing to trash his own mother, but it's going to be a million times worse for you when every racist fuck goes after you even harder."

"I know." The criticism levied at her would always take on that dimension, another level of intensity. But she was far more prepared for that than Danny's betrayal.

"Then what the fuck do we do? Because we can't just let this happen."

"Maybe we can?" she said hopefully. "It's just a pitch with a spec paragraph at this point. Who knows if it'll even get picked up."

"Two months ago, I might have agreed with you. But given everything that's happened with Annie in the last few weeks—my love life is a hot commodity again. I know you sometimes accuse me of being overly cynical, but I have to think that's the reason that he's choosing now to try and make this happen."

She frowned. "I'm sure you're right. Danny might be lazy, but he's smart. I'm sure he saw the news about the New Year's Eve benefit and thought he had an opening."

"I already tried talking to our lawyer. That's why I came back early, to catch Mitch Bolton before church so I could walk him through it in person. He doesn't think we should file an injunction. Right now, it's just in editors' emails, but the court papers would be public record. It might actually drive up demand for stories about you. But we both know it's just a matter of time before someone leaks it."

"This is about media strategy. We have to call Gwen."

"That means Ben's going to be in on it, too, and he's going to hit the roof."

"His protective meter goes up to an eleven about you—I know."

"About you, too."

"I hate, hate, hate that this is going to take up bandwidth for anyone on staff. It doesn't even deserve the time of day, but I just don't see another way."

"Jasmine, everyone is going to think protecting you is important. Do you really not understand how much we all care about you?"

"I'm a junior communications staffer, I'm not..." she muttered.

"You're family," Trip insisted. "And if there's one thing the Ashworths and everyone in their orbit takes seriously, it's that."

Jasmine exhaled slowly. "Then let's make the call."

"Let me do it." Trip rolled over to pick up his phone. "You FaceTime Addison and fill her in, I'll talk to Gwen."

Before she could climb out of bed, Trip pulled her back to him.

"I love you," he said, repeating the sentiment with a new air of solemnity. "No matter what happens, we've got that."

She smiled and placed a kiss on his cheek. "I love you, too." And she got up to call Addison.

They gathered in the conference room just over an hour later room in Senator Ashworth's office, Ben joining them via Zoom from Scranton. If rage could permeate through a screen, Jasmine could feel Ben's ire all the way from northeast Pennsylvania.

"Who does this little fucker think he is, anyway?" he fumed, shocking Jasmine with the coarse language from Ben's normally careful mouth.

"He's not a bad guy," Jasmine said. "He just—the situation with his mom really screwed him up."

"That doesn't give him license to lie about you," Gwen said, equally incensed.

"No, but it's all 'he said, she said' at this point. We all know whoever gets their side of the story out first is the one who gets to decide what the truth is."

"Okay—we need to get out in front of it," Gwen said. "Is there some way to accelerate the feature with Lauren, let Trip talk about what happened with the two of you before Danny can sell his story?"

"That sends the message that this office thinks Trip's love life is fair game. Is that a precedent we feel comfortable setting?" Ben asked.

"Who cares?" Trip said immediately. "If it'll help, I'll do it."

"I'm not sure your father will agree that that's the best course of action, son."

"You think I fucking care what he thinks?" Trip shot back, his own anger rising.

"We all have to care about that, dear," Gwen said, not unkindly. "But in this case, not because he's worried about the impact on him or any campaign. He's genuinely concerned about both of you. I'm not sure he'd be comfortable essentially making it open season on your relationship. He knows how hard that is."

Ben was nodding on the screen. "I filled him in before I came on here. The only thing he wanted to know was if you two were okay. And that means he'll want us to tread lightly."

"I just wish there was some way to prove nothing happened on that Denver trip," Jasmine said, exasperated. "If we could credibly take down one part of the story, it casts doubt on the whole thing."

Addison—who'd been keeping Tess up to date on the issue—sat upright, almost dropping her phone in the process. "But we can prove that."

"Addison," Trip said. "No one was in that hotel room other than me and Jasmine. It's our word against his."

"But did *he* sign a sworn statement about it? Because *you* both did, when you filed the compliance paperwork declaring nothing happened between the two of you before Thanksgiving. You did that over a month ago when there was zero reason for some kind of cover up."

"Wait, Addison is right..." Gwen said before rushing from the room.

"Trip, Jasmine," Ben began seriously. "Please know I'm not attempting to question your integrity, but I need to know, to be one thousand percent certain. Please tell me everything you said on those disclosure forms is true."

Trip nodded earnestly. "I think I even said something to the effect of 'despite having traveled together previously' on mine, actually."

"I'm not a cheater, and I'm definitely not a liar, Ben," Jasmine said, equally seriously. "We told you the truth the first time, and every time thereafter."

Gwen came bounding back into the room, Jasmine's personnel file in hand. "I think Addison's onto something. We have independent statements from both of you on the nature of your relationship, signed and dated the Monday after Thanksgiving. They directly contradict the story that Danny is trying to sell."

"I never thought I would say this, but God bless HR red tape," Ben said, not without a hint of sarcasm.

"So what do we do, then?" Addison asked. "Wait until he publishes and then sue him for libel?"

"That's one approach," Ben agreed.

Jasmine shook her head. "Let me talk to him, see if I can get him to agree to back off."

"Jasmine, are you sure you want to do that?" Gwen asked.

"I was with him for years, Gwen, I don't want that reduced to him being anonymously served with a lawsuit. Plus, I want a chance to set the record straight. Let him know that he's wrong about me."

"I'm coming with you," Trip said immediately.

"Absolutely not. There's no way he'll even think about talking to me if you're there."

"Then I'll go," Addison quickly volunteered. "Bailey and me. We'll at least be nearby—in case you need us."

Jasmine didn't know what to say. Maybe Trip was right about how they all saw her. And that filled her heart in a way she couldn't have imagined.

"Okay, then. Let's do this."

Chapter Twenty-Eight

Danny had worked Sunday nights at Mac House since high school, doing dishes in the back before he graduated to delivery driving. Jasmine knew she'd find him there.

While Jasmine and Gwen copied the disclosure affidavits, Addison got Bailey on FaceTime to arrange for her to meet them at Mac House. According to Addison, Bailey was practically breathing fire about Danny's lies, and if Jasmine didn't get down there that evening, Jasmine was a little afraid Bay would go kick his ass herself.

They left the office and went straight to the pizza place, meeting Bailey outside. "You okay, girl?"

"I'll be better once we get this over with."

"Then let's get on with it," Bailey said. "Where's Trip?"

"I sent him home. I don't need him lurking in the background just waiting for a chance to punch Danny in the face."

"Bold of you to assume I won't," Bailey mumbled.

"I'm an Ashworth, I probably won't even catch a charge if you let me do it," Addison said.

Jasmine laughed, despite her anxiety rising about confronting Danny. "I'm both humbled that both of y'all are willing to throw down for me. And a little nervous about what will happen if I ever cross one of you."

"As you should be," Bailey said smugly. Addie nodded in agreement. With a deep breath, Jasmine pushed open the door.

Eddie was working the register, and his face immediately lit up. "Jasmine! Hi! It's so good to see you!" He ducked around from behind the counter and gave her a hug. When he spotted a pissed off looking Bailey over Jasmine's shoulder, he froze.

"Uh oh," Eddie said. "This can't be good. You heard about the article, didn't you?"

Jasmine pulled back in surprise. "You know about the article?"

"I've been trying to talk him out of it all week. Ever since the pictures of you two over New Years came out—he's obsessed with the idea that this is his ticket to landing a book deal."

"It's going to be his ticket to an ass kicking if we have anything to say about it," Addison snapped while Bailey nodded.

"Guys, please, chill." Jasmine turned back to Eddie. "Is he here?"

"He's on a delivery run, but he'll be back soon. Do you want to..."

"Yeah, let him know I'm in my usual spot."

She paused for a minute. "Does he really think...I mean, does he *actually* believe I cheated on him with Trip? Because I didn't."

"I believe you," Eddie said earnestly. "But Dan can't shake his suspicion, and once it was obvious you'd gotten together, he just let his worst fears run wild."

Jasmine sighed and shook her head slightly. "You'll tell him I'm here when he gets back?"

Eddie nodded, and she made her way back towards the booth. She slid in and gestured to Bailey and Addison. "You two wait over there where he won't see you when he comes out from the kitchen. I don't want him to feel ambushed."

"I don't know why the fuck not?" Addison mumbled, but followed Bailey to a table out of the line of sight from the swinging door.

Jasmine fiddled with her rings, unwilling to look at her phone and see any anxious texts from Trip wanting an update. Every time the kitchen door swung open, she practically jumped out of her skin. It was either the third or fourth time when she looked up and finally saw Danny.

Eddie grabbed Danny's arm, leaning into his ear and gesturing back to the booth where Jasmine was waiting. Danny's expression hardened, but after Ed talked to him for a few more seconds, he seemed to sighed and stalked over to Jasmine.

"What do you want?" he asked coldly as he approached the table.

"To make sure you know the truth about Trip and me before you blow up your career trying to drag mine. You going to sit?"

He hesitated for a minute before he slid into the booth opposite her, his face unreadable.

"I saw the spec you're querying, and you should know, you have it wrong."

He barked out a sarcastic laugh. "Yeah, okay. Nothing happened between you and Trip while we were together, that's why he's the one who picked you up the night you moved out."

"The night *you told me* to get out," she clarified. "And yeah, he came to get me, but I called Addison. Not him. They just happen to live together."

"How convenient for you both," Danny practically sneered.

"Regardless, nothing happened between Trip and I until the end of November."

"And I don't know why you expect people would believe you, especially with all the shit about Trip and Mariana. People already think he's a lying jackass, no matter how she's trying to change the spin."

"They'll believe it because it's the truth,"

"So says you."

"So says this."

She placed the file with their affidavits on the table and flipped it open for Danny to read.

"What the hell is this?"

"Disclosure that Trip and I filed with Senator Ashworth's office as soon as our romantic relationship began. Signed and dated the Monday after Thanksgiving. Telling the whole story of when things changed between us—three days prior. It's all there, under penalty of perjury."

"Why does this even exist?"

"I work for the Senate, Danny, there are rules about everything. We consulted counsel and this is what they recommended."

"Lawyers getting involved, how romantic."

"That Trip wanted to protect me and make sure that I was covered right from jump? Yeah, it actually is," she shot back. "But that's not the point. These documents clearly spell out the timeline of our relationship, and it's completely different than what your story implies."

"This doesn't prove anything." He shoved the file back across the table at her.

"Maybe not, but it begs the question, why lie? What would either of us have to gain by faking the dates in a disclosure document months before we knew we'd have to defend it? Why would I risk my job like that? My *reputation* like that?" She paused. "And it doesn't really matter, anyway."

"What do you mean?"

"Now that you've seen these documents, *you* know that there's a credible way to demonstrate your claims are false. If you publish an article that alleges differently, you're not only being unethical by ignoring it, but you're also opening yourself up to a lawsuit for libel. You have no grounds for deniability at this point."

"Sure you don't want to go to law school with that little speech?" Danny asked half under his breath. Jasmine gave him a pointed stare.

"And once you have a reputation for stretching the truth? It's going to dog you your whole career, way longer than it's ever going to affect me or Trip once the news cycle moves on."

"So now you're trying to threaten me into dropping the story."

"No, Danny. I just want you to tell the truth when you do."

Danny froze. "Wait, what?"

"You want to tell people I was a shitty girlfriend who refused to support your need to get out of the town that ruined your parents' marriage? Do it. You want to tell them I moved on too quickly after we ended it and how that made you feel? Do it. That's your truth, I'd never tell you not to share that. But you don't need to make up lies about me to prove your point."

"I—I don't get it. Those things are still going to make you look bad."

"At least they're honest," she explained. "The most important thing I've learned from this job is that there are no pure villains or victims. People are complicated, Danny, more complicated than we can ever imagine from the small slivers they let us see." She continued, "And when we try to reduce things to snapshots and soundbites, we miss the story. And that's what matters. The story is what you're good at, Danny. You're a really talented writer. You just need to get out of your own way and trust the truth in what you're telling—not give in to the pull of a salacious lie that you think makes you more appealing."

"You really think I'm talented?" That insecurity of his was always bubbling right beneath the surface.

"I always have. But you're your own worst enemy. You let yourself get stuck, blaming the place or the time or the people around you for why you're not writing. When really, you just need to believe in your own talent. Your own voice. Tell your truth, that's enough."

"Where was this pep talk a few months ago?" he sighed.

"I don't know, why did you agree to stay in D.C. for a year just to make us both miserable?" she snapped, before pausing to take a breath and collect herself. "Honestly? I was too afraid," Jasmine admitted. "Just like I was too afraid for months to tell you that I didn't want to leave D.C. I knew that being honest about those things might break us, and I didn't want to lose you. Even though I knew deep down I had to."

"But once you had Trip..."

"It had nothing to do with him. I never wanted to fall for Trip. It's like the worst idea in the world, to date my boss's son—never mind when that boss's son is Trip Ashworth. But love doesn't always make sense."

"So you love him."

"I do. And it doesn't mean I didn't love you. It just means... Hell, I don't even know what it means. It's feels right. Just like staying in D.C. feels right. While I'm sorry that those things hurt you because of how they happened—and I hope you know I truly am sorry for that—I'm not sorry that they did. That's my truth. So, go ahead and tell yours. I owe you that much."

Danny closed his eyes and exhaled. "I'll pull the spec paragraph back and revise it to take out any indication that you had cheated. And I'll send you the final copy before anywhere publishes, let you figure out if and how you'd respond before it goes to press."

"Thank you. For real," she said quietly. "You've always been a good guy."

"Too bad that wasn't enough for you," he said, still bitter but without the harsh edge of anger.

"That's never what it was about," she said, starting to understand that herself for the first time. "We ended up wanting different things, and that's no one's fault. It would have been a bigger mistake to try and force it and end up resenting each other. You actually did a brave thing by pushing us to end it."

"Maybe I'll believe that someday."

"I hope so, too." She gathered the folder she'd laid out for Danny back into her bag and stood up. "Bye, Danny."

He said nothing, just waved and looked down at the table. She stopped for a second, wanting to say more, but found she didn't have the words for what she'd want to say, anyway. So she walked towards the door. Bailey and Addison followed, all of them silently waving to Ed on their way out.

Once they were safely on the sidewalk, Addison wrapped her arm around Jasmine's shoulders tightly.

"You okay, girl?" Bailey asked.

"I hurt him—badly. But I can't change that. He agreed to tell the truth about the timeline."

"But he's still going to publish this?" Addison asked incredulously.

"If someone will buy it," Jasmine shrugged.

"Jasmine, you can't let him—" Addison began, but she cut her off.

"I have to let him, Addie. You know better than I do that we can't control what other people say about us. I can't deny him the opportunity to tell his own story. I'd be a huge hypocrite if

I did. I just want him to be honest about it. That's enough for me."

"Trip is going to hate this," she said under her breath.

"So's Gwen," Jasmine said. "But they're both going to have to figure out how to live with it, because I'm not going to compromise my integrity just to protect my ego."

"Girl, you really are something," Bailey said with a smile, and Addison moved to hug her tighter.

"Come on," Addison said. "Let's get you home."

Chapter Twenty-Nine

The three of them returned to the brownstone, and walked into an expectant Trip, pacing back and forth in the entryway.

"Well?" he pounced as soon as they were inside. "Did he agree to pull the article?"

Jasmine exchanged a glance with Addison, who just nodded at her.

"We need to talk," Jasmine said. "Can we go upstairs?"

He looked uneasy, but turned and headed up the stairs. Jasmine looked at Bailey. "I may be a while, I'm sorry that I can't—"

"Go work this out with your man. Let me know how it goes." She wrapped her in a fast hug. "Addison can drive me home."

"You got it, Bay," Addison said. "I'll be around after if you need me, but I hope you'll be otherwise occupied."

"Same." She hoped she'd get Trip to understand, and they'd be able to move on.

Once Bailey and Addison left, Jasmine walked slowly up the stairs, turning over in her mind exactly what she would say to Trip about everything that had happened in the last day and a half.

Trip was sitting on the edge of the bed, bouncing his knee when she entered the room. She walked over and knelt on the floor between his knees, putting one hand on his leg to get it to still, using the other to put her fingers to his chin to get him to look her in the eye.

"Hey, Trip, are you okay?"

"I will be once you tell me this is over and Danny's dropping the whole thing."

"I—I can't tell you that."

"That asshole," Trip swore, before he started talking a mile a minute. "Well, okay, then we'll just have to call Mitch Bolton tomorrow. Find out what the options are now that we have proof he's lying. It might make sense to take another look at the injunction, when we can—"

"Trip," she broke in gently. "I need you to stop being a lawyer for a second. He's not dropping it because I told him he didn't have to."

"Wh—what?"

"I told him to go ahead and tell his story, just do it without the lies. He agreed."

"What do you mean, tell his story?"

"I broke his heart. That part is true. I can't ask him not to talk about that. That's his story."

"But you didn't do anything wrong, you just—"

"Come on, Trip. Isn't this kinda like what happened with you and Mariana? And I clearly remember someone saying that she had the right to her truth—so does Danny."

"You're using my own logic against me," he protested.

"No, I'm saying you were right then, and you're right now. You just wish that you weren't."

"Can you even trust him, that he won't renege and lie anyway?"

"He promised me he'd send me the final copy before it goes to press if he sells it. And if he doesn't, then we know we've got the whole libel suit in our back pocket. Just in case. But that's the scorched earth, last line of defense approach. I want to give him a chance to be good for his word. We were together for two years, Trip, I have to believe that I meant enough to him that he'll try."

Trip closed his eyes. "None of this would be happening if it weren't for me, it's *my* fault that—"

"Stop," Jasmine said sternly. "I'm not going to let you blame yourself for my mistakes. I'm the one who needed to be honest with Danny about what I wanted. And I wasn't, so I have to live with the consequences. I'm okay with that. I'm not perfect, and I don't want you to pretend that I am."

He cupped her face, bringing her forehead to his. "But you are—at least to me. And I know I don't deserve you, but—"

"No, Trip. You can't—that's the attitude that made you keep this from me in the first place. I love that you feel like I'm worth protecting. I haven't felt that often in my life, honestly."

Tears built in his eyes.

"But what I really need from you is to treat me as your equal. You've never made me feel less than, but I can't be on a pedestal, either."

Trip was quiet for a moment, taking in what she had said. "I was just so afraid I'd lose you, that you'd see what being with me was going to cost you—and you'd..." His voice cracked.

Jasmine couldn't take it any longer. She tilted her face up to kiss him softly, gently on the mouth.

"I'm not going anywhere. I went into this with eyes wide open—knowing better than most what to expect since it was literally my job to stalk you on the internet for months," she joked. He chuckled.

"We need to be upfront with each other. I kept things from Danny, and it was the reason we fell apart. You kept things from Mariana and that's why you fell apart." Jasmine took a deep breath before continuing. "I want to make sure we learn from that—that we get it right. I want to get it right with you. Because I think we could—" She stopped short, unsure if she should finish that sentence.

But the way Trip looked at her told her she didn't need to. "Yeah, I think we could, too."

She kneeled up further to kiss him again, that unspoken but very much understood sentiment lingering in the air between them. And her hands went to his waistband, taking advantage of her position on her knees to show him just how much he meant to her.

Before she knew it, Jasmine awoke with a start to the sound of someone banging on their bedroom door.

"Trip, Jazz, you in there? You need to see this!"

Jasmine fumbled around for her phone on the nightstand, the room still dark. 6:30 a.m. She really should be getting up for work, but she couldn't make herself move before Addison came barging in. The light from the hallway landed squarely across Trip's annoyed face.

"What the fuck, Addie? We're not even decent," he complained, as Jasmine sat up, tugging the sheets with her to cover her bare chest.

"You think I didn't expect that when I came in? My default assumption is that if the two of you are alone together, you're naked."

"Not a bad assumption, to be fair," Jasmine joked. Trip shot her a look—somewhere between *please stop talking* and *it's too early for this*.

"Anyway," Addison said, pushing her phone into his hands. "Annie just posted a new video on TikTok that I think you need to see."

"Seriously? Danny yesterday, Annie this morning. Can we not catch a break from ex drama for like, a day?" Trip grumbled.

"Huh, Danny and Annie. You guys ever noticed that your ex's names rhyme?" Addison quipped.

Trip shot her a murderous glance.

"Right, not really the time," she said quickly. "Anyway, this clip, it's a little different."

Trip sighed as he tapped the screen to un-pause the video. Jasmine leaned over his shoulder to watch.

The first thing that caught her eye was the caption at the bottom.

TFW you're actually happy for an ex who's found their soulmate. Tour has already been WILD, y'all. #inspiration #growth #almostus

The video was Annie sitting behind her keyboard, playing a snippet of a song. It didn't sound like anything Jasmine recognized. Given how well she knew Annie's discography, it had to be new. She homed in on the words Annie was singing in her distinctive honeyed soprano.

And I think for a minute, that was almost us
It was almost me you were giving your love
But I realize something when I watch you touch her...
It was never meant to be me
Cuz she's the only thing you need

"I mean, that's obviously about the two of you, right? After she saw you at the show on Saturday?"

"Maybe she invites all her exes and their new girlfriends to her tour gigs," Trip said as Jasmine laughed.

"She really came out here and said, 'stop hating on Trip, he's found the one,' huh?" Addison said, taking her phone back with a wide smile on her face.

"Well, one thing's for certain. Gwen will be happier about this than the news about Danny," Jasmine said with a sigh.

"I'll be right there with you," Trip assured her, before turning to Addison. "Can you, uh, get out of here so I can get dressed?"

Addison grabbed her phone from Trip and scurried out of the room. Jasmine and Trip quickly got ready for a busy day. Jasmine once again cursed Bailey for convincing her to leave her hair natural and simply wound it into a quick bun to save time. They rode to work in relative quiet, Addison giving both of them space to prepare for the conversation that awaited them at the office.

After a quick stop downstairs for coffee, they went up to the conference room to wait for Gwen to arrive. She was laughing as she walked in with Ben, his hand caressing the small of her back. Now that their relationship was out in the open, there were a lot fewer awkward moments of them trying to conceal their romance, but a lot more awkward moments of watching Ben be openly affectionate—Jasmine wasn't sure which was worse.

"Good morning, all," Gwen said brightly as she entered the conference room. "We'll get to this morning's TikTok news in just a moment, but first, I trust everything was handled last night?"

Jasmine let out an anxious breath. "In a manner of speaking."

"What does that mean?" Gwen asked sharply.

"I told him to go ahead with the article, as long as he told the truth about what actually happened with me and Trip," Jasmine said, not meeting Gwen's eyes. Trip reached over under the table and took her hand, giving it a squeeze.

"Jasmine, why on earth would you—We had him dead to rights to kill this whole thing!" Gwen exclaimed.

"And we don't need to. If anything, maybe it humanizes Trip a little more, if people know he's in love."

"But what about you, Jasmine?"

"I'm not ashamed of being ambitious or in love with Trip. If those are the worst things he accuses me of, I'll be okay."

Gwen looked to Ben for help, but he nodded.

"Gwen, let him out of the box. We can't control every last mention of anything Ashworth adjacent out there. If this is what Jasmine wants to do, I trust her."

"So do I," Trip put in.

"And so do I," Jack's voice rang out across the conference room.

Trip turned around to face his dad. "Got to hand it to you, Dad, you really know how to make an entrance. Do you ever just walk in and say *hello* like a normal human? Or is it always dramatically announcing yourself from the doorway?"

"Politics is theater, son. Jasmine and Gwen both understand that," Jack said, not without a smile on his face.

"You do the same thing, you know," Jasmine pointed out to Trip quietly. He just gave her a slightly smug smirk.

"Senator, we didn't expect you this early!" Gwen practically squeaked. "We haven't even made coffee yet."

"Don't worry about it, Gwendolyn," Jack said easily. "My son asked me to be here this morning, so I came in a bit ahead of schedule."

Jasmine looked at Trip in surprise, and he gave a small shrug. He clearly didn't expect that his dad would actually show up.

"All I'm here to say is that this is Jasmine's decision, and as long as she's comfortable with where things are, then I would like for this office to officially drop the matter—don't give it a moment more airtime than it deserves." He turned to Jasmine.

"Jasmine, I'm not asking you this as a member of my staff, I'm asking you this as someone who's important to my son...are you really fine?"

"I really am, sir."

"And this is how you want this to go?"

She nodded as Trip's hand tightened around hers, grounding her. Across the table, Addie looked at her with such genuine affection that Jasmine thought she might cry.

"Then let's move on, shall we?" Jack said, earning nods from everyone in the room, while Jasmine swallowed thickly to regain her composure.

"It's not all bad news on the media front this morning," Addison offered, pulling up the video Mariana had posted on her phone and playing the audio to the room. "This has a ton of views already. I think it's going to be a hit when she does release it."

"I can't believe this thing is going viral, too," Jasmine muttered quietly while Trip squeezed her hand under the table.

"Buckle up, babe, this is just the beginning."

"Good thing you're worth it, Ashworth."

Jasmine could feel Jack watching them carefully, a cryptic smile playing at the corners of his lips.

"If we're all set here, I've got a committee hearing to prepare for," Jack said. "Trip, do try not to inspire any more pop songs before lunch? I have a very busy day."

"I make no promises, Dad," Trip said with a chuckle. This was easily the most lighthearted interaction Jasmine had ever seen between father and son.

Jack departed with a slight laugh, motioning for Ben and Gwen to follow him as Ben finished writing something down. Ben got to his feet, handing Trip the note on his way out. Trip opened it up and smiled.

"What's it say?" Jasmine asked, craning her neck to look at the scrap of paper Ben had torn off his legal pad.

Trip tipped the paper her way, and Jasmine wanted to cry all over again reading Ben's messy scrawl.

You can tell she reminds him of your mother.

Chapter Thirty

As winter melted into spring across D.C., and Trip's law school graduation inched closer, so did Jasmine's anxiety about what came next.

By the end of March, when tourists descended on the city for the famous cherry blossoms, Jack still hadn't told the staff when he was planning to announce his candidacy. Spring was usually when the front runners would come out of the gate, stretching into early summer with more dark horse candidates emerging. Jasmine didn't understand why he was waiting—he should've started fundraising yesterday. Successful presidential campaigns were expensive, and Gwen was-not-so-quietly fretting about the financials whenever the Senator wasn't around.

Surprisingly, a lot of other high-profile prospective Democratic hopefuls, including Governor Martinez, were also holding off their announcements as well. Jasmine wondered if they were waiting for Jack to come out of the gate first—so they would have something to run against immediately.

It seemed like a very high stakes game of chicken to her.

It gave everything an air of uncertainty, and she hated not knowing if she'd be packing her bags to hit the road with the campaign staff, or if she'd be asked to help hold down the fort in D.C. while others took up the mantle of getting Jack Ashworth elected President. Which of those she wanted, she hadn't quite decided yet. Each came with its own kind of pressure—and its own kind of distance from Trip.

He was in a holding pattern, too, unable to commit to anything knowing he could be crisscrossing the country campaigning for his dad. They were all in limbo, trying to live in the moment and enjoy the cocoon of relative simplicity in their brownstone in Georgetown.

As simple as it would ever get for them, anyway. He was still Trip Ashworth, after all.

Things had settled down on the tabloid front once it became clear that Trip was in a lowkey long-term relationship with a non-famous person. And they had rarely gone out these last couple months, giving the internet very little to gossip about.

Trip was busy getting the final two issues of his tenure as editor-in-chief of the *Law Journal* ready for print before his last round of finals started. Work had ramped up for Jasmine, too. With the Trip situation under control, Gwen had expanded Jasmine's portfolio substantially, and she had taken on messaging around a few different high-profile bills coming up in the spring.

The long days of working melded into nights with their friends—Addison initiating endless rounds of board game marathons and dinner parties with Alex and Nigel, Bailey and Hakeem, with Tess down every couple of weekends as well. Even Jasmine's mom had come around on Trip after she agreed to have Jasmine bring him around for Sunday dinner. She'd been won over not by his charm, but by how he clearly loved her daughter.

Mary *had* been a little surprised when pictures of Jasmine and Trip accompanying her to church showed up on the internet, though. Despite the occasional bit of media attention, it seemed like all the pieces of Jasmine's life were finding a way to fit together. It was the most content Jasmine had ever felt.

And she was just waiting for it to blow up when Jack's announcement came down.

It looked like today was going to be the day. Jack had personally reached out to each staff member individually via text early Saturday morning, inviting them to a meeting at the office at eleven a.m. It wasn't unusual to have weekend meetings, but Jasmine was certain he'd chosen a day when Congress wouldn't be in session to create some distance between his Senate office and the campaign.

She came down the stairs, ready to ride over to the office with Addison, and was surprised to find Trip standing at the bottom of the stairs, also ready to go. "You need to head to the library while we do this thing?" she asked as she gathered up her work bag.

"I missed it when I was in the shower, but Dad texted me, too, asking me to be there."

Jasmine stopped short. "So...this is really it then?"

Addison nodded. "Looks like it. Come on, let's get over there."

The three of them were all a little uneasy as they drove across the city. It was exciting, sure, but it also meant their entire status quo was about to change in a major way, and what that meant for each of them would be different. They parked and went up. Ben and Gwen were already in the conference room when they arrived.

"Trip, I didn't realize you were coming," Ben said. "You here for moral support?"

"Dad asked me to come. Do you know if he's going to..."

Ben shrugged. "He didn't tell me anything, either."

Jasmine glanced at Trip, unsure what to think. Ben always knew what was going on with the Senator before anyone else. That even he hadn't gotten confirmation what the meeting was about was surprising.

They filled mugs with the coffee Gwen had brewed and took their usual seats around the conference room table. Trip nudged his chair so close to Jasmine that the leather clad seats bumped together under the table. His palm rested on her leg, and his fingers tapped on her knee as they waited for the Senator to arrive.

Just before eleven, the door opened, and Jack walked in alone. "Good, you're all here, I wanted to tell everyone at once."

"Shouldn't Elizabeth be here, then?" Addison asked—the first time Jasmine had ever heard her refer to Jack's second wife by name.

"That might be a little awkward, given what I'm about to tell you," Jack said, sitting down at the table while the rest of the room exchanged confused glances. "The reason I called this meeting is to let you all know before it leaks to the press. Elizabeth and I are getting a divorce."

The confusion on their faces turned to shock. This was not the news any of them expected Jack to share.

He looked specifically to his son. "Trip, I'm sorry to tell you with everyone else, but I couldn't wait. The final decision was made last night, and the papers will be filed Monday. She'd like to get this done quickly and quietly—well, as quietly as possible. And I'm going to do my best to make that happen, I owe her that."

"Uncle Jack, what happened?" Addison asked.

He sat back with a sigh. "It's not easy, being married to a widower—knowing that there's always going to be a part of them that belongs to someone else. We could make it work as long as I kept the past put away. But when we started meeting with the campaign consultants, they wanted to know my story, why I am who I am. And it's impossible to understand me without bringing up Fancy."

Trip's hand closed tightly over Jasmine's knee, and she placed her hand on top of his, giving it a squeeze. He'd told Jasmine about his dad's pet name for his mom, how Francesca was always 'Fancy' to him. It felt hugely intimate for Jack to use it in front of them all.

"That's the first time I've heard you say her name like that in years," Trip said softly, tears threatening to escape the corners of his eyes.

"I know, and I'm sorry, son. I had to put the past away—it was too painful for so long. I know my inability to talk about her hurt you all over again. I don't want to live like that forever. I want to be able to remember her, who she was and what she meant to me—to all of us. I'm ready for that now."

Jasmine looked over at Ben, who was also tearing up. She couldn't fathom how special this woman had to have been, to see all these powerful, stoic men misty at her memory.

"And that was all too much for Elizabeth," he continued. "She hated feeling like she was competing with a ghost. And I understand where she's coming from, truly. So, it's for the best that we part ways."

Gwen spoke up softly. "Sir, forgive me for being the one to turn this back to politics..."

Jack let out a chuckle. "That's what I pay you for, Gwendolyn."

"First of all, please accept my condolences about the divorce."

"Thank you, but they're not needed. We'll both be better off, I believe."

"Of course, sir. But, um, I think you know we were all expecting quite a different announcement during this meeting, one that probably just got a bit more...complicated."

"I don't think I need to tell any of you that the middle of a divorce isn't exactly the ideal time to launch a presidential campaign."

"So are you going to delay the announcement until after the dust settles?" Gwen asked.

"I'm not making the announcement at all. I'm not running for president."

If they looked shocked moments before, it was nothing compared to how they looked now.

"But Dad, it's what you've always wanted—what you and Mom talked about..." Trip said.

"It's what I thought I was destined for, but that's not enough to make it worth it," Jack said. "I don't need to spend time and money on a vanity project campaign just to put a target on my family's back for the next fifteen months. I'd be the front-runner right now, which means everyone will want to take me—and by extension the people I care about—down. I can't do that to Elizabeth, and I won't do it to you, Trip."

"Do you really think you wouldn't get the nomination?" Addison asked. "We've all seen the polling..."

"At this stage in the game, polling is more about name recognition than anyone's actual opinion," Jack said, shaking his head. "For all practical purposes, I'm the leader by default. But this is Martinez's year. Once people get to know him, he's going to win the nomination. And he deserves it—he'll be a great president. We've been talking quite a bit over the last few weeks, and I'm planning to throw my full support behind him and his campaign."

"What's in it for you, sir?" Gwen asked immediately.

"The knowledge that I'm supporting the best candidate for the job," Jack said, but there was a mischievous twinkle in his eye.

"What's in it for you?" Ben repeated with a knowing smirk.

Jack chuckled. "Well, Ramon Martinez is a very capable chief executive, as his overwhelming reelection margins for his second term as the Governor of New Mexico would demonstrate. But he only spent a handful of terms in the House, and he's going to need someone on his team to help him navigate the complexities of Washington. Not to mention he's thin on foreign policy experience. The Senate might be uniquely prepared to offer up a vice-presidential candidate who could bolster his credentials on both fronts."

"He's putting you on his VP shortlist," Gwen said bluntly.

"I *am* the VP shortlist," Jack clarified. "Nothing official until much closer to the convention of course, but we have a handshake agreement that I do believe he'll honor."

"You're going to be his Biden," Trip said.

"That's the plan," Jack confirmed.

Jasmine glanced at Trip, his expression caught somewhere between pride and disbelief. For the first time in weeks, she could almost see the boy he must've been—watching his father talk about duty and destiny, and believing in both.

"Isn't the party going to pressure him to pick a woman?" Addison asked, Jasmine snapping back to attention.

"That's why he'll also publicize his shortlist for Secretary of State when he names me his running mate," Jack explained. "All women, all extraordinarily capable."

"Smart move," Gwen commented.

"He's good, his team is good, you'll like working with them," Jack agreed.

"Wait, Dad—what about Hank Kensington, and the deal with Tess?" Trip chimed in. Jasmine looked to Addie, who looked slightly panicked as she realized this might mean Tess had to wait even longer to come out.

"Hank gave me his blessing to speak with Ramon, and the deal is still on. He's not wild about Hank for Energy, for obvious reasons, but Ramon thinks Hank would sail through confirmation for Labor Secretary, and I have to admit, I think that's probably an even better fit, given how union friendly Kensington Energy has always been. I should have thought of it."

"So Tess will still..." Addison trailed off, unable to finish the thought.

Jack nodded. "She will." Addison gave an audible sigh of relief. "Truly, I think this is the best move for everyone involved, including the party. But I do want to apologize for letting you all down by deciding not to run."

Ben just smiled. "Sir, I've never been prouder to work for you than I am right now."

And every single person on the payroll nodded.

But Jack then turned directly to Jasmine. "Jasmine, I'm sorry you won't have the opportunities you thought you'd have when you took this job. There will always be a place for you here, but if you want to go work on the Martinez campaign before we officially join the ticket, I would completely understand and give you the absolute highest recommendation."

"Thank you, sir, but I like life here in D.C. just fine," she said, looking over at Trip. Trip's smile faltered slightly, and Jasmine drew her brows together in concern. "What is it?"

"I just—Jazz, you shouldn't feel like you need to turn down any kind of opportunities for me. We'll figure it out if you want to get out there."

"I'm not missing out on anything. Look at what's on the docket for this legislative session. Healthcare, student loan reform, an updated Voting Rights Act? Our work's not done here. I'm proud of what I do for the Senator, for your dad.

That's what I want to keep doing, making a difference. Right now, not *maybe* after another election. And I'm so excited to see where that will take me, take us, next."

"Us?" Trip asked with a smile. "Does that mean you're finally going to listen to what I have to say about that half-ass healthcare bill you're trying to convince Dad to co-sponsor?"

"Oh, I've listened. You're just wrong," Jasmine shot back with a smile of her own.

"It's death by a thousand cuts," Trip argued. "Comprehensive reform is the only way to fix such a broken system, but we'll pat ourselves on the back for slapping a Band-Aid on a bullet hole?"

"Two Taylor Swift references? Really? And until we have the political will to make that kind of sweeping reform happen, this at least increases access to care for Medicaid recipients, even in the states that refused ACA expansion grants. And it includes addiction treatment. I seem to remember *someone* championing that in multiple interviews that *I* set up for him..."

"They do this all the time, forget there's anyone else in the room when they start talking policy. It's like some kind of weird foreplay," Addison mumbled to Gwen, who gave a halfhearted shrug. Jasmine assumed she and Ben had a similar dynamic.

For his part, Jack smiled at Trip. "She's so much like your mother."

"Just one of the things I love about her," Trip agreed.

The spell of the moment was broken when Gwen chirped "Well, then, we should probably get to work on the media strategy for the divorce announcement, then?"

Addison jumped to her feet. "I'll get my laptop and order lunch."

"I'll start a draft of a statement." Jasmine leaned down to pull her own laptop from her bag.

"And I'll walk my son out," Jack said, getting to his feet. "I'm sure you have editing to do today."

"Do you—do you want me to stick around?" Trip asked, an unspoken anxiety behind his eyes.

"I'm really okay, son. I'm not going to drink," Jack said. Trip's face relaxed with relief. "But thank you, that you want to…" Jack trailed off, before adding, "Oh, and not for nothing, but the Naval Observatory seems a much better spot to host a wedding than the White House, don't you think?"

Jasmine swore the whole room would be able to hear her heartbeat, with how intensely it was hammering in her chest. It was one thing for Trip to joke about them getting married one day, but to hear it come from Jack as well took on another layer of importance.

She glanced uneasily at Trip, who met her eyes with that slightly crooked smile. "What makes you think I'm going to wait until you're sworn in to make an honest woman out of her?" he teased, tipping Jasmine a wink. "After all, you proposed to Mom after just six weeks. By your standards, I'm already behind schedule."

"Then I suggest you get on with it, before this amazing young lady wises up about you. Why do you think I locked Fancy down so fast?" Jack said with a laugh, leaving Jasmine's head spinning as Trip and Jack walked out together for the first time Jasmine could remember.

Epilogue

Jack had been right. Number One Observatory Circle, otherwise known as the official residence of the Vice President, was indeed the perfect spot for a wedding. Chairs lined the grassy area beside the pool, where the cocktail hour would be held before the party moved to the tent out back in the garden. It promised to be a hell of a party. Over three hundred guests had RSVP'd—this was the hottest invitation inside the Beltway.

"How does everything look?" Addison called from behind her, as Jasmine took in the scene from the windows.

"Absolutely perfect," Jasmine said, turning just in time to see the stylist pin the short net veil to Addison's hair. She was still in the white satin robe, matching with the floral ones she'd gifted the bridesmaids, but she looked so much like a bride already, Jasmine immediately teared up.

"Jazz! You can't start that this early, you're going to make me cry!" Addison said, waving frantically at her face. "Bailey will be so pissed if I wreck this makeup!"

"She can touch you up when she's done with Tess," Jasmine said, glancing towards the door. Bailey was down the hall putting the finishing touches on the other bride. "She has to come back here to get dressed."

The past six months had been absolutely wild—more so than even the campaign, election, and transition. An hour after Hank Kensington was sworn in as labor secretary, Tess posted an emotional Instagram post where she officially came out, and was absolutely flooded with support from all over the country. Two days later, in the middle of the National Arboretum, she proposed to Addison, surrounded by all their friends. After they'd spent so long having to deny or conceal their love, Tess hadn't wanted to wait another minute to make good on the promises she'd whispered to Addison in secret. Pictures were all over social media from onlookers who recognized them and what was happening.

Now, on a bright June day, the Vice President's niece and the Labor Secretary's daughter were about to be married by a Supreme Court Justice who'd voted to legalize same-sex marriage on the federal level.

Jasmine had thought when she took a job working in the Senate, she might be a witness to history, but she didn't expect it to look quite like this. And she couldn't have been more thrilled to be a part of it.

Addison, ever a fan of quirky fashion, had asked Bailey to design her and Tess their looks for the big day, opting for the jumpsuits that had become a staple of her collections after designing Jasmine's viral New Year's Eve look.

Tess's was simple and relaxed: wide legged with a deep V-neck and flutter sleeves. Addison's was of course more dramatic—a strapless bustier style top that tucked into a high waisted cream satin faux cummerbund with matching tuxedo style stripes down the sides of the pants. Tess planned to rock her boho vibes all day, but Addison had a second look: a solid sequined romper with a crossover neckline and split long sleeves that she was changing into after the first dance.

Jasmine's own dress hung on the back of the door: a simple gold charmeuse floor-length cowl-neck slip dress—demure yet sexy, a feat only Bailey could pull off. Next to it was Bailey's, a ruched one-shoulder dress, fitted impeccably despite weeks of sewing struggles. And though Trip and Tess's two brothers wore standard tuxes to stand up on Tess's side, Alex and Nigel were wearing the coordinated brocade suits Bailey designed for their wedding two months prior. Every detail of this wedding was a fashion moment.

Which was precisely why they hadn't told Bailey yet that rights to the photos of the event had already been sold to *People* to raise money for The Ashworth Family Foundation's LGBTQ impact fund. They didn't want her to pass out from the nerves.

It was a major coup, and Jasmine was thrilled to have landed as one of her first big fundraising wins. She'd taken over leading the Foundation's advancement team right after the inauguration, having left her senate job the previous summer to spend the final months before the election crisscrossing the country in support of the Martinez/Ashworth ticket. The grassroots nature of the foundation appealed to Jasmine's desire to make immediate, tangible, if incremental, change. And she was determined to prove that she was just as much an asset to the foundation as she had been to Jack's Senate team. In the lead-up to the wedding, she leveraged the connections she'd cultivated with reporters on the campaign trail—the ones who'd run glossy features on her and Trip—to secure top dollar for the Foundation.

Shortly after Bailey returned from finishing Tess's makeup, Jasmine and Bailey had just gotten into their dresses and were about to start dressing Addison when there was a knock on the door.

"We're not ready yet!" Bailey practically screeched.

The door cracked open, and Trip poked his head inside. "Sorry, I just need to borrow Jasmine for a minute. Addison already cleared this."

Addison nodded curtly. "Make it quick, Ashworth. I need my matron of honor!"

"Can you please stop calling me that?!" Jasmine cried. "It makes me sound a thousand years old."

"You're the one who decided you were in a rush to marry my idiot cousin."

"Hey!" Trip cried, offended.

"I say that with love!"

"I'm going to let that slide since it's your wedding day, Trip said. "But just remember who's giving the best man toast later!"

Sorting out who claimed who in the wedding party had been a whole thing. In the end, Tess got Trip as her best man, while Addison claimed Jasmine—and they were giving a joint toast at the reception later.

"Jasmine will protect me," Addison said.

"You want to keep calling me a matron and find out?" she joked before ducking out into the hallway with Trip.

Once they had stepped into the side hallway with a bit more privacy, Trip pressed Jasmine back against the wall. "Oh my God, babe," he breathed in her ear. "That dress is…"

He didn't even finish the sentence before his mouth was on her neck.

Jasmine laughed and pushed his shoulders back. "Hey now, not really the time or the place, my dude."

"Can you blame me? You look incredible."

"Well, thank you. But I don't think that's the reason you came to see me?"

"Of course not." He reached into his pocket and pulled out a small white box. "I know I'm a day early, but happy anniversary."

The next day marked one year since Trip and Jasmine had exchanged their vows in a small ceremony on the beach in Stone Harbor. They'd gotten engaged the previous Thanksgiving, a year after they'd begun dating. Some questioned the rush, but to them, it made perfect sense—they both wanted the certainty of forever.

They had put off planning their wedding initially, assuming they'd have to wait until after the election. But the more they thought about it, the less they wanted their wedding to be a political spectacle. By the time they decided to go ahead, they had a narrow window of time to pull it together. In the end, it was an intimate ceremony of about thirty people, just days before Jack was announced as Ramon Martinez's running mate.

And because of that, Jasmine knew just what was in the box Trip had handed her.

Once they decided to try and get the wedding in before the announcement, Trip drove them the three hours to the house in Gladwyne to talk to Jack about it, who'd been spending significantly more time at the house when he was back in Pennsylvania. Not only because his second wife had gotten the Rittenhouse Square condo in the divorce, but he was slowly growing able to look back and remember Francesca in a way that was less bitter than sweet. He'd been spending time in places she loved rather than running from those memories. The relationship between Trip and Jack still had a long way to go, but it was getting better the more they acknowledged and honored the woman who linked them.

They explained their plan to Jack, who immediately understood their desire to make it happen sooner rather than later, and to do it in Stone Harbor where Trip had memories of his mom. He promised to make some phone calls to help them.

Later, he pulled Trip aside to talk to him in private in his study. Trip emerged, looking tearful but happy, and asked Jasmine to come in. Jack quietly exited as Trip went to a panel in the wall that was swung open. "Wall safe," he explained, as he withdrew a box from behind it. "It's where we've kept Mom's jewelry since..." he trailed off, and Jasmine reached out for his free hand.

"Dad and I were talking," he said, sitting next to her. "Mom wanted my wife to have her jewelry. Most of it is yours as soon as we're married—the rings, the bracelets, the necklaces, all yours. But the earrings...they're special."

Jasmine noticed there wasn't a single photo of Francesca without a pair of gorgeous gold earrings. Even just relaxing on the beach, she would have a pair of gold hoops shining in the sun.

"So if it's okay with you," Trip continued. "Rather than give them to you all at once, I'd like to save them, so I can give them to you one at a time. Like, for every major occasion, I can pick out just the right pair, tell you the story behind them and why they're the ones for that moment."

Jasmine's eyes were swimming with tears.

"Is that okay?" he asked.

Jasmine recovered her voice after a moment. "I think that's the most wildly romantic thing I've ever heard in my life. I would love that." She paused. "Is your dad okay with it?"

Trip smiled, looking at the box in his hands. "It was his idea."

The box he gave her that night contained the ones that she'd worn on their wedding day. Similar white boxes had continued to appear for special moments: the pair with blue Murano glass beads for the night Trip introduced Jack for his nomination acceptance speech at the DNC, the twisted love knot studs for their interview and photo shoot with the "Vows" columnist for the *New York Times*, the simple hammered hoops for election night, the dramatic diamond chandeliers that complimented her strapless gown—another Bailey creation—for making the rounds at the inaugural balls. And now, for their anniversary and Addison and Tess's wedding, pearl drops on gold hoops with channel-set diamonds inlaid. They matched nicely to the pair Addison had on, the pearl and diamond cluster studs that 'Auntie Chess' had made sure that she passed onto Addison just for this occasion.

"They're gorgeous," Jasmine breathed as she lifted one out of the nest of cotton in the bottom of the box.

"I asked Addie to pick out a pair from out from the collection for today. She wanted to coordinate with her sister for her wedding day."

"I'm going to melt into a puddle and Bailey is going to kill me," Jasmine laughed, holding back tears.

"I love you so much," Trip said softly, kissing her.

"I love you, too." She placed the lid back on the box. "But now I do really have to go help Addie finish getting ready."

"Duty calls." He nodded. "Thank goodness Tess's mom is helping her—you know I'd be absolutely hopeless at tying that thing."

Jasmine laughed. "I can't wait to see you out there. The reception is definitely going to go until after midnight, so we'll be able to properly celebrate our anniversary afterward."

"Jasmine Ashworth, the things you do to me..." he said, shaking his head.

"Including keeping you in line. Go make sure Tess is ready!"

"Yes, ma'am," he said with a smirk, watching her walk back down the hall.

Acknowledgments

AMERICAN ROYALTY marks my first traditionally published novel, and it's a milestone I never could have reached on my own.

Thank you to my editor Shakera Blakney and publisher Kelly Moran at Rowan Prose Publishing, who took a chance on this one. I am forever grateful for your help in bringing Trip & Jasmine's love story to the world. And thank you to all the Rowan Prose authors for your friendship and encouragement as we navigate the wild world of publishing together. It's a lot more fun with all of you!

Thank you to everyone who's touched this book on its way to publication, including Britt Belle, Sarah Vance-Tompkins, Kate Clayborne, and Laura Brown, as well as all my early readers, you know who you are! Your feedback made this a better book, and I don't think it would have made it this far without each of you.

Thank you to my family for their unending support in my dream of being an author. Not everyone has the kind of husband who will copyedit for free, or kids who love to tell anyone who will listen that their mom wrote a book. I am forever grateful that I do.

And finally, thank you to the readers who take chances on new stories. There's a million different happy ever afters out there, thanks for picking up this one, and believing in the power of love to change the world.

CHECK OUT THESE OTHER EVER-AFTERS FROM ROWAN PROSE:

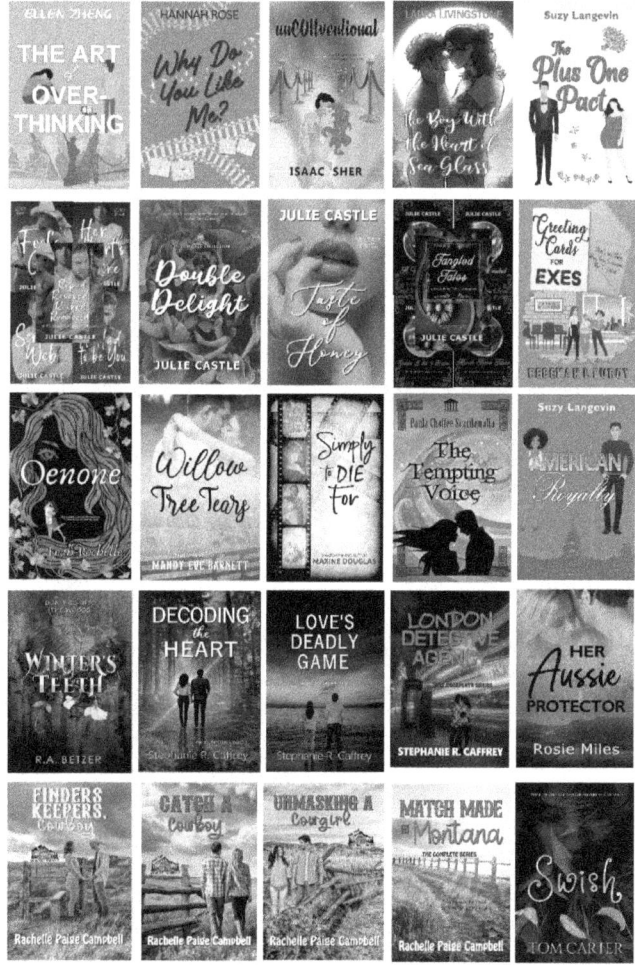

Suzy Langevin loves love, even though she forgot how to say it in Latin when she was a contestant on *Jeopardy!* Her career as a clinical social worker, along with her own experience living with autoimmune disease and ADHD, allow her characters to embrace the tough stuff without it becoming a cliche, incorporating themes related to mental health and addiction with authenticity, heart, and humor. She is a 2024 RWA Golden Heart Winner. Suzy lives and writes in central Massachusetts.

www.ingramcontent.com/pod-product-compliance
Lightning Source LLC
LaVergne TN
LVHW091803030426
835323LV00039B/322